CLAY BRENTWOOD SERIES
BOOK NINE: COMANCHE JUSTICE

CLAY BRENTWOOD: BOOK NINE: COMANCHE JUSTICE
by Jared McVay
Published by Creative Texts Publishers
PO Box 50
Barto, PA 19504
www.creativetexts.com

ISBN: 978-0-578-56388-6

COMANCHE JUSTICE
By
JARED MCVAY

An imprint of Creative Texts Publishers, LLC
Barto, PA

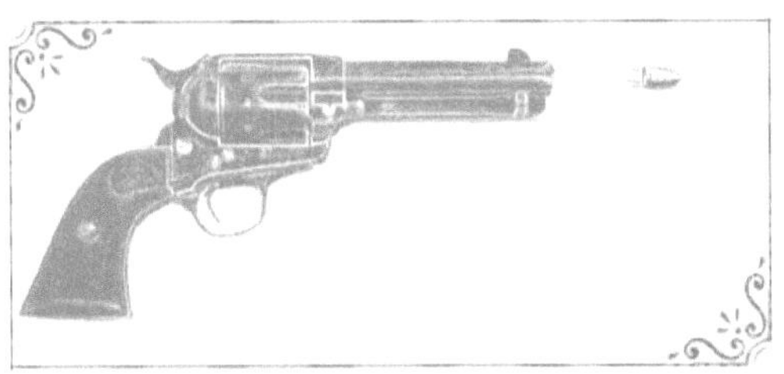

CHAPTER ONE

-

It was late afternoon when Clay Brentwood rode the black stallion away from the front gate of his ranch like his tail was on fire, racing across the wide expanse of prairie until he was far out on his range and the ranch house could no longer be seen. Slowing the black stallion down to a walk to give him a breather, he stopped close to a lone elm tree standing not far from a small lake where his cattle and horses drank.

He stepped down from the saddle and removed it, dropping it next to the tree, and then slipped the harness from Midnight's head. "Go on down to the lake and get yourself a drink and a good roll; you've earned it." Clay never used a bridle on Midnight, or any of his other horses – he didn't like them. He couldn't imagine someone putting a bit in his mouth and pulling it between his teeth and gums.

He used a halter with the reins attached to a ring on the bottom, which worked just fine. Most of the time he knee-reined the big horse, which allowed him to use his hands for other matters, like shooting his pistol or rifle.

The black stallion shook his head up and down, nickering his agreement, then trotted down to the lake where he bent his head and drank deeply.

Clay dusted off his pants and shirt as best he could with his hat, then sauntered over and sat down with his back against the tree and sighed. He needed some time and space to mull things over in his mind. Everything had gotten way too complicated.

While watching a cloud that looked like the head of a unicorn floating slowly across the sky, he rolled and lit a smoke, then blew a smoke ring into the air that disappeared with the cool breeze making its way across the Texas prairie.

A crow landed on a limb near where Clay sat and stared down at him.

Clay looked up at the crow and asked, "How in blue blazes did I get myself in this mess? There are two women back at the ranch house and both of 'em want to marry me and the truth is, either one would make me a good wife - so how can I choose one of 'em without hurting the other one's feelings?"

The big crow shook himself as though he didn't know what to say, then cawed loudly and flew away.

Clay's mind suddenly became filled with the images of the two women.

First, there was Loralie Benson, the fiery red head from Tennessee he'd brought home with him. He'd gone back to Tennessee to help her with some trouble she was having with horse rustlers, and when it was all over, he'd asked her to marry him – and she'd said, yes. Not only was she a woman to ride the river with, but she looked mighty good all dressed up and hanging on his arm at a barn dance or just walking down the street. Plus, Ol' Son took to Loralie like they'd been together all their lives.

Back in Tennessee, Loralie owned six hundred and forty acres of prime timberland, along with a horse ranch where she raised and trained Tennessee Walkers that were highly sought after. A lot of men would have thought that alone would make her a fine catch, but not him. He wasn't after her ranch or her land. He had a perfectly good ranch of his own right here in Texas and he for sure didn't need her money. Due to an inheritance he was a wealthy man, so it wasn't that. He just liked the way she made him feel.

So... with that in mind, how had he had the audacity to ask her to give all that up and move out in the middle of Texas where there weren't many trees and the wind blew on a constant basis? His land was miles and miles of flat land where hers was all mountain country. But he had asked her to do just that, and she'd said she would. She'd told him she would go anywhere he wanted to go and live anywhere he wanted to live. She'd told him it didn't matter where they lived as long as they were together.

Her idea was to bring her horses out to Texas and train them here. As far as her land was concerned, she would hire a caretaker to watch over it and they could go back for visits from time to time to make sure everything was all right. She had been emphatic about never wanting to sell off the timber. She wanted to save and preserve the land into posterity – maybe someday, she would turn it into a park.

Clay smiled as he remembered the train ride from Tennessee to Texas. Loralie Benson had definitely been a handful.

He knew she loved him with a fierceness that wouldn't quit and that she would stick by his side through whatever came up, but it still bothered him that she'd have to give up the place where she'd been born and raised. Her parents were buried on that land. It was the only place she'd ever lived.

Clay blew another puff of smoke into the air and watched it disappear, then turned and looked out across his land that held several thousand head of cattle and at least two hundred or more horses. Could he give all of this up to go live in Tennessee, or any place else for that matter? He didn't think so, but in truth, he'd never been asked.

Somehow it was different for a man. They didn't have to make choices like that. He wasn't quite sure why that was, but it was the way it had always been, right or wrong, the woman usually just followed the man. His thoughts turned to his first wife, Martha, and he felt an ache in his heart. She had left her home and her father up in Wichita to come out here in the middle of nowhere so he could follow his dream and because she had, she had died at the hands of outlaws.

Clay turned his hat over and over in his hands. Could he ever love a woman enough to give up everything for her? Women did it all the time, so why couldn't a man if he was a mind to?

Clay sat his hat on his head and snubbed the butt of his cigarette into the ground and reached for the makings of another one. Loralie was not the only one he had to consider – there was the Senora Victoria Marie Christina Claire Ontiveros. She was tall and beautiful, with a Spanish aristocrat background, she was well educated and also a woman to ride the river with. She was a few years younger than Clay and a widow.

She'd been forced to marry a man that she'd never met and didn't love. When her father died, her new husband took control of the ranch and almost ruined it. When he was killed by the very rustlers he'd been dealing with, Victoria had taken over and tried her best to run the ranch, but she soon realized she needed help. Her vaqueros were loyal to a fault, but she needed a Segundo – a foreman who knew cattle – a man who could take control of the ranch and was not afraid to stand up against rustlers.

Clay had come along just when she was about to give up and she hired him to run her ranch. She'd even allowed him to introduce whiteface cattle to her herd of longhorns. During his time there, he'd not only averted several attempts to rustle her cattle, but when slavers had abducted her, he'd gone after her and the other women who had also been abducted. The chase had taken him down into Mexico before he was able to rescue them. From that time on she had looked at him differently - even hinted several times about him becoming Patron of the ranch, which meant they would have to get married for that to happen. They had never had an actual affair during the time he worked for her as Segundo, but she had kissed him, once. And now she was down at the ranch house, stating flat out that she was here to marry him.

Did that mean she wanted him to go back to New Mexico with her and be the Patron of her ranch? He was sure he couldn't handle both her ranch and his at the same time. Both ranches were large and needed constant looking after. Moving to New Mexico was out of the question.

Clay stood up and looked out over his land. It was wild, untamed land, with hot, windy summers and harsh, cold winters that brought heavy snows and temperatures that dropped well below zero. And in the fall, they could expect a tornado at any time of the day or night. But even with all of that, this was his land and he'd worked hard to turn it into a paying ranch. He brought in whiteface and short horn cattle and mixed them with the longhorns, and they were thriving better than he'd ever expected. Where the wild horses came from, he wasn't sure, but come they did, and after capturing and breaking them, he had a good horse business to go along with his cattle business. Other than losing Martha, life had been all he'd asked for, with only a few deviations from time to time. Bill McDaniel, head of the Texas Rangers, had not only been the one who arrested him, but had also saved him from hanging for a murder he hadn't committed. Instead, Bill got him sentenced to two years as a Texas Ranger, which turned out to be much longer – several years longer.

Clay shook his head, remembering his time as a Texas Ranger and all the dangers it had brought with it. "At least that's over and done with now," he said to himself. He'd done his time and brought many an outlaw to justice and had the scars to prove it. But now it was time to get on with his life before his luck ran out. Living the life of a rancher with a wife and maybe a son or daughter was where he saw his future.

In the distance, Clay saw a small dust cloud rising into the air. He dropped his cigarette butt on the ground and rubbed it into the dirt with the sole of his boot. He reset his hat on his head and stood there, hoping and praying it wasn't Loralie and Victoria. He didn't want to deal with that right now. As the dust cloud got closer, Clay could see it was three men and gave a sigh of relief.

Shortly, he could distinguish two of them – Running Coyote, his number one foreman, and Riley, his number two foreman. But the man in the middle was still a mystery to him.

As they got closer, Clay saw the sun glisten off something shiny on the man's chest and guessed it to be a badge.

A slight chill ran down his spine. Why was the law coming to see him? He hadn't broken any laws that he could think of and he felt he no longer had any obligations to the Texas Rangers. Another look told him it wasn't Bill McDaniel.

The three men reined up in front of Clay and stopped.

"Out here hiding, are you, boss?" Running Coyote asked with a big grin spread across his face.

Not being one to be left out of the fun, Riley said, "There surely is two mighty purty women waitin' on ya back at the house. You out here cause you ain't got the gumption ta face 'em? Them bein' just ah couple of poor little innocent females and all." Riley said, laughing at his joke, and as an afterthought he said, "Maybe you should become ah Mormon and marry both of 'em."

"Not funny," Clay said, knowing it had been said good-naturedly.

Looking up at the man in the middle, Clay took his measure. He was a tall man, over six feet, Clay guessed. His skin was pale, like the men who worked inside a store in town. His dark brown mustache was thick and well-trimmed. The man's eyes told Clay he was not a man to be trifled with, but the gun hanging on his hip seemed out of place. To Clay, the man didn't fit the image of a western sheriff.

"If I was a guessing man, I'd say you are the new sheriff in Seymour." Clay said.

The man stepped down from his horse, a speckled mare with white and brown spots. He let the reins drop to the ground, then walked over and stopped in front of Clay and stuck out his hand. "Name's Rice Cooper, and I guess you are the famed Texas Ranger, Clay Brentwood."

Clay shook the sheriff's hand and said, "You're right about me being Clay Brentwood, but I've retired from the ranger business and I never looked for fame - just did my job."

The two men stood staring at each other for a good half a minute before Clay asked, "What brings you out here? If you're looking for a Texas Ranger, you're gonna have to contact Austin. Like I said, I'm retired – I'm just a rancher now. And just so you know, I'm sorry about your predecessor, Hank, getting shot in the back. He was a good man – we were friends."

Clay looked over toward Running Coyote, who just hunched his shoulders, then looked back at the new sheriff. "If you're here to ask what I think you are, you've wasted your time coming all the way out here. I don't chase outlaws anymore," Clay told him.

Rice Cooper was a man used to getting his way but knew arguing with Clay right now would get him nowhere. He didn't plan on going back empty handed, so he just stood there, staring at the man he'd come to recruit.

Clay looked up at the sky and noticed the sun was getting lower in the west. "Seeing as it's getting onto dark and it's a long ride back to Seymour, you're welcome to stay for supper and I'm sure we can find you a place to spend the night in the bunkhouse. You can go back to Seymour after breakfast in the morning."

The sheriff smiled to himself as he touched his fingers to the brim of his hat and said, "Much obliged, I'd like that. Maybe we can talk on the way back to your ranch house. And just so you know, I've already contacted Austin and your old boss, Bill McDaniel. He's the one who said I should come out here and talk to you."

Clay looked down at the ground, wondering why McDaniel had told him to come out here when he knew he didn't want anything more to do with chasing down outlaws. "All right, I guess talking won't hurt anything," Clay said at last. "But, like I said, I'm retired."

Clay turned and looked toward the lake and gave a whistle. The black stallion turned his head and looked in their direction, then reared up on his hind feet and pawed the air before racing up and stopping just in front of Clay, putting his chin over Clay's shoulder.

"That's quite a horse you got there," Rice Cooper said, admiring the big stallion.

Clay stepped back and rubbed the horse's forehead and said, "Yeah. We've been together for a few years now and have gone down the river more than once."

Clay slipped the halter over Midnight's head and tightened the clasp, then threw the blanket and saddle on Midnight's back. After tightening the cinch, Clay put his foot in the stirrup, grabbed the saddle horn, pulled himself up and swung his leg over and settled onto his saddle, then turned and headed back toward the ranch at a leisurely lope.

When Running Coyote and Riley pulled alongside of him, Clay told them to go on back to the ranch and let Mrs. McIntyre know the sheriff would be staying for supper.

After they'd ridden away, the sheriff rode up next to Clay and they slowed the horses to a walk.

The sheriff scratched the back of his neck and said, "I guess you're the only rancher I know of that has Indians working for him."

"You have a problem with that, do you?" Clay asked, sensing this new sheriff might have some animosities toward Indians like a lot of white people did, especially the ones close to Seymour, who had lost cattle and horses.

The sheriff looked at the sky for some time before he spoke. "When I took this job, it was with the understanding that I would do what I could to stop the cattle and horse stealing that's been going on. Now, I've talked to most of the ranchers around here and they all say the same thing, Indians are stealing their cattle and horses. All of them except you, that is. Why do you suppose that is?"

Clay felt a strong dislike for this man building up inside him and he took a deep breath before he answered him. "There has been attempts by would-be rustlers, but I have hands who ride for the brand, all good men, including the Indians who work for me. Like I said, there has been attempts, but they've been taught not to come around here, so we don't get bothered much. And when we do, we take care of it ourselves."

Rice looked over at Clay while rolling what he'd just said around in his mind. "You say, would-be rustlers - but you never mentioned the fact that they were Indians."

Clay stopped the black stallion and took his time rolling a smoke and when he had it going, he said, "That's because they weren't Indians."

"And you know this how?" the sheriff asked as he sat staring at this man who had a reputation for honesty.

Clay blew a smoke ring into the air then looked directly at the new sheriff. "I know this for two reasons. First, I went out to speak with Walks Tall, chief of the Buffalo Chasers Tribe. They're Comanche. I asked him point blank if they were behind the rustling that had been going on and he told me no. The buffalo have been good to them this season and they had enough meat to last through the winter. Plus, when the buffalo hunting is not good, he comes to me and I cut out enough stock to last them through the winter, which gives them no reason to steal any cattle.

And second, He Who Bites, one of the Comanche Indians who works for me, checked the tracks of the would-be rustlers and each time, said they definitely weren't Indians."

"And you believe him and this Walks Tall?" the sheriff asked.

"Why shouldn't I? Unlike white men, Indians don't lie," Clay, answered.

Rice Cooper wasn't sure what to make of this man who everyone had said was an honest and forthright man – the most respected man they knew of. Not only did he visit the Indians in their village – he had Indians working for him. Rice sat, taking in the look of the man, trying to guess how far he could push him and judged not too far. But none of that mattered. He had a job to do. He was here to gather information and get the man's help if possible. He didn't have to like him to use him.

"It just seems strange that all the other ranchers swear it's Indians who are stealing their stock, and yet you can walk right into their village and talk to the chief."

Clay thought long and hard about what he was going to say next. He wasn't about to tell him that Walks Tall was his half-brother – it would not bode well with what the man seemed to believe. Clay rubbed out the stub of his cigarette on the top of his saddle horn and scattered the remains into the wind, then touched his feet against the sides of the black stallion.

When the sheriff rode up next to him, Clay said, "Those Indians are not the savages they've been labeled. Most of them have more common sense than many of the white men who look down on them – and are also more religious than a good share of those hypocrite white people who claim to be Christians. One of the things I like about them is that they don't lie. Now it was you who asked, so here it is. You need to be looking for white men, not Indians. They're the ones stealing the rancher's stock."

"Somebody told me you were an Indian lover, but I reckon I needed to see it for myself," Rice Cooper said with a bit of hostility in his voice. How could everyone be so deceived by this man? He was an Indian lover through and through. "Seems you're a bit biased when it comes to Indians."

Clay looked at the new sheriff and said, "You can stay the night but come morning I suggest you go back to Seymour and start looking for the white men who are making you all look like a bunch of fools."

With that, Clay slapped his heels against the sides of the black stallion and rode off at a high lope in the direction of the ranch house and the conflict that awaited him there - leaving the new sheriff to make his own way to the ranch, if that's what he chose to do. To Clay, it made no difference one way or another.

Anger rose in Rice Cooper as he watched Clay ride away from him.

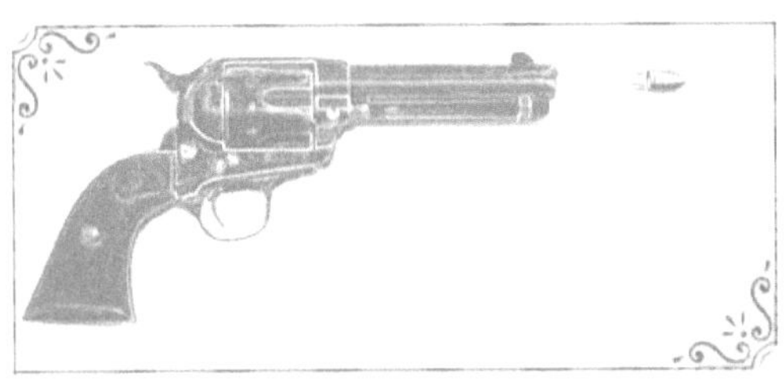

CHAPTER TWO

-

As Clay rode up next to the barn and stepped down, He Who Sleeps A Lot stood looking in the direction Clay had just come from and said, "It looks like the man who came to see you does not wish to stay for supper."

Clay turned and looked behind him and in the far distance he saw the sheriff riding back in the direction of Seymour. "Reckon not," Clay said and handed the reins to his top horse wrangler. "Just as well," Clay said without further explanation.

Clay was standing there, watching as the sheriff disappeared into the growing darkness when Loralie Benson came running up to him and threw her arms around his neck and kissed him full on the lips while Ol' Son jumped around at his feet.

"What was that all about?" Clay asked, looking around for Victoria, after Loralie released him and stepped back.

As Clay stood there, scratching Ol' Son's ears, Loralie said, "Well, me and Victoria, we had us ah what you might call, a talk, and I convinced her I was the one who should be mistress of this ranch and so she and them men who ride guard on her up and left. Said she was goin', I mean going, into Seymour and catch a train back to New Mexico and for us to have a good life."

"What do you mean, you talked?" Clay asked as he allowed himself to be led into the house where Loralie informed him supper was almost ready.

Inside the house, Loralie climbed the stairs to her bedroom, saying she was going to get cleaned up and suggested Clay do the same. She was proud of herself at being able to speak better English and not sounding so much like a hillbilly, plus evading Clay's question.

Clay watched her go and shook his head, wondering what she'd said to Victoria that had convinced her to leave? Women. He wasn't sure he would ever understand them, but they sure were nice to have around. They somehow seemed to be somewhat more levelheaded than men, and smelled better, too – along with having with conniving ways.

Clay continued to watch as Loralie went into her room and closed the door. On the way out from Tennessee, they had agreed that until they were actually married, they should stay in separate bedrooms so there wouldn't be any improprieties.

After cleaning up and changing shirts, Clay went to the kitchen where Mrs. McIntyre and her daughter, Cindy, were putting food into large bowls. The ranch hands were already sitting at the long kitchen table eating their supper – only nodding their heads as he came in.

Mrs. McIntyre and Cindy busied themselves, giving him only a smile.

Clay asked, "Anyone know what Loralie said to Senora Ontiveros to make her take off like she did?"

Mrs. McIntyre and her daughter looked at each other and rolled their eyes.

Mrs. McIntyre shrugged her shoulders and said, as she lifted a platter filled with fried steaks and headed for the dining room, "How would I know? I'm just the housekeeper." Her daughter, Cindy, quickly followed her mother with bowls of gravy and mashed potatoes, saying nothing.

The ranch hands all sat around the kitchen table with their heads bent down, studying their food and eating, but no one was saying anything. Clay saw a bowl of corn sitting next to the stove and picked it up on his way to the dining room, knowing Mrs. McIntyre was not telling him everything she knew.

The two foremen normally ate their meals with Clay, Mrs. McIntyre and her daughter, Cindy, and tonight was no exception – Running Coyote and Riley were already seated at the table when Clay walked into the room.

Clay sat the bowl of corn on the table just as Loralie came walking in. The two foremen jumped to their feet and stared openly at the beautiful red head. She was dressed in an emerald green dress that fit her like a glove and her red hair hung down over her bare shoulders, making her look stunning. After seeing Victoria, she wanted to look good in Clay's eyes.

Clay stared at her and the only thing he could think of to say was, "You look stunning."

Loralie smiled. She could get used to these kinds of compliments. She liked being mistress of the house as long as she could still take the time to work with her horses. Recovering, Running Coyote stepped over and pulled out a chair so Loralie could be seated and said, "You look positively radiant, Miss Benson."

"Why thank you, Mister Coyote," Loralie responded as she sat down, trying to be very much the lady of the house.

Running Coyote smiled as he returned to his chair. He was proud of being able to speak the white man's language so elegantly. He had taken his studies seriously when he had been sent to the Jesuit's school.

When everyone's plates were filled, Clay looked at the women who were busy cutting their pieces of meat, and asked, "So... is someone going to tell me what happened to make Victoria rush off in such a hurry, or am I going to have to drag it out of you?"

Both Mrs. McIntyre and her daughter busied themselves putting salt and pepper on their meals, leaving Loralie to answer Clay's question.

Loralie started to take a bite of steak, then put it back down on her plate. "Well, if you really want to know..."

Before she could go further, there was a knock on the front door.

Cindy jumped to her feet and hurried out of the room, shouting over her shoulder, "I'll get it!" They heard the door open, then heard Cindy say, "Won't you please come in." Clay turned in his chair and watched as Cindy came back into the dining room, followed by Sheriff Rice Cooper. The sheriff had his hat in his hands and was turning it around and around.

Clay stood up and faced the sheriff. "What can I do for you, Sheriff? Do you need more convincing that it isn't the Indians who are stealing the rancher's stock?"

"No. No, that's not why I came back," Rice said after clearing his throat. "First, I'd like to apologize for how I acted. I guess I got caught up in the way the ranchers and the people of Seymour think. Every time something goes wrong; folks seem to think it must be the hostiles that did it. No offense intended," he said, nodding his head at Running Coyote.

"Then I got to thinking about what you said, and it made sense. If the rustlers wanted to throw us off their trail, what better way to do it than to make us think it was somebody else." Running Coyote stood up and walked over to the new sheriff and stuck out his hand and said, "Now that you have your head back on your shoulders, I believe we have a lot to talk about."

Running Coyote looked over at Clay and rolled his eyes in the direction of the table. Clay grinned and said, "Now that you're here, why don't you pull up a chair and join us for supper. We can talk about this while we eat."

"If you're sure, yes, thank you," the sheriff said as he pulled out a chair and sat down.

Mrs. McIntyre was already up and placing a plate and silverware in front of him. During the meal, the rustlers were discussed at length, leaving the Victoria Ontiveros matter until a later time, to which Loralie gave a sigh of relief. Clay turned down the sheriff's request for him to join a posse to go and look for the rustlers, but told him he would allow He Who Bites to go along, and assured him he would find no better tracker.

Rice swallowed the mouthful of food he was chewing and looked across the table at Clay and said, "I would be tickled pink to have him along as my tracker, but I'm not sure what the men in the posse will say. They're all from town and the nearby ranches, and they believe it's the Indians who are doing the rustling. And I guess if I have an Indian tracker, why wouldn't they think he would lead us in the wrong direction?"

Clay nodded and said, "I suppose you're right. Too bad. He's the best tracker I've ever seen – even better than me."

He Who Bites could hear the conversation in the kitchen where he was seated with the other ranch hands. He lowered his head and smiled at Clay's compliment. The sheriff nodded his head and said, "I'm sure he is, but if you were along, they might accept him, but other than that..."

Riley, who had been silent so far, looked at his boss and said, "You know he's right, but maybe if'n I went along I could talk to 'em and make 'em understand."

Clay looked at Loralie who smiled and said, "Clay, maybe it's not my place to say anything, but in my opinion, you need to go along, too. They're your neighbors and they'll listen to you. We can take care of the ranch just fine while you're out chasin' down them rustlers, I mean, chasing down those, outlaws. Can't we Mister Coyote?"

Running Coyote looked down at his plate, a smile crossing his face, and said, "Yes ma'am, I'm sure we can."

After some more discussion, and Clay's strong demands, it was decided that adding men from town to the posse would only delay matters and save some possible disagreements about He Who Bites being the tracker.

The following morning, right after breakfast, Clay, the sheriff, Riley, and He Who Bites rode off in the direction of a neighboring ranch owned by Clay's friend, Marion Sooner. "If he's lost any cattle it will be a good place to begin our hunt." Clay assured the sheriff.

The sheriff wasn't sure he liked the idea, but decided he had no choice but to go along. This was, after all, their territory and they had told him to recruit Clay, if possible.

Before they went through the gate, Clay had to stop and tell Ol' Son he wouldn't be going this time. Ol' Son looked at him, but wasn't convinced until Loralie ran up and squatted down next to him and put her arm around his neck, hugging him close to her and speaking softly, "We need you to stay here and help take care of the ranch while Clay is gone."

Ol' Son rolled his eyes so he could see Loralie, then whined and wagged his tail. Loralie looked up at Clay and said, "You go along, now. He'll stay here with me."

CHAPTER THREE

-

Marion Sooner was walking out of the barn, leading a saddled horse and a pack horse when Clay and the others rode up and stopped in front of him. "I was just coming to see you," Marion said, looking up at his friend.

"Lose some cattle, did you?" Clay asked.

"Nigh on to sixty head as far as I can tell," Marion told them.

"See who it was?" the sheriff asked.

Marion looked over at Rice Cooper with a questioning look on his face. "He's the new sheriff in Seymour, Rice Cooper," Clay stated. Marion looked at Clay, "Oh, yeah, I heard about Hank. I'm real sorry, he was a good man," Marion said, extending his hand toward the new sheriff. "What was your question, again?"

"Did you see the rustlers?" the sheriff asked for a second time.

"Oh sure, but they weren't who they wanted me to think they were," Marion said with a wide grin.

"And just who did they want you to think they were?" the sheriff asked, patiently.

"Indians," Marion told him straight away. "They wanted me to think they were Indians, but they weren't. No-sir, not by a long shot."

"And what makes you think they weren't?" The sheriff queried, still trying to make sense of this whole thing.

Marion looked over toward Clay, who nodded his head.

Marion looked back at the sheriff and said, "Because they were white men dressed up like Indians, only they didn't do a good job. They might' a fooled the folks in town, but not me. Especially since we know most of the Indians who live around here, don't we, Clay?" Marion asked, looking back at Clay.

"That we do, my friend. That we do," Clay answered.

"Anything else?" the sheriff asked.

"Now that you mention it, there is," Marion told him. "They were riding shod horses and had good looking saddles. I can't ever remember seeing an Indian who had a nice saddle except for the ones that work for Clay, here. Plus, the Indians don't have any shod horses in their herds that I know of. And if they did, they don't have a blacksmith to keep the horses shod, and the rustler's horses were all shod."

"That's very interesting," the sheriff said to Marion. "Anything else?"

"Well there might be one more little thing that you might find important. They were speaking English when I rode up on 'em, and only a few of the Indians I know of, speak decent English," Marion said with a grin.

"You say you rode up on them. When was that?" the sheriff asked.

"Couple of hours ago. I yelled at 'em and fired my pistol in the air and they took off like scalded dogs, yelling words most Indians don't even know. I fired a few more shots at them and I'm pretty sure I hit at least one of 'em, maybe two."

"And you say they got sixty of your cows?" He Who Bites asked.

"Yeah, that sounds about right. They were already heading them toward the south when I come up on 'em. I reckon they may have run off ah few pounds by now the way they stampeded them. I knew I couldn't take them on alone, so I came back here to get a fresh horse and some supplies before I went to ask Clay for his help. Like I said, I was on my way over to see about Clay helping me track them down, but now I don't have to, do I?"

"No, I guess you don't," Clay said with a grin.

"Want me to show you where I came up on 'em?" Marion asked him. "Maybe with He Who Bites along we can track 'em down a whole bunch sooner."

Clay looked over toward the sheriff and asked, "Well?"

Rice chewed on the inside of his cheek for a moment, then said, "I don't know. Maybe we should go back to town and get a few more men. If these are white men we're talking about – not a few starving Indians…"

Marion looked at the new sheriff and asked, "Can you use that hog leg you got hanging on your hip?"

The sheriff looked down at his pistol, which in reality had been the property of the late sheriff, Hank, then back at Marion. "I've been known to hold my own," he said, trying to make himself look better than he was. "And I'm a fair shot with my rifle. But what does that have to do with anything?"

Marion stepped up onto his saddle and settled himself. "The way I see it, if we go back into Seymour and take the time to put a posse together, those rustlers could be halfway to Mexico. But, since there are only four of 'em and there is four of us, maybe if we start now, we just might catch up to 'em before dark. That's why I was asking about your shooting ability – just in case me or Clay might need to take care of more than our share."

Clay had to turn his head so the sheriff wouldn't see him grinning.

Rice could feel the anger building inside him. He wasn't used to being talked to like that, but quickly realized he couldn't compare these two men with the men in town, or the men where he came from. "I said I can carry my own weight and I can. If He Who Bites can track them down, we'll get your cattle back and I'll see they get what they deserve."

Thirty minutes later He Who Bites looked down at the ground and said, "You don't need me, even a child could follow these tracks."

Clay had to agree. Hiding the tracks of sixty or so cattle and four horses would not be easy. Instead of catching up to them by dark, for the next two days they followed the herd that increased with each day. Cattle came from several directions to join with the herd they were following.

"What do you make of this?" Rice asked of Clay over supper of the second evening.

Clay, He Who Bites, and Marion Sooner had been discussing this very topic and Clay looked over to where the sheriff was squatted next to the fire, eating a plate of beans and dried meat. "He Who Bites thinks there's more than one group. He believes they are banning the cattle together into one large herd. He also said he thinks they're headed toward the Colorado River, and I have to agree with him."

The sheriff stirred his beans around in his plate with his fork and said, "I came out here from Missouri and I haven't acquainted myself with this part of the country yet, so bear with me if I ask stupid questions."

Clay, Marion and He Who Bites sat looking at the sheriff, waiting for him to continue.

After a moment the sheriff said, "Of course it's important that they're headed for a river. Seems to me a river would make a good place to water a large herd of cattle and maybe put a little weight back on them."

"That would be true if it was just any ole river, and that's the only reason they were headed there," Clay informed him. "But we're talking about the Colorado River. Not only is it a good-sized river, but it runs all the way down to the gulf."

The sheriff had a puzzled look on his face and asked, "So, what are they going to do, make the cattle swim all the way down to the gulf?"

Marion Sooner stood up and walked over to the fire and refilled his coffee cup, then went back and sat down next to his plate. "Some years back, a group of rustlers were stealing cattle over west of here. They herded them to the Colorado then shipped them down to the coast on barges. It's said there are people down there who will buy them for top dollar and ask no questions. I also heard these people have ships that haul the cattle away to only God only knows where."

"But they no longer do that, do they?" the sheriff asked.

"Not for several years, now," Clay told him.

"Who put a stop to it?" Rice asked.

"Texas Rangers," Clay said. "Before I came along."

"And you think that's what they're planning on doing – a repeat of what worked some years back?"

"Kinda looks like it," Clay said.

"So, what's the plan?" the sheriff asked, feeling like a fish out of water.

"Get a good night's sleep and come first light, ride like the devil is chasing us and hope we can get to the river before the cattle are loaded onto barges and gone," He Who Bites stated.

The sheriff nodded his head and said, "I think it comes down to how many cattle they now have - along with how many barges they have to haul them away. But you're right we needn't waste daylight. How far is the river from here?"

Everyone turned and looked at He Who Bites, who studied the sky for a moment, then said, "Maybe five, maybe six hours if we ride hard."

The sheriff nodded and headed for his bedroll, grateful for the chance to get some rest. He wasn't used to riding a horse all day, chasing outlaws.

.

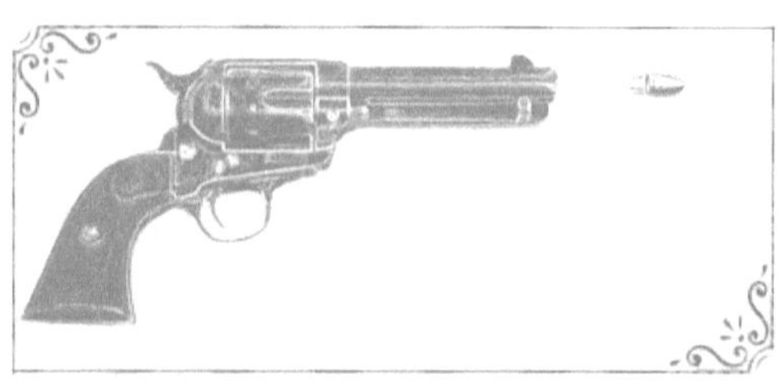

CHAPTER FOUR

Loralie Benson came down to breakfast dressed in Levi pants, a man's work shirt, and wearing worn down boots. She carried a cowboy hat in her hand and dropped it on the kitchen table as she entered the kitchen.

Mrs. McIntyre looked up and said, "The hands have already eaten, but the skillet is still hot if you want some bacon and eggs, I was about to fix some for me and Cindy."

"Sure, I would like some breakfast. Is there any coffee?"

"Almost a full pot. Clean cups are in the cupboard, Miss Benson," Mrs. McIntyre called over her shoulder.

"I would prefer you call me, Loralie, if you don't mind," Loralie told her as she poured herself a cup of coffee.

"Of course, and my first name is Colleen. But I hope you realize that when the men are around, and with you soon to be the mistress of the house, I'll be addressin' ya as Miss Benson or ma'am and of course, Mrs. Brentwood after the weddin'."

Loralie sighed and said, "I'm not sure I can ever get used ta that. Back home I did most all the cookin' and can't remember being called, ma'am, or Miss Benson, in ah coon's age – but I have to admit, Mrs. Brentwood does sound real nice."

Cindy came in about that time and took one look at Loralie and said, "You look like a ranch hand. Are you planning on working outside?"

Loralie looked at Cindy who was dressed in a pale-yellow dress, with her hair hanging down around her shoulders.

"I break and train my own horses," Loralie told her. "And I brought six with me that are in various stages of training."

"Really?" Cindy asked, her eyes wide with excitement. "I love the horses we have here and sometimes I get to ride ones that need exercising."

"You like ta ride, do ya?" Loralie asked over her coffee cup, slipping back into to her old, familiar way of speaking.

"Oh yes. And Riley says I'm getting pretty good at it, too."

Loralie sat her cup on the table and grinned. "Riley, isn't he that boy Clay seems to think a lot of? The one I'm told you've been steppin' out with?"

Cindy turned a bright shade of red. Her face felt flushed and found it hard to swallow. Trying to regain her composure, she said, "Well, he has asked me to a few socials they hold in town... but mama is always there, too. She and Running Coyote, that is."

Loralie turned and looked at Colleen McIntyre, who was busy filling the plates with their breakfast as though she hadn't heard a word.

"Mama and Running Coyote are talking about getting married," Cindy said.

"Is that a fact?" Loralie asked, smiling at Mrs. McIntyre.

"Well then, you're in luck. If yer ma ain't set... I mean, if your mother hasn't set a date yet, maybe we could hold a triple wedding when me and Clay get hitched. Yes-sir, we could all get married right here at the ranch and invite folks from town to a big whing-ding."

Mrs. McIntyre stuttered and stammered saying, "Well, I don't know about that. I would need ta talk with Running Coyote. Besides, we still ain't too sure gettin' married is such ah good idea. People will talk, ya know – him being an Indian and all."

"Oh posh," Loralie said walking up to Mrs. McIntyre. "If you love the man then don't let nobody stand in your way – especially not them uppity folks in town. Look what I did to that Victoria gal."

Mrs. McIntyre smiled, knowing Loralie had said the one thing that would make any woman leave. "Are ya really carryin' Mister Brentwood's child?" she asked.

"Not so's anyone would notice," Loralie said with a mischievous grin. "But Miss Victoria didn't know that. I'm in a war that I don't plan to lose, so I told her the one thing I knew would make her leave. And it worked, too!"

Mrs. McIntyre studied the woman who would soon be her mistress and decided she was not some willy-nilly female who could be run roughshod over. She liked her and decided right then and there, they would be friends.

Brave Eagle and He Who Sleeps A Lot were standing with their arms on the top rail of the corral, inspecting Loralie's horses when she walked up. She looked at Brave Eagle and said, "I'm guessing you are Brave Eagle, and you are He Who Sleeps A Lot," she said to the other Indian standing next to the corral fence.

"I am, and you are the woman from Tennessee who rides and shoots like a man. The one who will soon be the mistress of the ranch," Brave Eagle said with a smile. "I am the unofficial veterinarian and my friend He Who Sleeps A Lot is in charge of wrangling," he told her, waving his hand toward his friend.

Loralie smiled and stuck out her hand. "I'm very pleased to meet you both. Clay told me I should ask the two of you to look over my horses and make sure they made the trip safely. I need to start working them as soon as I can."

Brave Eagle smiled. "Mister Brentwood mentioned that I should give them a look-see, so I took the liberty yesterday of checking each one. They are fine horses and in good shape. You can start your training anytime you want."

Loralie was surprised that he'd already looked at them, but happy that he had. She was also surprised at how intelligent the Indians that worked for Clay were. She knew from the ones back in Tennessee that they weren't the savages everyone thought them to be, but these men had more schooling and spoke better than most of the people she knew.

"Well now, thank you," Loralie told him. "I'm surprised you've already checked them over and more than pleased you didn't find anything wrong with any of them. I'll begin this morning, then. First off, I think they each need some riding to stretch their legs and let them know who's in charge. They tend to get a bit feisty when they've had a few days off. Cindy said she'd like to help and if the two of you aren't doing anything..."

He Who Sleeps A Lot glanced over at the horses and smiled. They were different from the wild horses they trained as cattle ponies here in Texas, and he'd already wondered what it would be like to ride them. "I would be honored to help," He Who Sleeps A Lot said, turning back to his new mistress, as Brave Eagle nodded his head in agreement.

Loralie looked around and liked what she saw. Everything was clean and well kept. Before she had a chance to say more, Brave Eagle pointed toward the house.

Cindy came bounding out to the corral with a big smile on her face. She was dressed in canvas pants, a cotton shirt, boots, and a well-worn, wide brimmed hat. Nothing looked new.

"So, which one is mine?" she asked stopping in front of Loralie, then turned to the two Indians and said, "Good morning, Brave Eagle. Good morning, He Who Sleeps A Lot. Aren't Miss Benson's horses beautiful?" There was no question she liked these new horses.

Both the Indians liked Cindy - she was full of life and was always polite to the ranch hands, and always ready to pitch in with whatever needed to be done. And she didn't look down her nose at Indians, which in their view put her a step or two higher than most of the young ladies from town.

"Yes, they are beautiful animals and I am anxious to see what they do that makes them different from our ranch horses," He Who Sleeps A Lot said.

Turning back to Loralie, Cindy asked, "Are we going to ride all of them today?"

Before Loralie could answer, Running Coyote came walking up and said, "We've got company coming. Maybe you ladies should go back to the house until we see who they are. It appears to be four men and they're riding kind of steady like and four abreast, like they're looking for trouble."

Loralie looked in the direction of the front gate and saw what Running Coyote had just said was true. Taking Cindy by the arm, she said, "Come on."

Cindy started to resist, but Running Coyote looked at her and said, "You go on, now, Miss Cindy. We can't watch you and those men at the same time."

Loralie looked at Running Coyote and asked, "Where are the rest of the hands?"

Running Coyote had stepped to one side, a little away from the rest of them and Loralie noticed he was wearing a gun belt and pistol that he hadn't been wearing a few minutes ago. He looked at her and said, "Out tending the cattle and horses. Now please, do as I ask, and go into the house."

The four riders were getting much closer now and Loralie could see they all had stern looks on their faces and all were wearing pistols on their hips. Loralie had seen trouble more times than she liked to talk about and these four fit the images that popped into her mind.

As soon as they were in the kitchen, Loralie ran into the living room and took down a lever action rifle from the gun rack and checked to make sure it was loaded. Satisfied, she went to the front door and eased it open just enough to see out. The riders were just coming through the gate and she watched as they rode up and stopped in front of Running Coyote, Brave Eagle and He Who Sleeps A Lot.

The one who spoke was a hard-looking man with several days stubble on his face, mean looking blue eyes and unruly black hair sticking out from beneath his tall, wide brimmed hat. His pants, shirt and short jacket looked as though they'd seen better days, but the pearl handled pistol riding on his hip looked like the kind gun slicks wore and appeared to be well used.

"Can I do something for you, mister?" Running Coyote asked - looking up at the man who'd stopped his horse just a little in front of the others.

"Yeah, I reckon you can," the man said, looking at Running Coyote. "You can go bring out the other cattle thievin' Injun you got hidden around here somewhere. We was tole there are four of ya."

"And just who might you be?" Running Coyote asked.

"Name's, Ranse Boswell, and we're the necktie party who's been hired by the ranchers ta see all four of you cattle thievin' redskins swing for what you've been doin'. And ta give yer Injun lovin' boss ah warnin' not ta take sides with stinkin' redskins. It ain't healthy."

Running Coyote stepped back a couple of steps, putting a little more distance between himself and the four riders, then spread his feet apart and let his hand drop down a little closer to his pistol.

"I think you've been misinformed mister," Running Coyote told him, keeping his eyes on the four men. "The Indians who work on this ranch don't need to steal cattle or horses – we have plenty here already. Besides, it isn't Indians who has been stealing the cattle. Its white men dressed up like Indians to throw everyone off their trail. So, you go on back to wherever you come from and tell your boss he's made a mistake."

Ranse Boswell was a man who didn't like opposition and had his own notions on how to deal with it – kill anyone who stood in his way. He'd already dealt with six, so far.

Ranse looked over his shoulder and grinned at his companions, who up to this point had sat quietly, waiting for Ranse to start the dance. Turning back, he looked at Running Coyote and asked, "You know how ta use that gun you got hangin' on your hip, Redskin?"

Running Coyote swallowed and stared up at the man who he was sure was trying to bait him into a gunfight. "I'm not looking for a fight, mister, but this is private land and you and your friends are trespassing. I'm the foreman here and I'm ordering you to leave."

"Well now ain't you actin' all high and mighty, but it don't draw water with us. We ain't leavin' and you're gonna die like the cattle thievin' redskin you are and then we'll take care of them stinkin' Injun friends of yours."

Ranse swung his horse around so he could have a clear shot at Running Coyote. As he did, he heard a voice call out from the direction of the house. "Hold it right there, Mister. You go for that hog leg and you're a dead man."

Ranse swung his horse back, looking in the direction of the house, but the sun was just high enough so he couldn't make out who was standing in the doorway, but he could see enough to make a good shot and he reached for his pistol. It was just clearing his holster when he felt the stab of pain hit his chest and felt himself being propelled off his saddle. He was dead by the time he hit the ground; a bullet lodged in his heart. At the sound of gunfire, Ranse's three companions drew their pistols and began firing.

Mrs. McIntyre had come out the back door with a rifle in her hands and saw Ranse lifted from his saddle, then saw the men with him draw their weapons and begin to fire. With a calmness she didn't quite understand, she lifted the butt of the rifle to her shoulder and sighted down the barrel and squeezed the trigger. She watched as a second rider left his saddle.

The loud roar of weapons being fired, and the smell of gunpowder filled the air as a third rider was knocked off his horse from a bullet fired by Running Coyote, leaving only one rider left. The last remaining rider threw his pistol on the ground and raised his hands high above his head. "Don't shoot! I quit! I give up!"

"Hold your fire!" Loralie yelled.

There were no more shots, but no one put their guns away – not yet.

"I reckon I took up with the wrong people," the last rider said.

He was a man of around forty with gray hair showing below his hat. He was a tall, thin, rawboned man who looked as though he'd lived a hard life. "I'd be much obliged if you'll let me turn around and ride out of here – and I promise you'll have no more trouble out of me."

Loralie walked up close enough to study his face, yet far enough away to shoot him if he had a hidden gun and tried to draw on her. "If you want to live to see another sunrise, you'd best listen up and listen up good. I'm the mistress on this ranch and we don't hire thieves of any kind or any race. The men we have riding for us are good, honest men, both white and Indian. So, you go on back and tell whoever hired you that they were wrong. And while you're at it, you can tell 'em if they send any more men out here, they'd best come along and bring a wagon to haul the dead bodies away."

The lone gunman sat staring at the red headed woman and knew she meant business. She'd already killed Ranse and he had no doubt she or all of the others would start throwing lead at him if he made a stupid move. "You understand what I've just told you?" Loralie asked.

"Yes ma'am," he said, doffing his hat.

"Then load up your friends so's you can take them with you, then skedaddle out of here before I change my mind."

As the man stepped down from his horse, Running Coyote walked over and helped him load the dead bodies belly down across their saddles. While they were loading the bodies, Brave Eagle slipped into the barn and returned with pieces of rope so he could tie the dead men to their saddles so they wouldn't fall off during their return to wherever they came from.

When he handed the rope to the man, the man looked at him for a long moment, then said, "Much obliged. And... I'm truly sorry about all of this. Maybe when this is all over, I can come back and see about a wrangling job. I'm really not a gunman and I am good with horses and cattle. I just came along because of the money."

Brave Eagle stepped back and nodded his head but said nothing. Loralie, Running Coyote, Brave Eagle, He Who Sleeps A Lot, Mrs. McIntyre and her daughter, Cindy, stood quietly and watched as the man rode away, leading three horses with their silent passengers. Running Coyote walked up to Loralie and lifted his hat and asked, "Are you all right, Miss Benson?"

Loralie's hands shook slightly and her heart was beating faster than normal, but other than that, she was trying to stay in control of her emotions. She had, after all, just shot a man.

"Of course, I'm all right. I told Clay we could handle anything that came up and as far as I can tell, we did," Loralie said, turning to look at Mrs. McIntyre. "Is there any whiskey in the house? I think we could all use a drink."

Brave Eagle walked up and smiled at Loralie and Mrs. McIntyre. "You are brave women – and you, Miss Benson, will truly make a fine mistress of the ranch, and we will happily join you in a drink, but if you don't mind, we prefer buttermilk or coffee. You know what they say about whiskey and Indians."

Loralie frowned and said, "Thank you for the compliment, but no I don't know what they say about whiskey and Indians."

As they walked toward the house, Mrs. McIntyre walked alongside Loralie and told her about Indians and alcohol – how it made them want to go on the warpath.

Loralie thought that might be an old wives' tale, but she would not dissuade her three brave Indians from their drink of choice.

-

While all of this was going on, The Southern Pacific Railroad labored its way across the wide-open plains of Texas with a destination of Albuquerque, New Mexico. Black smoke lifted from the chimney of the train and the wheels made a clickity clack noise. Along with the noise and the rocking motion of the train, many of the passengers had drifted off to sleep.

Instead of making the long trip from Clay's ranch, all the way back to New Mexico by buggy and horseback, Victoria Ontiveros and her vaqueros were enjoying the train ride as far as Albuquerque. From there, they would travel by horseback and buggy, back to Victoria's ranch in the southern part of New Mexico.

With their horses and the buggy riding safely in a boxcar, Victoria's vaqueros were having a drink in the train's lounge car, enjoying this new mode of travel. Victoria was sitting in her private sleeping quarters, enjoying a glass of wine. She was looking out of the window, wondering how things might have turned out if she had gone to see Clay during the time when she first began thinking about the trip. Maybe it would be her who was carrying Clay's child.

All of a sudden she choked on the wine and when she finally got her breath back, she said to no one in particular, "That dirty little liar. She is no more with child than I am. She just said that to get me out of the picture."

Victoria Ontiveros was so angry for allowing herself to be fooled by the redheaded vixen she almost pulled the emergency cord to stop the train so she could go back and scratch her eyes out, but caught herself before she made a complete fool of herself. They were out in the middle of nowhere. She would have to wait for the next town before they could get off the train. Hopefully there would be a train headed back to Seymour coming through soon. She just hoped she wouldn't be too late.

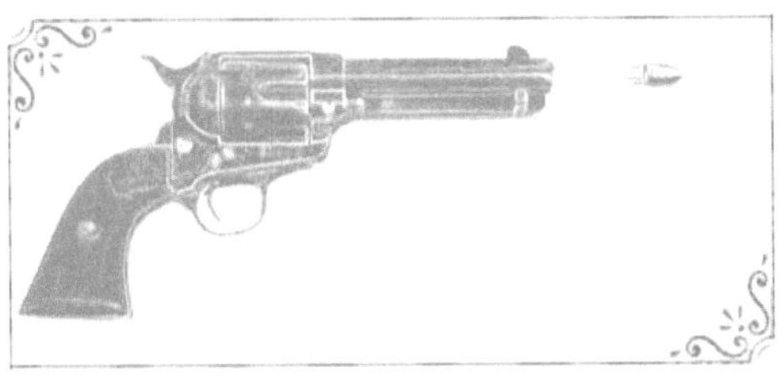

CHAPTER FIVE

-

The small posse was up at the crack of dawn, before the sun had barely climbed into the sky. They breakfasted on coffee, biscuits and bacon and within less than an hour they were riding hard toward the Colorado River.

The day before, they had seen storm clouds crossing the sky in front of them and knew a hard rain would be soaking the rustlers and washing away most of the tracks they were following.

Even without any tracks to follow, He Who Bites knew where the old docks were and led his small posse in that direction.

The sun had not yet reached its zenith when He Who Bites raised his hand and called the men to a halt - and when they rode up next to him, he said, "We must go slow from here on. We should be able to see the river and the docks from the top of that hill," he told them, pointing at the rise directly in front of them.

They dismounted and ground hitched their horses and made their way on foot to the top of the hill, keeping a low profile as they peeked over the top.

Less than a quarter of a mile in front of them, the Colorado River flowed to full capacity and jutting out from the nearby bank were two long, wooden docks. Tied up to the docks were four large barges – each one capable of carrying at least fifty cattle.

A short distance up the river, maybe a hundred yards, in among some elm trees, smoke lifted into the air from the rustler's camp. It looked like they were having a noontime meal. Clay put his field glasses to his eyes and counted twelve of them in the camp, but he could see no one keeping a lookout for anyone to come up on them. In fact, they didn't even have anyone riding herd on the grazing cattle.

"Do you think they can get all of those cattle on the four barges?" the sheriff asked.

"It's possible, if they crowd them," Clay ventured.

"And what are we gonna do about them no goods sittin' around the fire with not ah care in the world?" Riley asked his boss, which rankled the sheriff to no end since he felt he should be the one in charge and making the decisions.

"Aren't you askin' the wrong person, young fella? I'm the sheriff and this is my posse."

Clay looked at the sheriff and asked, "All right, Sheriff, what is the plan?"

Now that the question had been posed, his mind went blank. He was a town sheriff and knew little to nothing about this kind of work. Thinking quickly, he looked back at Clay and Marion and said, "Well now, I do have a couple of ideas in mind, but since they are your cattle and this is your part of the country, I'll defer to your thinking."

Pleased with himself for getting out of an uncomfortable position, the sheriff looked at the two men and smiled. One day he might turn to politics.

Both Clay and Marion almost broke out laughing but managed to stifle their urges.

Clay looked over at Marion and said, "I've been studying the situation and I think we have a good chance of recovering our cattle and taking the rustlers prisoners, for the sheriff to deal with. We get our cows back and the sheriff can keep his promise to the people of Seymour by bringing the rustlers in and thus, avoiding any trouble with the Indian population."

The sheriff smiled to himself. If Clay's plan worked, whatever it might be, he would look like a hero to the people of Seymour, but if it didn't, he would bear no blame. It would all rest on the shoulders of Mister Clay Brentwood. "So, what's your plan?" Rice asked in a whisper.

Clay motioned for them to move back down to the bottom of the hill so they could speak without being detected by the rustlers.

At the bottom of the hill, Clay laid out his plan, telling each man what was expected of him.

Again, the sheriff smiled to himself. According to the duties given him, his part in this wouldn't involve any danger to him, but could be embellished somewhat when he got back to Seymour.

As they went about preparing for getting the cattle back, Marion Sooner eased up to Clay and said in a low tone, "I see you left the sheriff out of the main part of the raid."

Clay scratched the back of his neck and said, "I guess I did. There's something about the man that worries me. He seems more like a man who's used to sitting behind a desk or telling a city council what they want to hear than a man who you want to ride the river with. So, with that in mind, I put him in a place where he would be out of the way and not be a hindrance to us, and still be able to get that part of the plan done."

Marion thought this over and then said, "Couldn't agree with you more."

Clay, Marion and Riley each ground hitched their horses and climbed the short hill overlooking the campsite and studied their prey. They had already discussed what each one was to do.

After a little more whispered discussion, Clay, Riley and Marion circled around to come at the rustler's campsite from three different directions - each having a good place to shoot from, while He Who Bites and the sheriff moved to a location near the cattle, but still out of sight, and waited.

Before setting out, Clay reaffirmed their plan. Clay whispered to Marion, "You take the high side of the camp and I'll take the cattle side. Riley, you circle around to the far side and find a good spot to shoot from."

Marion nodded his head and moved quietly off to his right. When he was in position, he gave a soft whistle that sounded like a dove, to which Clay answered with the same sound. It wasn't long before they heard the caw of a crow, indicating Riley was in place. These were signals they'd learned from their Indian friends.

It had been decided Clay would open the ball and he took off his hat, then stretched out on his stomach. He stuck the butt of his rifle against his shoulder and took aim on the campfire – actually, the coffee pot. He took a breath, then as he let it out slowly, he squeezed the trigger and watched the coffee pot explode, sending hot coffee into the air and on anyone close by. The rustlers jumped and grabbed for their pistols, and with guns in their hands they looked for someone to shoot at, but saw no one. Confused, they milled around, looking at one another.

The next thing that happened was the sound of yelling and pistols being shot off, along with the protesting of the cattle as they began to run away from where they'd been pastured.

"Yee haw!" the sheriff yelled as he fired his pistol in the air.

"They're stampedin' the cattle!" one of the rustlers yelled.

Another rustler yelled, "Get to the horses!"

But before they could take action, two more shots rang out, kicking up dirt on each side of them, causing them to stop.

"You're surrounded!" a voice from the top of the nearby hill called down to them.

"We've got you coming and going," another voice came through the air from farther away, between them and their horses.

"You start for your horses and we'll see ya afoot," a third voice called out.

"Drop your weapons on the ground, all of you, and move back close to the fire. Anyone tries anything stupid we're gonna leave a bunch of dead bodies laying around."

The rustlers stood there, looking at each other, trying to decide what to do as their stolen cattle were being driven away.

Finally, one of the rustlers said, "Ahh hell, I ain't dyin' for no stupid cows," and tossed his pistol on the ground and stepped over close to the fire.

When the other men still hesitated, Clay took aim and squeezed the trigger of his rifle and watched as the hat of the nearest rustler went flying off into the air.

That decided things for the rustlers, and they all dropped their weapons and moved over next to the fire as they'd been instructed.

The sheriff and He Who Bites had driven the cattle only a short distance before they turned and rode back toward the rustler's camp.

They rode wide of each other in case there would be resistance, but as they got close, they saw the twelve men standing with their hands in the air with Clay, Riley and Marion walking toward them with rifles in their hands.

The sheriff was the first to step down from his horse, and with his pistol in his hand, he walked up to the campsite.

"I'm Sheriff Rice Cooper from Seymour, Texas, and you're all under arrest for cattle rustling."

At this point, Clay was happy to turn the rustlers over to the sheriff. They had their cattle back - the sheriff would soon have the rustlers tied up, and no one had been hurt.

As Clay turned and looked at the sheriff, the sheriff looked over at him and said, "Our plan worked just like we thought it would."

Marion started to say something, but Clay stayed his words by saying, "It sure did, Sheriff. It sure did. Now, would you like us to truss up these owl hoots so you can take them back to town?"

The sheriff nodded his head and said, "I think that's a fine idea."

Rice Cooper turned to the outlaws and said, "Everybody turn around with your backs to us and put your hands behind you back."

When the rustlers had complied, the sheriff turned and asked, "We do have some rope to tie them up with, don't we?"

He Who Bites reached into his saddle bag and pulled out a handful of leather straps —each around two feet long. "We call these, pidgin' straps," He Who Bites said, as he walked past the sheriff and began tying the wrists of the first rustler he came to.

Marion and Clay each took a few straps from He Who Bites and began helping while the sheriff and Riley kept their guns trained on the outlaws in case any of them tried anything.

After they were tied up and secure, Riley walked over to the rustler's horses and began looking through their saddlebags and grinned. He pulled out Indian headgear, along with the makings for war paint.

He walked over and handed it to the sheriff. "Like I said, it was white men dressed up like Indians."

The sheriff looked at Riley and nodded his head. He had a lot to learn about this part of the country if he was in fact planning on staying - of that, he still wasn't so sure. Being a sheriff out here was a lot different than St. Louis, where he'd come from. Back there, he had several deputies to do all the dirty work. His job was to command his deputies like a general and speak to the ladies groups and the city council.

Suddenly, a group of men came ridding over the hill with guns in their hands and rode right up to them. "Hold it right there!" a portly man on a big white horse barked at them.

As they turned to face these new men, the portly man's jaw dropped and he said, "Sheriff, I didn't expect to see you! Who are those men you have tied up? And where are the Indians who rustled our cattle?"

Clay stepped forward and said, "Mister Atkins, there were no Indians rustling cattle, just these white men, pretending to be Indians."

Carroll Atkins stepped down from his horse and walked up and stood in front of Clay. "What are you talking about? I saw them, plain as day and I say it was Indians who stole my cattle!" He was puffed up like a toad and ready for a fight.

"Then maybe you need to get your eyes checked because they're apparently playing tricks on you," Clay said, standing up to the portly rancher. "I can assure you; these are the men who stole your cattle. We caught them red handed and found their Indian costumes in their saddle bags."

At that point, the sheriff walked over and handed Carroll Atkins the things Riley had found in the rustler's saddlebags. "Like Mister Brentwood here said, it was white men, not Indians."

Carroll Atkins stood there, his mouth open, flabbergasted at this information. He had been so sure the rustlers had been nothing more than a bunch of hostile - thieving Indians.

"If you wouldn't mind," the sheriff said. "I could use some help taking my prisoners back to town. These men need to sort out their cattle and take them back."

Carroll Atkins looked at the sheriff for a moment, then said, "Sure. Sure. I'll ride with you, along with a couple of my men, while the rest cut out my cattle and take them back to my ranch.

Marion walked up and looked at Carroll Atkins and said, "You and the sheriff go on and take the outlaws back to town. Clay and I will help sort our cattle from yours and we'll take ours home and your men can do the same with your cattle and any other they find," confirming what the sheriff had just said.

Clay looked at the sheriff and said, "If you need another man to help, I'll send Riley along to help you. He's a good man with both cattle and a gun."

The sheriff stuck out his hand and said, "Thank you for all you've done and yes, I would appreciate it if Riley gave us a hand. An extra man might come in handy." Moving prisoners like this was something new to him and he was grateful for Riley's help.

"We could hang 'em right here and be within our rights. There's plenty of trees," Carroll Atkins put in.

The sheriff thought for a moment, knowing Texas law would allow them to do just that and no one would say a word. "No, we'll take them back to town and do this legal – in a court of law. We'll let a judge decide what's to be done with them."

Clay looked at the sheriff and decided there might be hope for him, yet.

The sheriff walked over to his horse and tightened the cinch, pleased with himself.

CHAPTER SIX

After sorting out the cattle, Clay, He Who Bites and Marion Sooner drifted their cattle back toward Marion's place first, in seemingly no hurry.

Marion rode over next to Clay, who was rolling a smoke as his horse ambled along behind the cattle. "I take it you're in no hurry to get back?" He'd heard about Clay's problem with having two women at the ranch and both of them with matrimony on their minds.

"No. I don't see the need to run weight off the cattle just so we can get back," Clay said as he struck the lucifer against the top of his saddle horn, then lifted the flame to the end of his cigarette.

"I guess it has nothing to do with those two women you have waiting on you back at your place, right?"

Clay swallowed the smoke and coughed. "How do you know about the women back at my place?" Clay asked, eyeing his friend, suspiciously.

Marion was enjoying his friends' discomfort and took his time, rolling and lighting his own cigarette. After blowing a smoke ring, he looked off into the sky and said, "The way I understand it, there's money on which one you'll choose. Me, I got twenty dollars on the redhead."

"What?" Clay yelled. How in the..."

"Easy friend. Don't bust a blood vessel. I'm only teasin' you. I just happened to overhear Riley and He Who Bites, talking."

Clay breathed easier and shook his head.

"So, it's true then. There are two women back at your place and each one of them is expectin' you to marry them. One being that fiery redhead from Tennessee and the other one is the owner of that big ranch you worked on down in New Mexico?"

Clay sighed and said, "Actually, at this point, there's only Loralie, the one from Tennessee. I don't know the ins and outs, but it seems she convinced Senora Ontiveros to go back to New Mexico."

Marion laughed out loud and asked, "How in blue blazes did she do that?"

"Like I said, I don't know the details yet and the rest is kind of a long story," Clay told him.

Marion looked around and said, "Looks to me, like we have plenty of time for a long story."

Over the next hour, Clay told his friend about how he'd gone back to Tennessee to help Loralie with the horse rustlers and how one thing led to another and he'd asked her to come back to Texas with him and get married. Then, when they arrived at the ranch, Victoria was waiting for him and before Loralie got off the train, Victoria had proposed to him."

"Lord Almighty," Marion said. "So, what are you gonna do?"

Clay sighed and said, "Both of them are good women and I don't want to hurt either one of 'em, and from the sound of things, I won't have to make a choice. I've already asked Loralie to marry me and since she's the only one there..."

"Sounds like she's made the decision for you," Marion stated.

Clay ground out the butt of his cigarette on the top of his saddle horn and tossed the pieces to the wind. "You're right. I guess she has." And with that, he tapped his heels to the sides of the black stallion, grabbed his lariat, raised it in the air and yelled, "Yee haw, forcing the cattle to move a little faster.

He Who Bites rode up next to Marion and asked, "What put a burr under his saddle?"

Marion grinned and said, "I think your boss is about to try and saddle a tornado and he's anxious to see how it goes."

He Who Bites rode around to the far side of the herd and helped keep the cattle moving in the direction of Marion Sooner's ranch, not understanding what Marion meant by his comment. "White men talk in circles," he said as he brought a stray back into the herd.

-

Loralie was just leaving the corral when she looked up and saw Clay, Riley and He Who Bites riding toward the front gate. She smiled and her heart began to beat faster. She took a deep breath and stood waiting for her soon to be husband to come to her.

Clay saw Loralie standing in the yard and touched his heels to the black stallion's sides and felt the big horse leap into a run. At seeing her standing there with the sun shining off her hair and the smile on her face, an eagerness to hold her in his arms filled him with desire.

He reined the big horse to a sliding stop just in front of her and jumped down to the ground.

Loralie flung herself into his arms and kissed him boldly on the mouth. Not only was he pleased, but confused why she would do such a thing in front of everyone.

When they finally released each other, Clay looked around and didn't see Victoria or her vaqueros. "So, she really is gone?" Clay asked, expecting to see Victoria come out the door of the house at any moment.

Loralie sighed. She knew this time would come; she just wasn't looking forward to it. How was she going to explain the lie she'd told to get Victoria to leave? And what would Clay think of her for what she'd done? Sometimes her anger caused her to do things without thinking them through.

"You must be tired. Did you get everyone's cattle back? What happened out there? Did you capture the rustlers? I can hardly wait to hear the whole story," Loralie said, pulling Clay toward the house, trying her best to change the subject as Ol' Son jumped around, wanting some attention, too.

Clay reached down and rubbed Ol' Son's ears and forehead, then followed Loralie, still looking around, confused. Why was Loralie so anxious to change the subject about Victoria? She still hadn't told him what she'd said to make her leave, which made him somewhat suspicious.

They had just stepped onto the porch when Victoria's buggy came through the front gate with her vaqueros trailing along behind.

"Looks like she's back," Clay said without much excitement. Secretly he'd hoped she'd changed her mind and really had gone back to New Mexico, but apparently, she hadn't. Maybe she'd just gone into Seymour to do some shopping. There was a stack of boxes in the back of the buggy. He gave a deep sigh. Now he would have to confront her with his decision. Chasing down outlaws might be easier than what he had to do.

Loralie just stood there, staring. She couldn't believe the woman had come back. The fat would now be in the fire for sure, she thought to herself. Victoria would confront her about her lie, in front of Clay.

"Clay," Loralie whispered, cautiously. "There's something I need to tell you."

"Can't it wait," Clay asked, not wanting to face both Loralie and Victoria. He wasn't sure how Victoria would react and the last thing he wanted to do was to hurt her, but he didn't see any other way.

"No," Loralie said. "What I have to say needs to be said, now," she told him as she looked past Clay and saw the determined look on Victoria's face.

"Clay, I need to talk to you – both of you. I think you have been misled." Victoria said, stepping down from her buggy.

CHAPTER SEVEN

-

There wasn't room to house all twelve of the cattle rustlers in the small jail in Seymour and the newly appointed sheriff was at a loss as to what to do. For the time being he put all twelve men in the two small cells that were only designed for two each.

The mayor, Angus Dalton, was sitting at a table in the hotel dining room, waiting on his wife, Beatrice, to join him. They had supper here every Wednesday evening, but this evening was special. The waiter had brought him a whiskey with a glass of water on the side to drink while he waited.

This evening was special for more than one reason. First and foremost, it was the three-year anniversary from the day he'd been elected as mayor of Seymour, Texas, and he was proud of his accomplishments. With money Beatrice had inherited, they owned the mercantile store, which for the most part, his wife ran. They also had purchased a few pieces of property along the main street that they rented out to the barber, a Chinese laundry and the town's only attorney.

During his tincture, he had been responsible for the remodeling of the school and hiring a new teacher, which was turning out to be a major accomplishment. Cleaning up the storefronts in the downtown area had also been his idea. Well, maybe his wife's idea, but it was he that had pitched the idea to the city council and got their approval. He'd made a big hit with the Ladies Church League when he put a midnight closing time on all the saloons inside the city limits. And his latest accomplishment had been the recent hiring of this new sheriff who had just brought in a dozen cattle rustlers, which would make the ranchers happy and hopefully get them off his back.

He was enjoying his drink when his wife walked into the dining room and stopped and looked around. Why she did that Angus was not sure since they sat at the same table every Wednesday. Angus swallowed the last of his drink and sat the glass on the table next to them, then drank the water. Beatrice didn't approve of drinking alcohol.

As Beatrice walked toward where her husband was waiting, she saw him put the empty whiskey glass on the table next to theirs, but said nothing. Angus wasn't like a large number of the men in town who made a habit of frequenting the saloons, so… she supposed she could indulge him in this one small discrepancy from time to time.

Angus stood up and held the chair for his wife, and after a peck on the cheek, she sat down.

"Have you heard the news?" he asked.

"You mean about our new sheriff capturing the cattle rustlers?" Beatrice asked, knowing full well that was what he was talking about. Angus Dalton was nowhere near the man of her dreams, but he was faithful, and she could control him easy enough... And he was after all, the mayor. She'd made sure of that during election time.

"Yes. Yes, isn't it exciting?" Angus asked, hoping she was as happy as he was.

Beatrice got a questioning look on her face and asked, "Wasn't it everyone's belief that it was Indians who were stealing the cattle? And if that's true, why did he bring in white men?"

Angus beamed. "It was, my dear, it truly was. But it was the new sheriff, whom I chose, that discovered the truth. It was white men posing as Indians to throw the law off their trail. But our new sheriff was far too smart to be fooled."

Beatrice smiled and accepted the tea the waiter brought. She always had the same thing whenever they dined here, which was always Wednesday – including the pot-roast. As she stirred sugar into her tea, she wondered just how the new sheriff had accomplished capturing the cattle rustlers. In her opinion, he was not the assertive kind and had been puzzled by her husband's choice of men to act as sheriff of Seymour. She guessed there was more to this story than the new sheriff was telling. She wasn't sure just how she would go about it, but somehow, she would uncover the real story.

The waiter had just brought their dinners and they had taken only a few bites when the new sheriff and the rancher, Carroll Atkins came striding up to their table. The sheriff took off his hat and said, "Pardon me ma'am," then turned to the mayor, "I hate to interrupt your supper, but I need to speak to you on an urgent matter."

Angus swallowed the piece of meat he'd been chewing, then looked up at the sheriff. "Can't it wait until I've finished my supper?"

Carroll Atkins looked at the mayor's wife, who was scowling at him for the interruption and doffed his hat, knowing she was really the one calling the shots in their family.

"Begging your pardon, ma'am. I see we've come at a bad time. We'll just wait at the bar until you've finished your meal."

With that, he grabbed the sheriff's arm and hurried off in the direction of the bar, where they could get a stiff drink, or two.

"What was that all about?" Beatrice asked her husband who had gone back to eating as though nothing had happened.

"What?" Angus asked. "Oh, you mean, the sheriff and Mister Atkins? I haven't the slightest idea. Maybe he's just a bit excited about bringing those rustlers in and wants to talk about it."

"Maybe you're right," Beatrice said and returned to her meal, not fully convinced.

Since the sheriff didn't have to pay for his drinks here at the hotel bar, he and Carroll Atkins were on their third drink when Angus walked up and accepted his second glass of whiskey of the evening from the bartender.

"So, what's so urgent you had to interrupt my meal?" Angus asked with a bit of touchiness in his voice.

The sheriff finished off his drink and waved for the bartender to bring him another one. "You've got to do something, Mayor. You surely do."

"What in God's name are you talking about, man?" He was at a loss as to what the sheriff was talking about.

"The jail, Mayor, the jail. You've got to do something."

The mayor looked at the sheriff and could see he was very agitated. "What about the jail?"

The sheriff took a long pull of his fourth drink and said, "Mayor, that jail is too small. I've got twelve men crowded into two cells that shouldn't have more than four men in them. I need a place to put eight prisoners until the circuit judge decides what to do with them. And didn't you say he wouldn't be here for another two or three weeks?"

Angus was taken back. He couldn't remember ever being inside the jail, so he'd never given thought to the number of prisoners it would hold. "Eight, you say?" the mayor asked, knowing they couldn't keep twelve men in that small of a space for any length of time.

"Yes sir, eight. Our jail was only designed to hold four prisoners at a time and right now I have an even dozen over there standing shoulder to shoulder in each cell. And I come to you because you're the mayor and you need to do something about it."

"I see your point," Angus said, as his mind ran rampant trying to come up with a solution to the problem.

Just at that time, Cyrus Clemmons came into the bar for his evening glass of whiskey. He liked the taste of whiskey, and because of that, he allowed himself only one drink a night to help him sleep. At least that was the excuse he gave himself.

"Evenin' Mayor, Sheriff, Carroll," Cyrus said as he sat down on a stool next to the other men.

"Good evening, Cyrus. How's business?" the mayor asked, being cordial.

Cyrus took a sip of his drink and sighed. "Not too good right now. Things are kinda slow, but I got enough blacksmith work ta keep me from starvin' until the horse boardin' business picks up again."

"Well, let's hope..." the mayor said when suddenly the seed of an idea popped into his head. He looked at the sheriff and grinned, then back to Cyrus. "Let me ask you, my good man, how large are the stalls in your barn?"

Cyrus Clemmons looked at the mayor and wondered why he would ask such a question and decided he would show off his knowledge about such things. "Well now, Mayor, that depends on the size of the horse. A normal, fifteen-hand horse can be comfortable in a stall ten by ten, or ten by twelve. But me, I have to contend with all sizes of horses, so I don't take any chances. When I built my barn, I had all the stalls built twelve by twelve. Why do you ask?"

The mayor looked over at the sheriff who was equally puzzled, and said, "I have an idea."

Looking back at Cyrus, the mayor asked, "How many empty stalls do you have at the moment, and how much do you rent them for?"

Cyrus thought for a moment and said, "I got twenty-four stalls, but only two of 'em are bein' used at this time, so I reckon that means I got twenty-two empty ones. Like I said, business is kinda slow right now."

"And how much do they rent for?" the mayor asked.

"Ah dollar ah day, which includes hay and water. If they want oats, that's an extra fifty cents."

The mayor smiled and asked, "Cyrus, what if I was to tell you the town would rent all twenty-two stalls for the next two or three weeks, could I get a deal?"

"The next two or three weeks, you say?" Cyrus asked, the wheels in his head running like dry cattle headed for water.

The mayor nodded his head. "Yes. The next two to three weeks – all twenty-two stalls and you would only need feed and water for twelve stalls," the mayor said, thinking of the rustler's horses.

"If I don't have ta provide hay, I reckon I can let 'em go for fifty cents ah day," Cyrus said, still puzzled.

A light came on in Carroll Atkins' head and he punched the mayor on the shoulder. "Now that's some creative thinking, Mayor. Yes sir, some very creative thinking."

The mayor smiled and said, "Thank you. I see you understand where I'm going with this."

"I do. And I like it," Carroll responded.

"Well I don't and if I'm gonna be involved, I'd like to know what I'll be dealing with," the sheriff said.

Before the evening was over, the town had rented all the stalls Cyrus had to offer and not only had the rustler's horses been put into stalls, but eight of the rustlers had been chained in the stalls, as well.

"Well I'll be hog swallered," Cyrus said, grinning from ear to ear. "That's the derndest thing I ever did see. But I do have one question. Who's gonna watch over 'em – you know, bring their meals to 'em and let 'em out to go ta the privy – that sort of thing?"

"Well I can't be here twenty-four hours a day. I have a town to look after," the sheriff said before the mayor had a chance to volunteer him.

The mayor gave a big sigh and said, "the town council isn't going to like it but I guess they'll have to hire a deputy or maybe, two – at least, on a temporary basis."

The sheriff liked the idea of having a couple of deputies, even if it was only for a short while, but it was Cyrus who came up with a good idea.

"Why does the city council have to hire the deputies? Why don't them rich ranchers pitch in and help pay for all this. After all, look at all the money the sheriff saved them by capturing the men who was stealin' their cows."

The mayor looked at Cyrus and shook his head. "You know, Cyrus, I don't understand why folks say you're not a very bright fella. I guess none of them ever thought about it but running the stable and being one of the best blacksmiths I've ever seen, with a steady clientele means you're a pretty good businessman. You have a thriving business, which is better than some that I can think of. Living in those rooms off your office like you do is smart too – saves renting a room or buying a house."

Cyrus Clemmons lowered his head so they wouldn't see him blush. It was true; folks didn't seem to give him much thought and when they did, they thought he was an uneducated buffoon because he stayed to himself mostly and didn't do much socializing.

But what they didn't know and most likely would have been shocked to hear was that he had two years of college from a school back in Georgia and was a silent partner in several businesses around the state – like a cattle ranch down south, near Houston, a thriving hotel and restaurant in Dallas, along with a gold mine up in Colorado. He was actually a wealthy man. In one more year he planned to sell his business here in Seymour and retire at the ripe old age of thirty-five. He'd been secretly seeing the widow, Gloria Travis, that owned the dress shop. They planned on getting married and traveling to all the places they'd only heard talk of. He could hardly wait to see the shocked faces when they found out.

"Thank you, Mayor. That's right kind of you," Cyrus said with as much humility as he could muster.

Since he was in town, which didn't happen very often, Riley had decided a good, hot bath and barber shave was number one on his priority list, along with some clean clothes before going to supper. He'd gone to the mercantile and purchased new jeans, a nice shirt, a pair of socks and new underwear before checking into the hotel for the night. It was too late to be riding back to the ranch. Uncaring that the jail cells were too small to hold all twelve prisoners, Riley soaked in a tub of hot water, while downing three mugs of cold beer – trying to enjoy every minute of his free time. He wished Cindy could be here with him, but that wouldn't be proper, them not being married, yet.

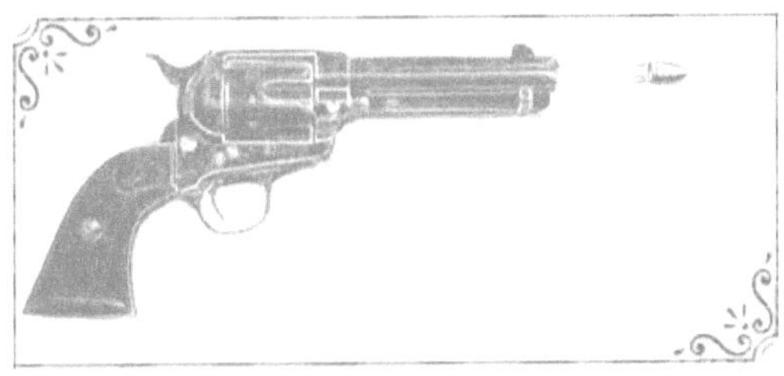

CHAPTER EIGHT

-

Victoria Ontiveros stepped down from her buggy and straightened her dress, then headed to where Clay and Loralie were standing on the front porch.

Loralie knew she didn't have much time and said, "I felt like I was in a war, Clay. Look at her. She's beautiful. She's educated. And she's rich. How am I supposed to compete with the likes of her? I was desperate and I had to think of something to make her go away – and telling her I was carrying your child was the one thing I thought would do it. And I could be, I reckon, but it's too soon to tell. I thought we would be rid of her for good, but now she's back and she will find out the truth. Are you mad at me Clay, for what I done?"

Clay looked down at the face looking up at him – a beautiful face whose eyes were filled with fear. How could he ever be mad at this crazy, impulsive redhead who cared that much about him? "No, I'm not mad at you. In fact, I came back with the intentions of telling

Victoria that I have no desire to marry her. It's you I want to marry and spend the rest of my days with."

"And the nights with, too," Loralie teased.

"Yes. And the nights too," Clay said with a big smile on his face.

Loralie threw her arms around Clay's neck and kissed him on the mouth with all the passion she was feeling – knowing Victoria would see them.

Victoria stopped halfway to the porch and watched as Loralie kissed Clay, and for just a moment, she was tempted to get back in her buggy and go back to Seymour and wait for the next train going to Albuquerque. But when the embrace ended and Loralie looked down at her and gave her a smug look like she'd just won some big contest, a stubbornness welled up inside her and she took a deep breath. If this hillbilly from Tennessee wanted a fight, she would get one.

Clay stood there and watched as Victoria walked toward them with a determined look on her face. At this moment he wished he could be anywhere but right here.

Victoria walked up next to Loralie and Clay, then, without a word, she reached up and took Clay's face in her hands and kissed him passionately.

When the kiss ended, Victoria released Clay's face and turned to Loralie, giving her a look that said, I am still here, and I haven't given up.

Loralie looked at Victoria and said, "I thought you went back to where you come from."

"As you can see, I have changed my mind."

"Why?" Loralie asked, already knowing the answer.

"I came back because I believe you lied to me. I don't believe you are carrying Clay's child – and I'm right, aren't I? You just told me that so I would leave. Well, as you can see, your lie didn't work."

Victoria turned and looked at Clay and said, "I have come back to get this settled once and for all. I want to hear it from you; but first, I have something I want to say to you in private."

Before he had a chance to say anything, Mrs. McIntyre walked out onto the porch and announced lunch was ready. She had been watching and listening from just inside the front door and decided this was something best taken care of inside the house in case the two women chose to get physical, which it looked like they might. She knew Loralie was just a hairs breath away from losing her temper. Things could get ugly and if it did, it shouldn't happen in front of the ranch hands.

Giving a sigh, Clay stepped aside and allowed Mrs. McIntyre, Loralie and Victoria to enter the house ahead of him. When they were inside, he was tempted to take off for the barn - get a horse and make a run for it, but Mrs. McIntyre saw the look in his eyes and turned back, taking hold of his arm. "Not so fast, you have two very agitated women inside the house and unless you want to see bloodshed, I suggest ya face up to 'em, and get this thing settled once and for all. After all, you're the one they're fightin' over." This last remark brought a slight chuckle that she tried to cover up with her hand.

Clay looked at her and knew she was right. He swallowed a large gulp of air and walked into the house. What was he afraid of? Victoria wouldn't shoot him if he told her he wanted to marry Loralie, would she?

The two women were already sitting at the dining room table, staring daggers at each other. Cindy had purposely placed them across the table from each other, making it harder for an actual fight to break out. Clay's place was at the head of the table where he always sat.

As Clay took his seat, Mrs. McIntyre spoke up. "I'm hopin' you'll be havin' your meal in ah civilized manner. When you're finished eatin' and you've had ah bit of time ta cool down, I'm sure Mister Brentwood will settle this matter once and for all, now eat."

Mrs. McIntyre had spent the morning making a pot of Irish stew and several pans of soda bread, which she served with the stew. Next to Clay's bowl was a small plate with several jalapeno peppers on it. She knew her boss liked a little spice with his stew. She'd thought of serving wine with the meal but changed her mind. Alcohol might not be the best option; even as low in alcohol content as wine was. Water with a slice of lemon in it would do just fine and have less of a chance for a drunken brawl.

This was the quietest lunch Clay could ever remember eating and when the dishes had been cleared, he looked at the two beautiful women sitting in front of him. Both sat with their hands folded in their laps, waiting for him to speak.

Clay stood up and looked at Victoria. "We can talk in my office," he said and turned and walked toward his one sanctuary.

When they were inside, Clay closed the double doors and asked Victoria if she would like a drink, which she declined. Even though Clay desperately wanted one, he too abstained.

Clay offered Victoria a chair, but she said she'd rather stand for what she had to say, so Clay walked over and sat down behind his desk and looked up at her.

"She is very beautiful and quite possibly more of a woman of the world than I am, but I think I would make the better mistress of this ranchero," Victoria told him.

Clay was surprised at this statement. He was sure she wanted him to go back to New Mexico with her and he was prepared for that argument, but not this.

Undaunted by the look on Clay's face, Victoria plunged ahead. "Since your leaving my ranchero, I have had much time to think about my priorities. I came into my holdings in New Mexico because of my father and husband dying – not because I saw the land and decided this would be where I wanted to spend my life. Before you came along, I was thinking of selling it. I wasn't sure where I would go, but you showed up and turned my world around, along with my ranchero. And when I was taken by the slavers, you came after me and the others they had taken. You saved all of us, but it was me you came after. I know that you felt something for me, that is why you did what you did. And even then, I knew I had feelings for you. I will make you a good wife." Victoria took a breath and sighed.

"Victoria," Clay said, but was stayed by her fingers on her lips.

"Please, let me get this out," she said. "After you left, my life became empty, again, and I considered coming to see you many times, but for the wrong reason. I wanted you to come back to New Mexico and be the Patron on my ranchero. Finally, I realized that wasn't what I wanted at all. I wanted to be with you. And it didn't matter where, as long as we were together. I will sell my ranchero and move here and be the mistress of this fine ranch."

Clay just sat there, staring at her, unsure what to say.

"Clay, I am young and hopefully I can bear you several sons and maybe a daughter for me. I am intelligent and would make an excellent mistress here at your ranchero. And I could not miss the fact that this ranchero was built very similar to mine. We have so much in common, Clay. I promise, you will not be sorry if you chose me. Plus, I will bring my vaqueros, which will add to your ability to keep the rustlers away. And they already know and admire you, so there will be no trouble."

Victoria walked around Clay's desk and reached out and took his hands in hers as if to validate her hopes.

Clay had just cleared his throat when Riley and Running Coyote came barging into Clay's office and stopped next to him. He looked up at his two foremen and said, "I'm kinda busy, so this had better be good."

"I think it might be, boss," Riley said. I spent the night in town and just got back a couple of hours ago. The sheriff and another man just rode through the gate and we weren't sure what ta do – you bein' in here with the ladies and all," he said with a grin.

"No sir, we weren't sure if we should interrupt you or not?" Running Coyote added.

By then, Loralie had also entered the office and stood off to one side.

Clay looked at Loralie and Victoria and said, "You'll have to excuse me. We'll continue this later."

As Clay walked out of his office, Mrs. McIntyre came walking toward him, leading the sheriff and the mayor of Seymour.

"I'm sorry, Sir, but the sheriff insisted it was urgent he talk to you," Mrs. McIntyre said.

"It's all right," Clay told her, then turned to the sheriff and the mayor, who he recognized.

"You say you have something urgent to speak to me about?" Clay asked.

Both men took off their hats and nodded toward the two women and Clay's foremen who were standing just outside the office. "Ladies," the sheriff said, and then turned to Clay. "Can we speak to you in private?"

"Of course. We can talk in my office," Clay said, leading the way, wondering what this was all about.

As the men left the living room, Clay heard Mrs. McIntyre say, "Ladies, I have some fresh apple pie, would you both join me in the kitchen?"

When they entered his office, Clay closed the doors and walked over and poured each of them a good measure of whiskey, then asked, "Now... what is this urgent matter you want to speak to me about?"

The sheriff took a long pull on his drink, coughed, took a deep breath and said, "It's the cattle rustlers."

"What about the cattle rustlers? You haven't let them escape, have you?"

Both the mayor and the sheriff looked down at their feet.

"The jail is only big enough to hold four prisoners, so I locked up the rest of them in the livery barn, but somehow..." the sheriff mumbled.

"They got loose and broke their friends out of jail," Clay finished the sentence for him.

"They dynamited the whole side of the jail," the sheriff said, raising his arms in the air.

"If you'll remember, I've already told you, I'm no longer in the ranger business," Clay explained, again, wondering why this new sheriff was having so much trouble.

"Yes. Yes, I recall you making that very clear, but there's more," the mayor said.

Clay felt the hair on the back of his neck stand straight up. "What do you mean, more?"

"They robbed the bank and took hostages," the mayor said, shaking his head.

"Hostages?" Who?" Clay asked. He still hadn't taken a sip of his drink, yet, but felt like he might need more than one.

"Three women," the sheriff told him. "The mayor's wife, Beatrice, Gloria Travis, who owns the ladies store in Seymour, and a young woman by the name of Barbara Peoples who just happened to be with Miss Travis at the time. She's new in town."

"And you want me to go after them." Clay stated.

The mayor swallowed the rest of his drink and said, "Technically, the way your boss back in Austin said in his telegram, you're still a Ranger. And you also have what the sheriff here tells me – is one of the best trackers he's ever seen. The town of Seymour would be very appreciative if you could help us. I surely do want my wife back, unharmed, if possible, but either way, I want her back, along with the other two. I'd be willing to pay for their return."

Clay remembered back to the time when Victoria and some other women had been kidnapped by slavers. "Running Coyote! Riley!" he called out and was surprised when the doors opened almost immediately.

"Yeah, boss?" Riley asked as he and Running Coyote entered the room.

"We thought you might need us, so we were waiting just outside the door," Running Coyote explained.

"Tell, He Who Bites to saddle four horses, two for him and two for me, along with a pack horse. I want to be ready to travel within an hour. I want Midnight and the buckskin mare, Lucy, for my two."

"You need either of us ta go along?" Riley asked, knowing his boss would probably say, no, but if there was a chance for some adventure, he wanted to be included.

"The cattle rustlers have escaped, and I need the two of you right here, watching over things in case they try stealing any of our cattle." Clay told him.

Clay walked into the kitchen and asked Cindy to fix bowls of stew for the mayor and the sheriff, and then turned to Mrs. McIntyre and asked her to put some supplies together for him and He Who Bites, stating they might be gone at least a week or so.

"What's wrong?" Loralie asked.

"The cattle rustlers have escaped, and they took three women hostages," Clay said.

Victoria took in a deep breath, remembering what it was like being a kidnap victim.

"You must go," Victoria said. "We will settle this matter when you return."

Clay looked at Victoria, then at Loralie, then back to Victoria. "No, it needs to be settled now."

Taking a moment before speaking, he finally looked at Victoria and said, "I'm sorry, Victoria."

Victoria felt as though she'd been kicked in the chest, but being who she was, she stood up and walked over and stopped in front of Clay, then reached up and kissed him on the cheek. "Bring those women back and be careful, Clay Brentwood."

And with that, she left the house, calling out to her vaqueros, "Get the buggy ready, we are leaving."

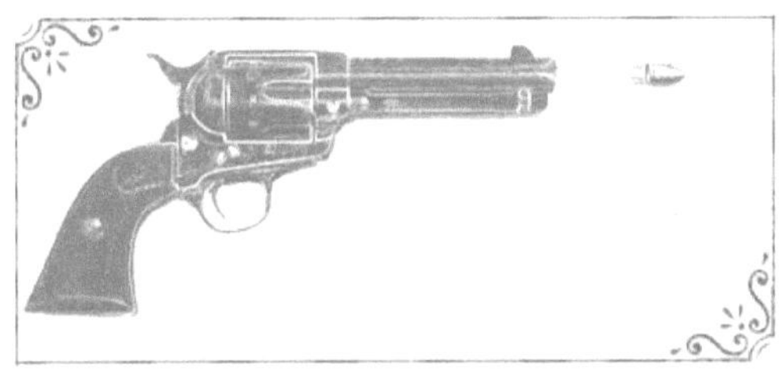

CHAPTER NINE

As they rode away from Clay's ranch, He Who Bites asked the sheriff, "How long ago did they make their escape?"

"Last night," the sheriff said. "At first, we tried to follow them, but the road was filled with tracks. There is a lot of coming and going in and out of Seymour."

"And you think I can find their tracks in among all those other tracks you speak of?" He Who Bites asked, shaking his head.

The sheriff just shrugged his shoulders, and the mayor smiled at He Who Bites, like he had all the confidence in the world in him.

He Who Bites rode up next to Clay and said, "Before we get into town, we should go off to the sides of the road and look for tracks. That many riders will be hard pressed to hide their trail. And maybe they headed this way."

Clay nodded his head and said, "You say when. I'll take the north side and you take the south side of the road. We'll meet up back at the edge of town if we don't find tracks, first."

He Who Bites dropped back and spoke to the sheriff and the mayor. "Before we get into town, Mister Brentwood and I will scout this side of town for tracks, out and away from the road. You two go on into town and we'll meet you at the sheriff's office."

"You think they might have left the road?" the mayor asked.

"That would be a reasonable assumption," He Who Bites told him.

The mayor shook his head and rolled his eyes. "For an Indian, you sure do speak well. I wasn't aware that Indians had such a good use of the Queen's language."

Giving the mayor a stern look, He Who Bites said, "There is a lot of things about Indians that might surprise you, Mayor. It appears to me that white people make a lot of assumptions without having any facts to back them up."

With that, he nudged his horse's sides and made his way back up next to Clay.

"What if they don't find their trail?" the mayor asked of the sheriff.

"Then I guess they'll have three more sides of town to check," the sheriff replied.

"Won't that take a lot of time?" the mayor asked.

The sheriff lit a small cigar and asked, "Do you have a better way of doing it?"

The mayor looked at the sheriff and said, "No. But my wife is out there with them and if we wait too long..."

The mayor's words trailed off into the wind. He was worried. He wanted his wife back safe and sound, if possible. But he also knew he was not qualified, nor brave enough, to go after them. That's why they'd gone out to see Clay. The man had a reputation of being tough and had brought many an outlaw to justice.

It was coming up on late afternoon by the time they reached the point where they would split off to each side of the road to look for the rustler's tracks – in case this was the way they might have come. No evidence of a large group of riders had been seen on the road coming out of town.

Clay hauled up close to half a mile from the edge of town and rode over next to the sheriff and the mayor, "You take our extra horses and go on into town. We'll be along soon. We can't waste much time. It'll be dark soon and their tracks will be even harder to find."

As the mayor and the sheriff rode on toward Seymour, Clay turned the black stallion off the road to the north and began hunting for sign.

South of the road, He Who Bites kept his paint horse at a steady pace as he watched the ground for any sign of a large group of horses traveling in this direction.

It was coming up on six o'clock when Clay and He Who Bites met up at the west edge of town.

"If they're riding to the west, they're riding on air and not leaving any tracks," Clay said as he brought the black stallion to a halt next to, He Who Bites.

"Other than a few wild animal tracks, I found no tracks made by horses on my side of the road, either," He Who Bites told Clay.

In the sheriff's office, Clay informed the sheriff and the mayor that there was not much else they could do tonight. "It's too dark and there isn't much of a moon to see by."

"But we can't just..." the mayor tried to protest, but Clay raised his hand and stopped him.

"I'm sorry, Mayor. I know you're worried and no one can fault you for that, but the truth is, we can't do anything more until daylight. If they followed the road, it's going to be very difficult to pick up their trail unless we have a shoe mark to follow. Our best hope is that they left the road and headed to a hideout somewhere. Come first light, He Who Bites, and I will go out again. If they left the road, we'll find their trail."

The sheriff asked, "And if they didn't leave the road?"

"Then we'll just have to second guess which way they're going," Clay said, matter-of-factly. "Now, if you don't mind, we'll see to our horses, then check into the hotel and after that, get something to eat. Will you be joining us?"

"We'll see about a table in the hotel dining room," the sheriff told them. Then as an afterthought, he asked, "Do you suppose they serve Indians?"

"Clay looked at the sheriff and the mayor as a grin began to spread across his face. "I happen to know the owner of the hotel, and let's just say, he has a few secrets he'd just as soon I keep, secret.

No, Sheriff, there won't be any trouble with He Who Bites eating with us or staying at the hotel."

The mayor sighed – relieved there wouldn't be any trouble or as head of the city council, he would wind up in the middle of it "So be it, we'll see you at the hotel. Then in the morning, I'll be going with you, if it's all right with you?"

Clay took off his hat and wiped the sweat from the inside band. "Sorry, but it isn't. No offense, but you'd just be in the way and to be truthful, because your wife is one of the captives, your emotions might get one or more of us killed. No, it's better if just He Who Bites, and I go."

"You mean you don't want me, either?" the sheriff asked, trying to act flabbergasted.

Clay didn't want him along either. He was a greenhorn in matters like this, but he was smart enough to know not to belittle the sheriff in front of the mayor. "You need to be here in case they come back. I have a feeling they'll be wanting some ransom money," Clay told him, hoping that would pacify him enough to keep him here. "They're cattle rustlers, not slavers, so I don't think they'll go far before asking for ransom money."

"But... but they already robbed the bank!" the mayor blurted out.

"And did they get it all?" Clay asked, knowing as a bank owner himself, the man he had running his bank for him always kept a large sum in a different, hidden safe, just in case of emergencies like this.

"Well, I suppose there might be some money they didn't get, but..."

"Mayor, these are men without scruples. They could care less if this town goes belly up because of them. The only thing important to them is the money. So, don't be surprised when they show up asking for it," Clay told him, looking back at the sheriff.

The sheriff tried not to show how relieved he was at not being invited to go along, and what Clay had said, gave him exactly the out he needed. "Yes, I think you're on to something. If they do send someone, I might be able to force him to tell me where the rest of them are hiding."

Again, Clay didn't want to embarrass the sheriff, so he said, "Yes, that's one way. But in my experience, whoever they send in will be someone who wouldn't talk if you took a blacksnake whip to him."

"Do you have a better idea?" the sheriff asked.

"I don't know if it's a better idea, just a different one," Clay said with a smile. "If it was me, I think I might agree to pay the ransom, but tell him it will take a couple of days to raise the money – then watch what kind of horse he's riding and make sure we have a good look at the prints his horse leaves. By then He Who Bites and I will be back and we can track him to their hideout; maybe even take a posse with us."

The mayor looked at the sheriff and nodded his head. "I think that's a splendid idea."

Later, at the hotel over their supper, Clay explained the next morning's plan. "As I see it, they're gonna need someplace to hole up until they get their hands on some ransom money, and with that many horses, they're gonna need more than just a waterhole. To the north, there's the Wichita River, but I figure that's too far way. The Brazos River is right south and west of here and their best bet. It runs all the way down to the coast, giving them plenty of water."

"What about the east?" the mayor asked.

Clay shook his head. "If they got any sense, they won't go that direction. There's no water for a long way that I know of, and not many places to hole up. Wichita Falls is the closest town and it's a good two-day ride. No, if it were me, I would head north for a few miles, then turn west toward the Brazos."

CHAPTER TEN

-

Cameron Longhand spent most of his life in the US Army and his last post was Fort Smith, Arkansas. At the time he was a sergeant with a wife and a son. Sergeant Longhand had never been a very good soldier and had only been made sergeant because of an incident when the patrol he was in was attacked and he happened to shoot an outlaw who was about to kill his commanding officer, thereby saving the colonel's life. The colonel was so appreciative that he raised Cameron's rank from corporal to sergeant, and then later, wished that he hadn't.

Shortly after being posted to Fort Smith, Sergeant Longhand fell in with a bunch of lowlifes at the saloon. In a short time, he was drinking, gambling and slapping his wife and son around while in a drunken stupor. When called to answer his deeds in front of his commanding officer, Sergeant Longhand's temper got the best of him and he ran around the desk and commenced beating on the colonel. Needless to say, Sergeant Longhand was court-martialed and drummed out of the army.

On his own, Cameron Longhand began hanging around with his friends from the saloon and shortly, was involved in a bank robbery for which he was never caught. In fact, the man was never seen again. Where he went was anyone's guess.

By now his son, James, was sixteen and running wild - and when his mother married a man James didn't see eye to eye with, James left home.

He was an even six feet tall and had a reputation for liking a good fight. In twenty-one barroom brawls, he'd never been beaten. During that time, James won a pistol and holster in a bare-knuckle fistfight contest where he beat the other man so bad the man had to be taken to the hospital.

Now that he was the proud owner of a forty-four caliber six shot pistol, he got it into his head to become a gun slick and began to practice in earnest. He was a natural and within a few weeks, he felt he was ready for his first shootout. He wanted to know what it felt like to kill a man.

His first gunfight was with a young man only a year older than himself, who came into the bar wearing a sidearm. James could see the young man was drinking heavily and faking a run-in with the young man, he challenged him to a gunfight. The young man had his pistol only halfway out of his holster when James' bullet penetrated his heart. And so, suddenly, James Longhand became a gun for hire.

James Longhand left Fort Smith, Arkansas at the ripe old age of seventeen, just ahead of the law. He was wanted for rape and robbery, along with six questionable shootouts. A few weeks later he found himself hiding in the badlands of the Oklahoma Territory. Being young and restless, he left the badlands as soon as he felt it was safe and drifted down into Texas. That had been ten years ago.

Since then, almost all of his time in Texas had been spent running from the law for one crime or another. He was wanted for four different charges of rape, several questionable shootings, cattle rustling and several other lesser crimes including robbery. During his time on the owl hoot trail he'd acquired a name for himself and had a following of young men who looked up to him for his fast gun and bluster about being so good that no man could best him with a gun or his fists.

Being jailed for cattle rustling made James even angrier than he normally was. If convicted, it would mean he would hang, and he was for damn sure, not ready to die.

As fate would have it, James was one of the ones held in the livery barn, which suited him just fine. He always kept a knife in a sheath inside his boot and was able to get to the knife and cut his bonds. After that, he released the other men, and on their way out of the barn, James noticed a case of dynamite sitting near the doorway. He grinned and said, "Boys, gettin' our friends outta the jail is gonna be ah piece of cake. He then assigned all of the men but his second in command, Bill Musgrove, to get their horses ready for a quick get-away.

When he was about to leave the barn with several sticks of dynamite, he happened to see three women going into the bank. And just like that, an idea filled his head. He would show that hick sheriff who was king of the roost.

"Saddle up three extra horses," he called over his shoulder. "And a couple of you go over to the mercantile store and get some food supplies ta take along with us. Be sure ta get enough ta feed all of us for at least ah week. And make sure whoever is in the store can't go yelling their heads off to the sheriff. And be quiet about it. We don't want ta bring no attention ta what we're doin' until we've helped our friends escape from that two-bit jail."

And with that, he and his second in command headed for the bank, walking along at a leisurely pace so as to not attract attention.

Again, fortune was with James. When they entered the bank, the only ones in there were the bank teller, the three women and the bank president.

James walked up next to Beatrice and stuck his pistol barrel against her ribs and said, "Be very quiet, lady and tell your friends to be quiet, too, if they want ta go on breathin'."

While James was taking care of the ladies, Bill walked directly into the bank president's office and slapped him alongside his head, knocking him unconscious. He then returned to the main part of the bank and did the same thing to the teller.

After filling several sacks with money, they hung a closed sign on the front door and left with the three women in tow. Bill locked the door with a key he found hanging just inside the door, on a peg stuck in the wall. As they passed a watering tough, Bill dropped the key in the water and watched as it sunk to the bottom.

Back in the barn, several of the men gagged the women, put them on the extra horses and tied them to the saddles while James and Bill headed for the jail to finish what they'd started.

The backside of the jail was facing an open field so there was no one to see what they were doing.

The explosion blew most of the wall away and the four outlaws rushed out and ran to the barn where their friends were waiting. The outlaw gang, with James Longhand in the lead, left the rear door of the barn like their tails were on fire and rode hard toward the north.

Three miles north of Seymour, James called a halt and sat for a minute, deciding their next move.

"We gonna have us some fun with them women?" one of the young outlaws asked, eyeing the youngest of the three women.

"What?" James asked him. He'd been concentrating on where to go and how to get some ransom money for the return of the women and had not given pleasuring himself any thought.

James looked at the three women and grinned. "Why not," he told the young outlaw. "But not til we get to ah place where we can feel safe from anybody followin' us."

"And when might that be?" the young cowboy asked. It had been a long time since he'd been with a woman and he was eager to get to it.

James felt anger well up inside him. He didn't like being questioned. His eyes turned mean and he said, "Don't push me. I'll tell you when it's time..."

The young outlaw, who had only been with the gang for a couple of weeks, saw death in his boss' eyes and backed his horse up a few steps. "Sure boss. Anything you say, boss."

When James just glared at him, the young outlaw pulled his horse around and went as far away from James as he could get.

James lit a small cigar. He could think better with a cigar, and by the time he was half finished, he'd put a plan together in his mind.

Looking over to his second in command, Bill Musgrove, he said, "Tell the men we'll ride on north for another mile or so, then cut back west. The Brazos ain't too far and we'll make camp there."

Bill Musgrove actually had more schooling than James did, but he didn't have the power over men that James did. He had two years of college and he'd been a bank teller who had gotten greedy being around all that money and had dipped into the funds up in Omaha. And when he was accused of the deed, after punching the bank manager, he'd stolen a horse and fled south.

He'd been with James for a couple of years now and his brains had earned him second in command of the group. Everyone seemed to like him and had no trouble taking orders from him. If the truth were known, they liked Bill much better than they did James. Bill was easy going, where James was as mean as a junkyard dog, and they were afraid of his temper.

True to his word, inside a clump of elm trees, James called a halt and told the men to look around and find some broken tree branches that still had leaves on them. He said they would be heading west and dragging the branches behind them to wipe out their tracks. If a posse was following them, the tracks would end here in the trees.

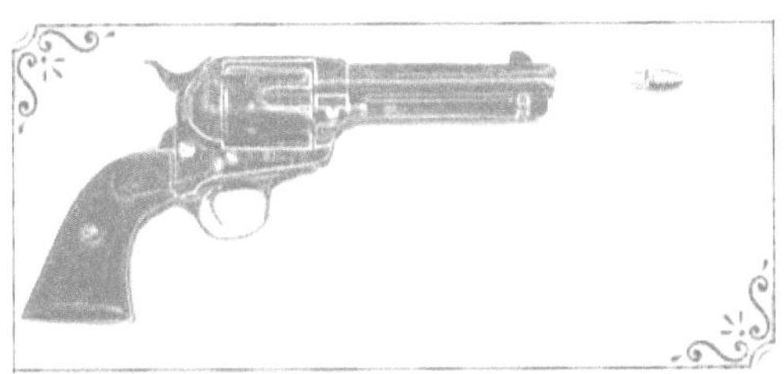

CHAPTER ELEVEN

It was Clay who found the tracks going north out of town and shook his head. They were doing exactly what he told the mayor and sheriff they might do. If they were gonna be this predictable they shouldn't be hard to catch up to.

He turned the black stallion around and rode back to town, but didn't stop and rode south of town, searching for He Who Bites. And when he'd caught up to him, they talked it over and both agreed at some point they would turn west toward the Brazos.

"No matter," Clay said, "That's the direction they went, and we need to follow them."

They stopped in town and informed the sheriff of their findings and then headed north, following the trail.

About a mile north of town, He Who Bites told Clay he had an idea. He would swing wide to the left and continue on, keeping Clay in sight. "If they turn to the west, I will see it, and if they turn to the east, you will see."

And with that, He Who Bites rode at an angle close to a quarter of a mile to the west, then continued north, keeping an eye on Clay, who followed the tracks heading north.

Close to an hour later, Clay followed the tracks into a small bunch of elm trees and pulled his horse to a halt. Inside the trees, the tracks stopped. Clay even turned around and looked to see if they had backtracked, but saw no evidence of that, knowing that if they had, he would surely have run into them. Clay rode further ahead to see if he could pick up the tracks farther on but had no luck. Next, he circled around to the east and rode back and forth – still finding no evidence of them. Riding back to the small group of Elm trees he rode through them and out toward the west. Looking around he saw He Who Bites riding toward him and rode out to meet him.

"When I rode north of the trees, I looked but didn't see you. What happened?" He Who Bites asked.

"Inside the trees, the tracks disappeared. I circled around to the east to see if I could find anything, but there was no evidence of them going that direction. What about you? Did you find any tracks?"

He Who Bites rubbed his throat, then said, "They could not just disappear unless the heavy wind that swirls in tall funnels came along and sucked them up into the sky. But I have seen no such wind funnels. The sky has been clear."

"So, where did they go?" Clay asked.

"There is a trick we have both used, and maybe they also know the trick," He Who Bites said, nodding his head up and down.

"You mean the one where they drag some brush behind them to wipe out their tracks?"

Clay asked.

"That is the one," He Who Bites replied.

"Then that means we have to widen the circles," Clay told his friend, who grinned and nodded his head.

An hour later, Clay heard two shots and came to a halt. He pulled his pistol from his holster and fired two shots in the air to indicate he'd gotten the message. He Who Bites had found the tracks. Clay touched the sides of the black stallion, and the big horse took off at a high lope, heading back toward the southwest.

A few minutes later, Clay saw He Who Bites in the distance. He had his arm in the air, waving it back and forth. Clay looked back over his shoulder and saw that the small stand of elm trees was directly behind him, but far to the east.

"Whoever is leading these men knows a little about hiding their tracks," He Who Bites told Clay when he rode up.

"Yes, but not good enough to fool a tracker like you," Clay said with a grin.

"It does not take great skill," He Who Bites said, "Only patience. Yes, I have found his trail, but he may soon have help from Mother Nature," he told Clay, pointing westward.

In the far distance, Clay could see a large black cloud heading their way and the heavy rain it was bringing with it. Looking around, Clay could see no place to get in out of the oncoming storm, which, he guessed, was no more than half an hour away.

"I think we should ride back to the stand of trees as fast as we can. It is not much, but it is better than no protection at all," He Who Bites suggested.

Nodding his head, Clay turned the black stallion back toward the elm trees and he and He Who Bites rode hard for the only protection they could see.

Longhand and his bunch had also seen the coming storm cloud and were looking for shelter and fared much better than the two men following them. As they topped over a small rise - in the distance they saw a house and barn sitting not far from the Brazos River. There was smoke coming from the chimney of the house and the barn doors were standing open.

A few minutes before the storm hit, in heavy, howling wind, the rustlers and their captives, rode into the barn and found a man pitching hay into stalls where several horses were standing.

Surprised at seeing a large group of riders that included three women, the man looked up and said, "Howdy. You got here just in time. There's a mean storm on its way."

As James stepped down from his horse, the man leaned his pitchfork against a stall and walked over, extending his hand. "I'm Simon McKenzie, and you're all welcome to step down. There's plenty of feed and water for your horses, and the missus has a pot of stew on the stove. I think there's enough for you, too."

James eyed the rancher and didn't like what he saw. The man looked to be middle aged, maybe around forty. He stood maybe five foot ten inches tall and was powerfully built. James guessed him to be in the neighborhood of two hundred pounds. The man was smiling, but there was something in his eyes that told James there would be trouble when he found out who they were. So, without a word, James jerked his pistol out of his holster and shot the man, dead center in the heart.

Simon McKenzie was pushed back two steps and stood there for a moment, a confused look on his face, then fell over backward. All three of the captive women, screamed.

Inside the ranch house, Cora McKenzie had been looking out of the window, watching the approaching storm and glancing back and forth between the dark cloud and the barn, hoping to see her husband come to the house.

When she saw the riders come across the yard and enter the barn, she noticed the three women riding with them and went to the door and opened it, intending to yell for the women to come inside, but the fierce wind pushed her back inside. She struggled to get the door closed and when she did, she went back to the window and watched the open doorway of the barn, hoping to see them come toward the house.

The howling wind carried James' gunshot and the women's screams to the ears of Cora and she jumped, bringing her hands to her mouth to stifle a scream. What kind of trouble had taken place in the barn, she didn't know, but something inside her told her Simon was in trouble. She ran over and took a rifle off the wall pegs and raced out the front door.

As she did, the wind did its best to knock her down and the pounding rain slammed against her face and body like shotgun pellets, stinging her everywhere they hit. Filled with fear for her husband, she bent into the wind and driving rain and ran for the barn.

"Company's comin'," one of the rustlers called out to James and the others as he stepped down from his horse and walked over to the side of the door.

Cora ran into the barn and pointed the rifle at the man standing not far away, with a pistol in his hand. "Drop that gun and put your hands in the air!" she yelled, looking for Simon.

The man grinned like an idiot and let his pistol drop to the floor of the barn and stepped aside so the woman could see her dead husband.

When Cora saw Simon laying on the barn floor with a small red spot in the front of his shirt, her eyes went wide and she yelled, "Simon!"

Before she could react any further, the man standing to the side of the door stepped up behind her and grabbed her with one hand, while he jerked the rifle from her hands with his other hand.

James bent down and picked up his pistol and brushed off the dirt, then put it back in his holster.

Cora was doing her best to get loose by kicking and twisting around, along with trying to hit the man with her fists, but he was strong and held her tightly. His real name was Arnold Williams, but he went by Stump, because he was short and built like a tree stump. Grinning, he asked, "What do you want me ta do with this hellcat, James?"

James Longhand got a vicious look in his eyes and said, "No names!"

Sorry, Boss. It won't happen again." Stump told him.

James Longhand walked over and slapped Cora across the face so hard, her head went back. It was the first time she'd ever been hit and she got a shocked look on her face. "Settle down, woman, or next time I'll use my fist instead of my open hand."

Feeling a stinging in her cheek, Cora quieted down and stared with hatred at the man standing in front of her.

"You want to live?" Longhand asked her.

At that point, Cora wasn't sure how to answer him. Her husband was dead and she wondered if there was anything left to live for. Reality slowly crept into her brain and she knew Simon would want her to go on. If she were dead, who would bury him? And who would raise the child she was carrying? Slowly, Cora nodded her head up and down.

"And if I tell the man holding you to turn you loose, are you gonna behave yourself?"

Again, Cora nodded her head up and down.

Longhand looked at Stump and said, "Turn her loose, but if she tries anything, break her neck."

Stump released his hold on Cora and she just stood there, glaring at the man standing in front of her. Not only was he an evil looking man, but he was looking at her with lust in his eyes that made her cringe. At that point she wasn't sure which would be worse, having to submit to this man, or death, which would amount to also killing her baby.

James looked at two of his other men and said, "Drag the man's body out the back door and leave it someplace where the coyotes can find it."

Cora couldn't control her mouth and she yelled at him, "You are a foul man. Have you no decency? At least let me bury him."

"What? And let the wild critters out there go hungry?" James said with mock concern.

Cora turned and glared at the rest of the rustlers who were all laughing at James' joke.

All, but the women. Not only were they standing there with their heads bowed, she noticed their hands were tied. They were not loose women - they were prisoners.

The oldest one raised her head and gave Cora a look that said she was sorry.

James saw the exchange and told his men, "Take the women in the house and hav 'em dish up some of that stew her husband was talkin' bout. And while you're at it, see if he has any whiskey. His missus and me are gonna stay here for a bit. We got some things ta settle between us, if you know what I mean."

The men were laughing and joking as they herded the women out into the storm. All of them broke into a dead run for the shelter and warmth of the house.

Cora watched them leave and wanted to beg them to stay, but knew it would do no good. They were animals, just like the man who gave the orders.

James stared at Cora McKenzie and felt a stirring. She was a fine figure of a woman, with wavy brown hair and large brown eyes. He guessed she was several years younger than her husband and wondered what she would look like without any clothes on? Which was something he hoped to soon find out. "Come over here, girl. We're gonna have us some fun in that hay pile over yonder," he commanded, pointing a small pile of hay nearby – the same one her husband had been pitching hay from.

Cora just stood there, gritting her teeth and glaring at him. She was filled with fear but tried hard not to show it.

"I said, get over here, now!" He yelled.

Still, Cora didn't move. She couldn't. It was as if her feet were nailed to the floor. She wanted to run, but where could she go? Nor was there anyone she could run to. She was at the mercy of this animal that had shot and killed her husband.

Tired of her resistance, James walked over and drove his fist into her stomach, driving her several feet back. She landed hard against the wall of a stall and felt a sharp pain in her back where the end of a nail penetrated her spine.

She grabbed her stomach and began to moan as she felt her body release her unborn child and at the same time, felt her own life slip away. Her last thought was that she would be with her husband, soon.

James looked down at her and saw what had happened. "Hell, lady, I didn't know you was pregnant."

After a moment, he grabbed her by the ankles and dragged her and her dead child out the back door of the barn and left them laying in the mud, next to her husband.

James was in a foul mood when he walked into the ranch house, but at this point he had lost his desire for female comfort. He sat down at the table and filled a bowl with the good smelling stew and began to eat. One of his men shoved a plate filled with home- made biscuits on it, along with a bowl of butter, over next to him.

He slathered a large amount of butter on one of the biscuits and savored the taste. It had been some time since he'd eaten food this good. Too bad the woman had to die.

Looking around, James told his men, "We'll hole up here till the storm passes. Come mornin', Bill will go back inta town with our ransom demand."

"What are we gonna do with the women in the meantime?" one of his men asked with a sneering grin on his face.

"Don't much matter ta me. We ain't gonna send 'em back, no how," James told him.

After filling his belly, James went back out to the barn and closed the doors, then laid out his bedroll on the small pile of hay and stretched out. He was tired and needed some sleep. If he'd stayed in the house, the women's screaming would have kept him awake.

If ever the devil created an evil man, it was James Longhand. He had not one bit of decency in him. He killed anyone and anything that stood in his way and never lost one minutes sleep over it

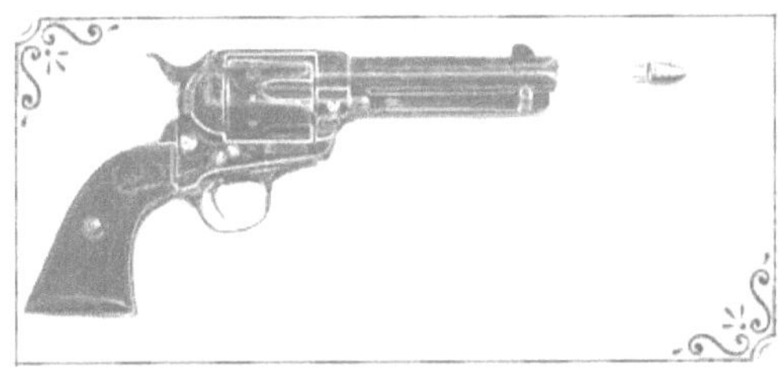

CHAPTER TWELVE

The following morning, Bill Musgrove saddled his horse and listened as James Longhand gave him explicit instructions. "There will be no trade other than money for the women. I don't want them ta be able ta lay in wait and ambush us. They are to give you the money, ten thousand dollars, in cash, today. You are to tell them you will leave a note at a place outside of town where there will be instructions as to where they can find their women. Pick a place that ain't easy to find and be vague about the instructions. We don't want them gettin' here too quick. Any questions?"

Bill finished saddling his horse, then turned and said, "No - none that I can think of."

What if they ask you if the women are still alive?" Longhand asked.

"I'll tell 'em, sure. They're alive and well – just waitin' for them to come bring them home."

"And is that true? Are they still alive and well?" Longhand asked.

Bill spit a stream of tobacco juice onto the floor of the barn and said, "Well, last I saw of them they were still alive. They were beat up some, and a mite sullen, but strong enough so's they fixed breakfast for us – after being threatened, of course."

"Good enough," Longhand said, laughingly. "Maybe I'll go in get some breakfast too."

Bill Musgrove stepped aboard his horse, put two fingers to his hat and put his heels against the horse's ribs.

"Remember ta tell 'em if they don't come up with the money, today, the women won't see the sun come up tomorrow," Longhand yelled after his second in command.

Bill waved his hand in the air as he rode away down along the Brazos River. They had doubled back, and the town of Seymour was no more than ten miles to the south.

Clay Brentwood woke up with a sore neck and aching hip. He was wet, hungry and cranky. The trees hadn't given them much shelter from the driving wind and rain, even though they had hung shelter tarps from the tree limbs. They normally used them as ground sheets, but guessed protection from the rain sounded like a better idea. They had tied one sideways between two trees and one overhead. They were protected somewhat, but the rain blew around and under the sheets soaking them from both above and below.

He Who Bites was already up and had a fire going. Clay could smell the coffee brewing and the bacon frying. After taking care of his morning necessities and putting his sleeping gear away, he walked out of the trees and stood in the morning sun, hoping he would dry off enough to ride.

Over coffee, bacon and hardtack biscuits, they discussed the plan for today.

"The storm has washed away their tracks, and unless they are very stupid, they will be hard to follow." He Who Bites stated. "I believe they are heading for the river.

"I agree," Clay replied. "But on the other hand, they also needed to find shelter and if memory serves me correctly, there's a small ranch directly west of here that sits right along the river. They could hole up there in the barn."

"Yes. That would be the McKenzie place," He Who Bites said, nodding his head.

"Correct," Clay said. "They came out a few years ago and started the place with only a half dozen young heifers and one bull. Nice couple."

Suddenly, both Clay and He Who Bites felt a chill run down their spines as the same thought entered their minds. The wife was young and very pretty.

In less than five minutes they had broken camp, saddled their horses and were riding at a high lope in the direction of the McKenzie place.

James Longhand had finished his breakfast and was enjoying a smoke to go along with his cup of coffee when the youngest of the three hostages walked past the kitchen table on her way to anyplace away from James.

Barbara was staring straight ahead and trying not to show her fear when she heard him say, "Hold on there, missy."

She stopped and stood very still. Her body went rigid when she felt his hands on her arms. "I didn't get ta have no fun last night like my friends did, but this mornin' I got me a hankerin'."

Something snapped inside her. She'd been repeatedly abused most of the night. She was in a lot of pain and now this man wanted to add to it. She just couldn't go through that again. She also felt the man she'd come out here to marry, when he found out about what happened to her, would no longer want anything to do with her.

Barbara Peoples had only been in Seymour a week. She'd come out to be a mail order bride, but the man she was to marry, Henry Gray, had been called away to Dallas to attend his mother's funeral. He'd left a note and had paid for a room at the hotel. On the morning she was abducted, she was accompanying Gloria Travis to the bank, then to

Gloria's shop where she was to be fitted for a wedding dress. Now this had happened and she couldn't expect Henry or any other man to wed her. She was soiled material.

When James spun her around, she saw the evil in his eyes and reached under the sleeve of her dress and pulled out the kitchen knife she had stolen just a few minutes earlier.

James saw only a blur before he felt the pain in his stomach as Barbara drove the knife into him and then stepped back, raising her hands to her face, horrified by what she'd just done.

James Longhand looked down at the knife protruding from his stomach and saw his shirt had turned red. He could feel blood running down his leg.

Anger welled up inside of him and he drew his pistol and shot Barbara, just below her heart.

The impact knocked her backward and she landed on the floor.

James walked over and looked down at her. Just before she left this world, Barbara looked up at him and said, "Thank you."

When his men heard the gunshot, they ran into the kitchen with pistols drawn and found James and the young woman laying side by side on the floor. Both were dead.

"This place is bad luck," one of the rustlers declared. "Let's get outta here."

"And just where might we be goin'?" another rustler asked.

"We'll head down the river and meet up with Bill. I reckon he's in charge, now," the man who thought the place was bad luck, said. And within a few minutes, the rustlers were headed south. In their haste, Beatrice Dalton and Gloria Travis were forgotten and stood watching as their captors rode away at a strong gallop.

"We need to bury Barbara, along with Mr. and Mrs. McKenzie," Beatrice said.

"What about the dead man on the kitchen floor?" Gloria asked.

Beatrice felt the anger rising in her and she wanted to lash out, but there was no one to lash out at, except the dead man. "As far as I'm concerned, we can drag him out and leave him where he left the McKenzie's bodies."

It was all the two women could do to drag the body of James Longhand out behind the barn and when they got there, both women got sick and had to leave. The vultures and other critters had already been at the McKenzie bodies and it was not a pretty sight.

When they'd recovered some, Beatrice said, "There's nothing we can do for them, but we can keep them from doing the same to Barbara. Let's go inside the barn and find a couple of shovels."

Being close to the river, the ground was fairly easy to dig, as they bent to their task.

He Who Bites and Clay, both saw the buzzards circling around in the far distance, then diving to the ground. Shortly the small ranch came in sight.

"There is something on the backside of the barn that the vultures seem to be interested in," He Who Bites said, as they cautiously approached the ranch.

Riding slow, with his pistol in his hand, Clay rode past the ranch house and noticed the front door was open. "We'll go slow until we see what's going on," Clay told He Who Bites, who already had his rifle in his hand.

Gloria Travis was down in the hole and had just pitched a shovel full of dirt out onto the pile next to the hole when Beatrice said, "I think..."

Before she could continue, Gloria held up her hand and whispered, "Shhh. Do you hear that?"

Beatrice stopped and listened, but even though she hadn't yet admitted it, she knew her hearing was not what it used to be. "What? I don't hear anything," she whispered back.

By that time, Gloria had climbed out of the grave and snatched up the rifle. "I hear two horses. Maybe a couple of them rustlers remembered leaving us here and have come back."

Clay rode around the edge of the barn and pulled the black stallion to a halt. He was looking at two women and one of them was pointing a rifle at him and from the look in her eyes, he knew he was just a hairs breath away from being shot.

Sensing these were the abducted women, slowly, and with great care, Clay put his pistol back in his holster and said, "Easy now. I'm not your enemy. My name is Clay Brentwood. I'm a Texas Ranger. I'm looking for the men who abducted you. Are they around?"

Both Gloria and Beatrice knew who Clay Brentwood was and Gloria lowered her rifle. "They've gone. The last we saw of them they were headed south down along the river.

After Barbara killed their leader, they went to meet the man who went into town to collect ransom money for our return, but as you can see, they left in a hurry and left us behind. Whoever comes to get us will have to come here if they want to find us."

As Gloria was speaking, Clay was letting his eyes roam around. First, off to his left, he saw the remains of what looked like a man and a woman, but it was hard to tell since the buzzards and other critters had been at them. Next, he saw a young woman on the ground next to the hole. She was dead. He'd been told three women had been taken, and guessed this must be the third one.

Beatrice noticed Clay's roving eyes and said, "The young lady on the ground is Barbara Peoples. Last night, the rustlers had their way with us, Barbara more than me or Cora, her being so young and all. And the best I can guess, the leader of the gang tried to abuse her some more this morning and she stabbed him in the stomach with a kitchen knife – and he shot her. He's laying over close to the trees. I hope he rots and goes to hell. Anyway, I'm Beatrice Dalton and this is Gloria Travis," Beatrice said, pointing toward Gloria.

"They shot and killed the owners of the ranch, Simon and Cora McKenzie. That's them over there - making a meal for the buzzards. We wanted to bury them too, but we were too late," Gloria told him, tears running down her cheeks.

Stepping down from his horse, Clay removed his hat and said, "I'm real sorry we didn't get here earlier."

Both women looked at Clay, then past him. Gloria had a curious look on her face. "You said, we, is there someone with you?"

"I'm right here," He Who Bites said, standing at the opposite side of the barn.

Both women jumped and turned around. When they saw He Who Bites, Gloria's hand flew to her chest and she exclaimed, "My God, you're an Indian!"

He Who Bites put two fingers to the brim of his hat and said, "Yes ma'am."

Beatrice turned to look at Clay, who was grinning, and asked, "He speaks English?"

"Probably better than I do," Clay said. "Plus, he reads and writes better, too. And on top of that, he writes poetry."

To say the women were stunned, would be stating it lightly. Gloria looked at He Who Bites and noticed what a fine-looking man he was. "You have my apologies," she told him. "I wasn't aware that Indians could speak the white man's language, let alone read and write it also. How is that possible?"

By now He Who Bites had walked up and stood in front of the two women. "I, and several of my brethren went to the Jesuit school, then we spent some time at the college up in Denver. We now work for Mister Brentwood on his ranch. It is my pleasure to make your acquaintance. I am He Who Bites," he said taking Gloria's hand and raising it to his lips where he kissed her hand softly.

At the touch of his lips against the back of her hand, Gloria felt a shiver run up her spine and knew her face was turning red. She'd never had a man kiss her hand, let alone an Indian.

Recovering, Gloria said, "I share the pleasure, Mister He Who Bites. That is an intriguing name. How did you come by it?"

After a quick explanation that involved his childhood, he said, "And that's what I've been called ever since."

Gloria Travis was transfixed by this savage who spoke so eloquently, and looked him in the eyes and said, "Well, with your education and breeding, I believe it's time for you to also have a white man's name. And since you write poetry, you should be named after a poet; so, from this day forward, I will address you as, Ralph, after the poet - Ralph Waldo Emerson. I've always admired the name, Ralph. How does that suit you?"

Clay would later swear He Who Bites was blushing.

He Who Bites looked at Gloria and smiled. "I think Ralph is a fine name, ma'am. I too admire his poetry. Thank you for the honor."

"It's Gloria. Gloria Travis, Ralph, and you may call me, Gloria," she told him. "And I hope to see you come to town from time to time."

"Yes, ma'am... I mean, Gloria. I will. And when I do, will you do me the honor of dining with me?"

Gloria smiled and said, "It will be my pleasure, Ralph," temporally forgetting about her association with the blacksmith.

Shaking her head, Beatrice said, "I don't mean to break anything up, but we've got a burying to do before the buzzards venture in this direction."

Jumping, Gloria said, "Oh my goodness. I didn't realize..."

"No matter," Beatrice interrupted. "Let's just get this done with so we can go home."

As Clay and He Who Bites finished digging the grave, he noticed the worried look on Beatrice's face and when Barbara was safely in the ground, Clay took Beatrice by the arm and walked her a safe distance away and asked, "What's wrong. Are you worried about facing your husband and the rest of the town?"

Beatrice sighed and said, "Both of us are. They were animals and the more they drank, the worse it got. I don't think I can face my husband. After what's happened, he surely won't want me back."

Clay scratched the back of his neck and said, "I can't say I know your husband well, but you don't look like the type of woman he could easily give up. Besides, why do you have to tell him at all?'

Gloria, who had been standing a short distance away had heard their conversation, and walked over to them. She stopped next to her friend, Beatrice. "I don't understand. How can we not tell them if they ask?"

Clay let out a small chuckle and said, "I guess you ladies aren't thinking straight just yet."

Both women had puzzled looks on their faces, so Clay continued. "For as long as I've ever known, women have been excellent at turning things around in their favor. No offense, but if they do ask, you might reply with, are you kidding me? I'm old enough to be the mother to any one of them; besides, Barbara was the young attractive one. She was the one they lusted after.

"And if either man has any sense, he will immediately reassure you that you are still attractive and desirable to them. Thereby turning the whole subject around."

Beatrice looked Clay in the eyes and smiled. "For a young man, you are very wise, Mister Clay Brentwood."

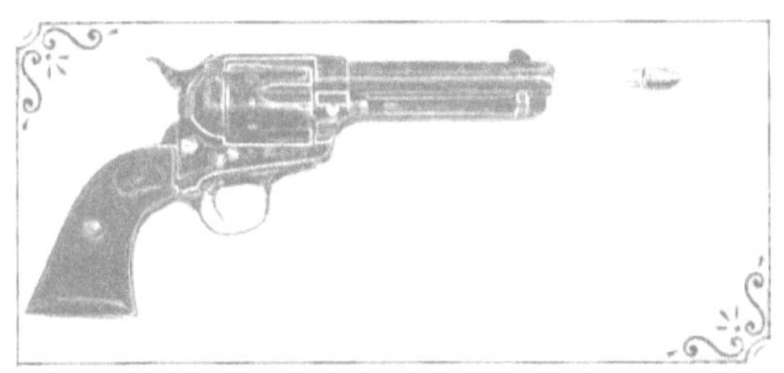

CHAPTER THIRTEEN

-

Bill Musgrove rode down the main street of Seymour at a slow, steady pace, his eyes searching both sides of the dusty main thoroughfare. Down the street on his left, he saw the sign he was looking for and guided his horse to the hitch rail in front of the sheriff's office. Still being cautious, he stepped down from the saddle and tied the reins to the hitch rail. The town was coming to life. Merchants were sweeping off the sidewalk in front of their business and Bill saw several women with baskets on their arms, out to do their morning shopping.

Through the window, Bill Musgrove observed the man inside, whom he guessed was the sheriff, since there was a star pinned on his chest. The man was drinking coffee and reading a newspaper. Bill looked up and down the street, again, but saw no signs of any threats, so he opened the door of the sheriff's office and walked in.

At the sound of the door opening, Rice Cooper laid the paper on his desk and looked at the man who had just entered. He was of medium height and weight. His clothes were dirty, and he had several days' growth of beard on his face. The pistol hanging on his hip looked well used and the look in the man's eyes sent a ripple down his spine.

"You the one they sent?" Rice asked, not wanting to waste time on small talk.

"I am," the man said, drawing his pistol and pointing it at the sheriff's chest. "And if you play it smart and keep your hands on top of your desk, you just might live through this."

Rice Cooper swallowed and took a deep breath. His heart was beating faster than at any time he could remember. "Just so we're straight, I don't have the power to negotiate any deals. That falls under the mayor's jurisdiction."

"And just where might the mayor be about now?" Bill asked, keeping his pistol trained on the man sitting at the desk.

Rice looked at the big clock on the wall and said, "My guess would be the hotel, having breakfast."

Bill Musgrove nodded his head and said, "I'm a mite hungry myself, so why don't you and I take a walk over to the hotel and join the mayor. Now stand up, real easy like and drop your gun belt on the chair, then step around so I can inspect you for any other weapons."

Rice Cooper knew that at this point, he had no other choice but to follow the man's orders. He stood up and unbuckled his gun belt and let it drop onto his chair, then walked around his desk, and with his hands in the air, turned around, slowly so the man could see he had no other weapons.

"Pull up your pants legs so I can see the tops of your boots," Bill said.

"What?" Rice asked with a questionable look on his face.

"I want to make sure you're not carrying a knife inside your boots. Now do as I told you!"

A knife inside his boot? What a novel idea, Rice thought as he raised his pants legs.

Satisfied the sheriff had no other weapons, he said, "We'll walk together over to the hotel, but know that I will have my pistol just inches from your back and if you try anything, you're gonna die."

"Look, mister, I'm not going to do anything stupid. Like I said, this is the mayor's call."

When they entered the restaurant attached to the hotel, Rice saw the mayor sitting at his usual table and headed in that direction.

Angus Dalton had just finished his breakfast and was enjoying a cup of coffee, but when he looked up and saw the sheriff and another man headed his way, he sat the coffee cup on the saucer and felt his heart begin to beat faster.

Without asking, the sheriff and the other man sat down, and Angus noticed a pistol in the man's hand as he pushed it beneath the tablecloth.

"You the mayor?" the man asked point blank.

"I am. And you are, sir?"

"My name isn't important. The sheriff here tells me you're the one to talk to about getting your women back. That right?"

Angus felt a tightening in his chest, and he took a deep breath before answering. "That depends," he said, trying to not show his emotions. "Are the women safe and, where are they?"

"Oh, they're safe, all right," Bill said, lying smoothly because he didn't truly know. "And as to their whereabouts, that will be revealed to you when I have the money in my hands."

"I'm sorry," Angus said, trying to brave out the negotiations. "But I need to see the women for myself and know they are safe and well."

Keeping his gun out of sight, Bill stood up and pushed his chair back. "No deal. Either I get the money, now or you'll have three dead women on your hands."

As he turned to leave, the mayor said, "All right! We'll do it your way. But please, don't hurt the women. How much do you want?"

Bill sat back down just as the waiter arrived. Bill looked up and ordered steak, eggs, potatoes, gravy and black coffee. "Breakfast is on the mayor," Bill said with a smile.

When the waiter looked at the mayor, Angus nodded his head.

The sheriff looked up at the waiter and said, "Nothing for me." He was actually, hungry, but his stomach was too upset at the moment to eat anything. He was wondering, again, why he had come to this God forsaken place, and like the mayor, he was helpless to do anything but go along. It was the women's safety that was important.

"Once again, how much money do you want for their return?" Angus asked.

Seeing the look in the mayor's eyes, triggered something in Bill's brain and he smiled and said, "One of those women is your wife, isn't she?"

Angus Dalton looked down at his plate. "Yes, one of the women is my wife and if you've done anything to harm her, I swear..."

"Take it easy, Mayor. Like I said, they're just fine. A little scared that maybe you won't pay the ransom, but other than that..." Bill lied, easily, again.

"All right. I guess I don't have any choice. How much?" Angus asked, again.

About that time, Bill's breakfast arrived, and he looked at the mayor and the sheriff and said, "I don't discuss business while I'm eating. Just sit tight while I have my breakfast, then we can get down to the details.

Angus and Rice sat there and watched as the man wolfed down his food like a man who hadn't had a decent meal in some time.

When he finished, he wiped his mouth with his napkin and took a sip of coffee. Next, Bill leaned back in his chair and said, "Thank you for the fine breakfast. The price is ten thousand dollars for each woman. That would be thirty thousand and no negotiation."

The mayor sat there with his mouth hanging open. He could maybe come up with twenty-five thousand dollars if he took a mortgage on his property, but that would still leave him five thousand dollars short. He finally looked at the outlaw and asked, "Why should I have to pay for anyone but my wife?"

Bill took another sip of his coffee, smacked his lips and said, "You don't, I guess. But any of them that don't get paid for will get their throats slit and left for the varmints to fill their bellies on. Your choice, Mayor."

By the look on the mayor's face, Bill knew he'd won. The man couldn't save his wife and let the other two women die and still face the people of the town. No, he would leave town with three times what James had asked for. Maybe he would pocket ten thousand for his trouble. James would be happy with twice what he'd asked for and he would be rich enough to leave the gang and go back east and open a business.

"I... I don't have that kind of money at my fingertips. It will take a couple of days to raise it, if I can," Angus pleaded.

Bill pulled a pocket watch from his vest, looked at it and said, "You have one hour or I ride out of here and you'll have three dead women to bring back and explain to the town what went wrong."

With Bill walking directly behind the sheriff and the mayor, they headed for the bank and arrived just as the bank president, Winford Hershel, was unlocking the door.

Once inside, the mayor related his plight in life and told the bank president he would empty his bank account and sign any kind of paper for whatever extra was needed.

The bank president looked at the man standing nearby with a pistol in his hand and knew he had no choice but to go along. He knew the mayor and his wife had close to twenty thousand dollars in their account and that the mayor would repay the difference.

"I'm not sure we have that much money. As I'm sure you're well aware, we were recently robbed."

Bill was becoming impatient and said, "Mister Bank President, I know they didn't get all of it the first time around, so just give me the money and worry about the paperwork later. I'm burning daylight and if I'm not back soon, my friends are going to think something went wrong and they'll kill the women and move on. Do I make myself clear?"

The bank president sighed and said, "All right. I'll get the money from the safe."

At the sight of all that money, which looked close to the amount James had already stolen, Bill suddenly got greedy. "Fill up three of them bags there on the side with big bills on top of the thirty thousand. I've decided I want to make a withdrawal, too."

The bank president started to protest until the man with the gun, cocked his pistol and pointed it at him.

"All right, all right, but please don't shoot me," the bank president pleaded.

With the ransom money and three extra bags of money, Bill told the bank president to hang the closed sign on the front door and then escorted the three men over to the sheriff's office where he recalled they had destroyed the cell walls, earlier.

Bill Musgrove ordered the three men to stick their hands through the bars and when they did, he handcuffed two of them and tied the banker's hands with his kerchief because there were no more handcuffs to be found.

Once they were secure, Bill gagged each man, but before he could gag the mayor, the mayor asked, "What about my wife? You have your ransom money."

As Bill tied a gag on the mayor's mouth, he said, "I'll leave a note on the desk out in the sheriff's office, telling you where you can find your women."

Bill wasn't sure any of them would be there, but that was not his concern because after thinking about it, he'd decided not to rejoin the gang. James might discover the money he had hidden in his saddlebags and take that, too. But if he headed east and kept going, he could disappear and never be heard of again. He might even change his name. He could go back to Boston and live happily ever after. And if anyone back there asked where he had acquired his money, he could tell them he'd found gold in a small stream south of Denver, and no one would be the wiser.

With that decision made, Bill drew a small map that would take them north along the Brazos River and indicated a small clump of trees where the women would be found.

He laughed to himself. When they arrived and demanded the return of the women, James would be furious when he found out he had taken the money and disappeared.

Taking a quick look at his prisoners, Bill decided he wouldn't even bother with locking the front door to the sheriff's office. He would be gone before anyone came looking.

Outside, Bill tied his saddlebags filled with money, behind the saddle, then stepped aboard his horse and rode up and stopped in front of the mercantile store and went inside, where he bought grain for his horse, two water skins to carry water in, along with some coffee, bacon and beans – a couple of potatoes and a handful of licorice, of which he was partial. After all, he could afford to indulge himself if he wanted to.

Bill told the proprietor he would be back for his purchases and walked out to his horse and looked around. The street was quiet with only a few people out and about. On the east end of town, he spotted a hostler sign and stepped aboard his horse and headed in that direction.

Shortly, he returned and loaded his supplies on the chestnut mare he'd purchased, which would double as a packhorse and a second horse to ride should anything happen to the one he was riding.

As he rode past the livery stable, he waved to the blacksmith who was standing in the doorway. The man smiled and waved back. He'd made a sound profit on the horse he had recently sold the man and was momentarily in a good mood. He was still worried about Gloria and hoped she was safe and would be returned soon.

After only a moment's thought, he headed for the sheriff's office to see if he had heard anything."

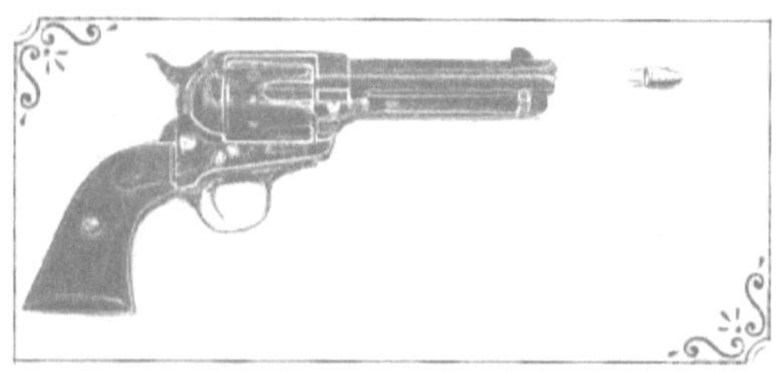

CHAPTER FOURTEEN

After Clay and He Who Bites, now called, Ralph, by Gloria, finished burying Barbara's body; they turned the stock loose and mounted up.

"We'll follow the river down to Seymour but keep your eyes on the lookout for the rest of the gang. They could be anywhere between here and town, waiting on the man they sent in to get the ransom money."

Gloria would have liked to have ridden alongside Ralph and learned more about him. He was an interesting man, along with being quite handsome – but he rode out away from the rest of them, looking for the outlaws.

Clay rode just in front of the two women. If there was trouble, he could send them scurrying for cover.

They had gone only a couple of miles when He Who Bites raised his hand in a silent command and pointing ahead of him and to the right.

Clay pulled the black stallion to a halt and looked in the direction He Who Bites had pointed. He saw a stand of elm trees and a small strand of smoke lifting into the sky.

Clay nodded and then turned to the women and said, "Ride slowly to the left maybe a quarter of a mile. We'll wait until you're in position before we act. And when we do, ride like the devil is chasing you. Head straight for town and don't slow down until you get there."

"I... I don't understand," Gloria said with a confused look on her face.

Clay pointed to the small column of smoke rising above the trees. "I think we've found the men who abducted you and I want you out of the way when the shooting starts."

"Shooting? Won't that be dangerous?" Gloria stated. "What if you or Ralph get hurt? Who will take care of you?"

Clay gave a sigh and said, "Please, ladies, just do as I ask. We can't be worried about you and those outlaws at the same time."

Beatrice, being levelheaded, turned to Gloria and said, "We'll do as he says. Now come on," as she urged her horse forward in the direction Clay had pointed.

With a worried look on her face and a last glance at He Who Bites, Gloria turned her horse and followed Beatrice.

Clay sat his horse, watching between the ladies as they rode away and the stand of trees to make sure they hadn't been spotted. The stand of trees was still close to half a mile away, so he felt relatively sure they didn't know he and He Who Bites were nearby.

When the women were in the far distance to the east, Clay turned the black stallion and rode over next to He Who Bites. "So, what's roaming through that mind of yours?" Clay asked.

He Who Bites shrugged his shoulders. "It will not be so easy this time. I took a closer look using the binoculars and they are having coffee, eight of them, but they're standing next to their horses like they are ready to ride at a moment's notice. Some are looking to the north, while the others are looking to the south."

Clay nodded his head. "The ones looking in our direction are looking for anyone who might come riding in their direction, and the others are waiting for the money man to arrive. Do you think the ones looking this direction has seen us?"

"If they had, I think they would have reacted, don't you?" He Who Bites asked.

"I agree," Clay told him, then said, "Maybe you could ease over to the river, then down close enough to their camp to be within rifle range. I'm going to ride up like I am someone just passing through, at least until I get close enough to talk to them. I'll place them under arrest and if that doesn't work, well I guess you and your rifle will come into play."

He Who Bites nodded his head and turned his horse toward the river, keeping a low hill between him and the outlaws.

Clay waited until He Who Bites was in position and he was sure the women were far enough away, then sent the black stallion into an easy lope in the direction of the trees.

The small group of elm trees was spaced wide apart and it was easy for Clay to see the outlaws. When he saw one of them place his hand on his pistol, Clay pulled the black stallion to a halt and yelled, "Hello, the camp."

"Hold it right there, mister. Who are you and what do you want?" the man with his hand hovering over his pistol, yelled.

Clay took his time rolling and lighting a cigarette, and when he had it going, he yelled back. "The name's Clay Brentwood. I'm a Texas Ranger and you're under arrest.

And just so you know, I'm not alone."

The outlaws all looked around, searching for whomever the man had spoken about, but saw no one.

"I think you're bluffin'," one of the other outlaws called out.

He'd no more than gotten the words out of his mouth when three rapid rifle shots tore up dirt at three of the horse's feet, causing them to rear up and go to bucking, causing a chain reaction among the other horses.

The outlaws were too busy trying to control their horses to see the two riders approach them with guns drawn and pointed at them.

When the outlaws finally got the nervous horses under control, they found themselves in an awkward position.

"Any of you not wanting to die today, reach down real slow like and unbuckle your gun belts and let them drop to the ground," Clay told them.

One of the outlaws who went by, Hawk, because of his lean frame and long nose that had a curve at the end, spoke up. "How'd you find us?"

"Hell, a schoolboy could have done the job," Clay said matter-of-factly.

"I thought we covered our tracks purty well," Hawk said.

"I will admit you did try, but my friend, here, He Who Bites can track a snake across bare rock - and when we arrived at the McKenzie place, we found two of the women alive. The third woman, a young lady named Barbara Peoples, was dead. The women said after he tried to have his way with her, she killed your boss, and then he shot her."

Ralph and I buried the woman and left your boss for the vultures to feed on," Clay said, pointing at He Who Bites.

"Ralph? What kind of a name is that for and Indian?" Hawk asked

"A right proper one, I think," Clay said, grinning at He Who Bites.

Clay was getting tired of the conversation and said, "Now, drop your gun belts and leave your horses where they are and walk over and stand in a circle, facing the fire. And just so you know, neither of us, is squeamish about shooting an outlaw in the back."

At this point, the outlaws looked at the two men holding guns on them and knew they had no choice but do as they were told.

A young man known only as, Crowder, spoke up. "So, if the young one is dead, where is the other two?"

Clay glanced off into the direction of town and said, "It would be my guess they're within a mile of town by now."

The outlaws looked at each other. If the women got back to town before Bill was able to get the ransom money and they couldn't somehow figure out how to get out of this predicament, they were all going to hang.

"While we wait to see if your man got the ransom money, I want all of you to sit down and put your hands on top of your head where I can see them.

When they were sitting, holding their hands on top of their heads, He Who Bites slid off his horse and gathered up the guns, then tied the horses in a string so they could be led.

When he was finished and back on his horse, Clay called out. "I think we've waited long enough. Everybody stand up and form a single line, then start walking toward town."

One of the outlaws moaned, "Walk? It's still several miles ta town. These boots I'm wearin' ain't made fer walkin'."

Clay smiled and said, "I understand. Any of you who don't like the idea of walking in your boots, feel free to take them off and walk back to town barefoot. Makes no difference to me."

To the man, all eight outlaws hung their heads and started walking.

Clay chucked. By the time they got back to town, their feet would be too sore for them to run.

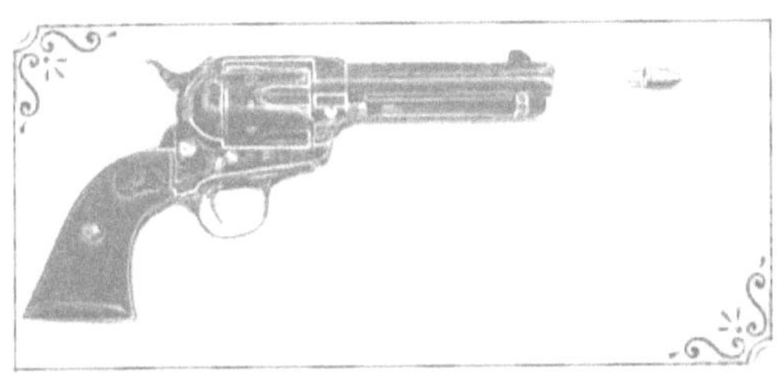

CHAPTER FIFTEEN

Cyrus Clemmons walked into the sheriff's office and called out, "Sheriff, you here?"

From back in the cell area, Cyrus heard several muffled, "Hummmp, Aggraaa, Aughhh sounds and hurried back where the prisoners were held and stopped abruptly when he saw the three men tied and handcuffed to the cell bars.

Cyrus made short order in removing the gags, then picked up the handcuff keys from the floor where they'd been discarded.

After releasing the three men, Cyrus asked, "What happened?"

The sheriff gave a quick rendition of what happened, then asked, "Did you happen to see a stranger this morning?"

Cyrus shook his head in disbelief and said, "Not only did I see him, I sold him a horse and he waved to me as he rode out of town."

"But your place is in the east end of town and he should have been headed west toward the river," the mayor said.

"Don't know nothin' about that," Cyrus said, 'but I do know for a fact he was headed east."

As the four men walked back into the sheriff's office, they were startled when the front door opened and in walked Gloria and Beatrice, looking a little worse for wear, but apparently unharmed.

The mayor was the first to react and ran over and pulled his wife into a bear hug. "I'm so glad you are safe, but how did you get away? Did they turn you loose? How did you get here? We thought they were north of town along the river, but the man who collected the ransom money left town going east."

Cyrus walked over to Gloria and took her hands in his. He wanted to do more, but since they weren't married, yet, he held back. He squeezed her hands, gently, trying to relay his happiness at her being back, but it was his eyes that told the story. "I've been so worried," Cyrus, told her as he continued to hold her hands.

Suddenly, Gloria got a rumbling in her stomach as the image of Ralph's face filled her brain. Taking a deep breath to regain her composure, she smiled and said, "It was a trying ordeal, but thanks to Mister Brentwood and his friend, Ra... I mean, He Who Bites, they helped us get back, but they put themselves in danger, doing so. I fear they are out there right now, shooting it out with that horrible gang of outlaws."

Cyrus turned to the sheriff and said, "We need to put some men together in a hurry. Gloria said the ranger and his Indian friend are out there right now, shooting it out with those cattle stealin', kidnappin,' outlaws, and the odds ain't in the ranger's favor – not by ah long shot."

The mayor, a man not known for his bravery, looked at his wife, who nodded her head. "You go along with them. I need some time to get a bath and into some clean clothes, along with a decent meal. I'll tell you all about it when you return with those terrible men in tow."

Luck was with the sheriff when he stepped outside his office. There were several cowboys riding down the street in front of his office, and when he told them what was going on, they immediately swung their horses around said they would help.

By the time the sheriff led the posse out of town, there was an even dozen of them, all armed and ready to shoot somebody.

They had gone barely a mile north along the river when the sheriff raised his arm in the air and called a halt to the posse.

"What's wrong, Sheriff?" the mayor said, riding up next to him.

The sheriff pointed and said, "I'm beginning to believe the stories I keep hearing about Mister Clay Brentwood, just might be true.

When they looked in the direction the sheriff was pointing, they saw eight men walking toward them, with their hands on top of their heads.

To the rear and off to each side rode Clay and He Who Bites. Each one was leading a string of horses. And each one had a rifle laying across his lap in case any of the outlaws got a notion to act like a jackrabbit.

As the outlaws walked up next to the posse, Clay called out, "Hold it right there."

It quickly became obvious that the outlaws would give them no trouble. All of them dropped down into a sitting position on the ground, groaning about how much pain their feet were in.

He Who Bites stayed off to the side, his rifle in his hand as Clay rode up next to the sheriff and asked, "Did the women make it back safe?"

The sheriff nodded his head. "They did, apparently thanks to you and He Who Bites."

Clay nodded his head and smiled.

CHAPTER SIXTEEN

-

Running Coyote stepped just inside the kitchen door and removed his hat. Loralie and Mrs. McIntyre were sitting at the long kitchen table having a cup of coffee and looked up.

The look on Running Coyote's face sent chills running down Loralie's spine. She stood up and asked, "What's wrong?"

"I think you need to step outside, Miss Loralie," Running Coyote said, opening the door wide so she could exit the room.

Mrs. McIntyre followed Loralie and gave Running Coyote a questioning look as she went past him, but he only nodded his head toward the back porch.

Outside, Running Coyote pointed toward a large dust cloud that seemed to be heading their direction. "I believe that man we ran off is coming back with reinforcements."

Loralie stepped back inside the kitchen and retrieved a pair of binoculars hanging on a peg by the back door and lifted them to her eyes. After adjusting them, she could make out what appeared to be close to forty men riding in their direction and none of them looked friendly.

After lowering the binoculars, Loralie sighed and said, "About now I kinda wish Victoria and her vaqueros were still here – and maybe, Clay and He Who Bites. We're gonna need all the help we can get."

Running Coyote looked at Loralie and said, "There's no need for any of you to get harmed. They want us, not any of you. We can go outside the gate and wait for them."

"No!" Mrs. McIntyre yelled, grabbing Running Coyote by the arm. "You can't do this. You are as much a part of this ranch as any of us."

"She's right," Loralie said. "You and all of the Indians, along with every man-jack who works on this ranch is the same as family and we don't sacrifice any of you to the likes of those idiots out there. Now, help me figure out what we're gonna do. With Clay gone you're the one we rely on, so tell us what you want us to do."

By now, every man, woman and child was standing nearby. Running Coyote turned to He Who Sleeps A Lot and said, "Take whoever you need with you and gather every rifle and box of ammunition you can find and bring it here, pronto!"

Brave Eagle and Loralie were already running for the front gate and when they got there they closed the huge wooden gates and placed the three bars across the back of the gates to hold them against almost anything you could throw at them, except maybe a large cannon.

The gates themselves were made of pieces of oak, eight inches thick, with steel plates, ten inches wide, running from the top to the bottom, holding them together.

Clay had designed the place in case of anything like this happening. The walls that surrounded the entire house, barn and other buildings were twelve feet high and three feet thick, of adobe, with a walkway on the backside where a person could stand and shoot over the top of the wall. The place was practically impregnable. Inside, they had food and water, along with enough ammunition to last for close to a week. Plus, in a shed not far from the barn, there were several cases of dynamite.

By the time the men who came to take the Indians away and hang them, got within hailing distance, they saw at least twenty rifles pointing at them.

A rancher named, Herman Langley was riding at the head of the mob and pulled his horse to a stop, raising his hand for the others to do likewise.

When the raiders were all gathered around him, Langley put his hand next to his mouth and yelled, "Hello the house!"

Loralie looked at the man who was yelling and yelled back, "I hear ya. Now my advice to you is, turn around and go back where you come from. I know why you're here and you've made a trip for nothin'."

"Just give us the cattle thieving Indians and no one else will get hurt," Langley called back.

"Ain't no cattle thievin' Indians here cause they didn't do it. It was white men dressed up like Indians ta throw you off the track," Loralie called back.

"I don't believe you," Langley yelled. "I saw them myself and they were Indians all right. Now I'll give you just one more chance. Send out them thievin' Indians and we'll be on our way. Otherwise, a lot of people are gonna get hurt, or maybe even killed."

Loralie looked down along the wall and saw her people, both men and women standing with a rifle in their hands, ready to defend the ranch and anyone inside the wall.

She looked at the man she'd been talking to and asked, "What's your name, Mister?"

"Langley. Herman Langley. My spread is a little southeast of Seymour and I say your Indians stole a good fifty head from me and I want them back, along with their hides. Cattle thievin' is a hanging offense here in Texas."

Loralie didn't want to get into a gun battle with these men, but she wasn't about to turn over innocent men to them, either. "Do you know who owns this ranch?" she called out.

"I do," Langley called back. "It's owned by that Indian loving Texas Ranger, Clay Brentwood. Before this is over, we're gonna settle with him, too."

"When it's all said and done, you're gonna find out just how stupid you've been, Mister Langley," Loralie yelled.

"Enough talk, lady. Either you send them thievin' Injuns out right now or we start shooting," Langley yelled, as he pointed with his hand toward the back of the enclosed walls, then raised four fingers. Four men swung their horses to the side and rode around to the back of the compound, which didn't go unnoticed by Loralie or Running Coyote.

Running Coyote nodded his head at Brave Eagle and He Who Sleeps A Lot, indicating they should go to the back wall.

Both men climbed down from where they were standing and ran toward the back wall, rifles in hand, their pockets filled with ammunition.

Loralie watched and smiled at Running Coyote, then turned her attention back to the men outside. "Shoot all you want, Mister Langley. These walls are thick enough to handle anything you got. Feel free to waste all the ammunition you want – but if you come any closer, you and your men are gonna feel the sting of our lead. It'll be like shootin' ducks on ah pond." She was slipping back into her old way of talking and was okay with that, at least for the time being.

Herman Langley studied the situation and decided the woman was right. The place looked stronger than an army post. Plus, he could see enough rifle barrels pointed his way to make him think twice about charging the place. Even if he were to kill a large number of the people, he still would be stuck outside and like she'd said, they would be like sitting ducks and he didn't want his men dying for nothing.

Langley sat, waiting to see what the four men he'd sent toward the back had found out, and he didn't have long to wait. He heard the report of two rifle shots, the sound of two yelps, and then the pounding of horse's hoofs.

From the far side of the compound, Langley saw two of his men riding his way, with the other two not far behind and when they reined up next to him, one of them yelled. "They shot Jake and Randy!"

"Are they hit bad?" Langley asked, looking at the two riders who had just reined their horses to a stop.

"We're both shot in the leg," Randy told him. "Either they're damn good shots or they got lucky. I'm bettin' on the first part."

Suddenly Loralie's voice came across the distance. "My men could have killed all four of your men, but decided they were only followin' orders from you, Mister Langley. But if you send anymore, our aim will be higher and you'll have horses with empty saddles."

Herman Langley knew when he was defeated, and it galled him to no end. "You may have won this round, but you can tell Brentwood, we'll be back, or maybe we'll just take fifty or so of his cattle to make up for the ones his no-good redskins took from me."

"I wouldn't even think about tryin' ta do that, Mister Langley. It'll bring you more trouble than you can handle," Loralie yelled at the backs of the retreating men.

Suddenly Loralie was tired – spent would be more like it. She wanted to go in the house and sit down and have a stiff drink. They had warded off another attack, but what if they came back and raided the cattle herd. The cattle were far out on the prairie - out of sight from the ranch house, and there were no cowboys out there, watching them.

Loralie's legs felt weak as she climbed down the ladder and handed her rifle to Brave Eagle.

Mrs. McIntyre took Loralie by the arm and said, "I'm thinkin' ah good stiff drink would hit the spot about now, don't you?"

Loralie patted Mrs. McIntyre's arm and said, "Great minds think alike."

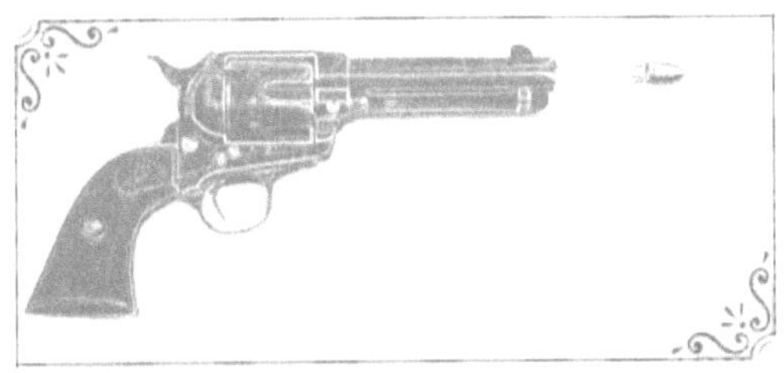

CHAPTER SEVENTEEN

-

Clay smiled as he handed over the rope that was tied to the string of outlaw horses. "Well, looks like our job is finished. I think you and these boys can handle it from here. It's time for me and He Who Bites to be heading home."

The mayor eased his horse up next to Clay and said, "Ahh, Mister Brentwood... there is one other small thing. Well, maybe not a small thing..."

Clay didn't like the way the mayor and sheriff were looking at him. "And just what is it that one other thing might be?"

"Well... ya see... it's like this..." the mayor stammered.

"What the mayor is trying to say," the sheriff said, "is that the man they sent in to get the ransom money, not only got the thirty thousand dollars ransom money, but also robbed the bank of what else they had. With the ransom money and the extra he took, he got away with over fifty thousand dollars."

"There was still that much money in the bank?" Clay asked.

"Several cattle buyers are in town and they put their money in the bank so they could buy cattle with a bank draft," the bank president said. "But now I have to face them and tell them there is no money – that is, unless you catch him and bring the money back."

"What happened to the first batch they stole?" Clay asked.

"I... I assume these men have it... don't they?" the bank president said.

Clay stepped down from his horse and went through all the saddlebags and searched each of the outlaws, finding only a few dollars on each one.

"If you're lookin' fer the bank money," one of the outlaws said, "we ain't got it mister. James Longhand was the leader of this gang and he always kept whatever money we got and doled it out after we was in the clear. That money is more'n likely still back there at the ranch."

Clay looked over toward He Who Bites and nodded toward the McKenzie place.

He Who Bites rode over and handed the lead rope of the horses he was leading to one of the cowboys in the posse, then headed back to the McKenzie ranch.

After He Who Bites had ridden away, Clay told the sheriff, "Guess we might as well get these men back to town. He Who Bites will bring the money to us if he finds it. In the meantime, you can fill me in on the details, like which direction he went because he for sure didn't come back this way."

"And you trust that redskin?" one of the cowboys asked with a sneer.

Clay looked the cowboy in the eyes and said, "A whole lot more than I would you."

Clay stepped aboard the black stallion and touched his feet against the big horse's sides and rode out toward town with the sheriff and the mayor riding up next to him.

-

He Who Bites rode into the McKenzie ranch yard and stopped his horse. He sat there for a moment and thought about what the cowboy had said, then turned his horse and rode up to the front of the barn and stepped down.

Inside the barn, He Who Bites found Longhand's things, along with an empty bag that still had six dollars inside.

Next, He Who Bites searched the barn, then the house but found no more money. He also looked for fresh turned dirt inside the barn in case the money had been buried in the hopes of coming back for it later. Outside, he found nothing but the grave where the young woman was buried.

He Who Bites led his horse over to the well and pumped a bucket of fresh water and allowed his horse to drink – then filled his canteen and drank deeply, then refilled it again and hung it on the saddle horn.

As he stepped aboard his horse and headed for town, he said to himself, "Someone has the money, but who?"

Could it have been one of the outlaws that took it before they left, he wondered? He didn't think so because the women had said they left in a big hurry when they found Longhand and the young woman dead on the kitchen floor.

So, who else could have taken it? Who had the time to search for it? The two women were the only ones here when he and Clay had arrived.

"Of course," He Who Bites said to himself with a slight smile creasing his mouth. "But which one? Or was it both of them?".

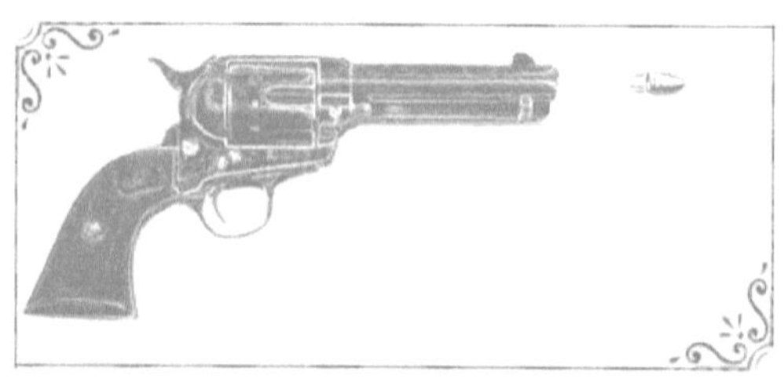

CHAPTER EIGHTEEN

-

Herman Langley was upset at not being able to hang some Indians. He'd lost a lot of cattle and someone had to pay. The Brentwood ranch compound had been out of sight for some time now, but they were still on the ranger's property.

Langley raised his hand and pulled his horse to a halt, and when everyone was around him, he said, "Maybe we didn't get to hang those thievin' Injuns, but we can still make that Injun lovin' Brentwood pay."

"What'cha got in mind, boss?" one of the men asked.

"It was those Indians he loves so much that raided and stole my cattle, so I'm thinking maybe if we ride over to where his cattle are, maybe we can find some with my brand on them."

"And if we can't," the same cowboy asked.

"Don't mean he don't have them hidden somewhere," Langley told them. "And if we don't, I plan to take a good fifty or sixty head to replace what he stole from me."

"I don't know, boss. The sheriff might look at that as rustlin', and they hang ya for doin' that here in Texas."

"You let me worry about the sheriff, unless you're not one to ride for the brand? If that's the case, then you can come by my place tomorrow and pick up what you got coming to you."

"Are you sayin' if I don't go with you, now, that I'm fired?" the cowboy asked, looking at his boss and seeing the man as he really was. He'd always run roughshod over his men but this was pushing it a mite too far. Yet, jobs were hard to come by and the man did pay well, and the grub was better than most places he'd worked on.

"You and any other man who don't have the guts to see justice done," Langley said, looking out over the men who sat their horses, staring back at him.

The men all felt what their boss was asking was pushing the limits of the law, but he was the owner of the ranch and when they signed on, they committed to riding for the brand and would do so, in the hopes he could handle the law if it came down to it.

-

Loralie was standing on the front porch of the ranch house with a glass of whiskey in her hand, but she had yet to take a drink of it. She was worried about what Langley had said about taking some of Clay's cattle.

"Brave Eagle!" she called out.

Brave Eagle had just walked out of the barn when he heard his name called and looked toward the house. Loralie was standing on the porch, looking in his direction, and with the sun where it was, there was a halo look around her entire body. He smiled, lifted his arm to signal he'd heard her, and then hurried in her direction.

As he got close, Loralie stepped off the porch to meet him. "I need you to go to town and try to find Mister Brentwood. He needs to know what happened here, today. I don't trust those men. They might be out there right now, trying to run off some of his cattle."

Brave Eagle thought she might be right, but another idea popped into his head and he said, "Finding Mister Brentwood in town might be a tough thing to do, Miss; plus, town is a several hours ride each way. What if I were to ride over to Mister Sooner's place. He's a lot closer. With him and his men and a few of our men, we could make sure those men don't make off with any of Mister Brentwood's cattle."

It took Loralie only a moment to realize Brave Eagle was right. "Yes, that is a better idea. Take a few men with you and ride over to Mister Sooner's place as quick as you can, but hurry, you might be too late."

Running Coyote walked up about that time and asked what was up? And after hearing the plan, he agreed and said he would also be going along if Loralie thought she would be all right."

"You just make sure he doesn't get any of Clay's cattle. We'll close the gates and post a couple of guards – but I don't think they'll be coming back."

On the way to Marion Sooner's ranch, Brave Eagle rode up alongside Running Coyote and said, "Mister Sooner has only a few men working for him."

"What are you trying to say?" Running Coyote asked with a sly smile on his lips because he felt he was having the same idea Brave Eagle was.

"I was just thinking, since the outlaws have somewhere in the neighborhood of forty or so men, we could use some more help."

Running Coyote lifted his hat and wiped the sweat from the band, then placed it back on his head. "I think you might be right. Walks Tall and his people were camped not far from here, yesterday. Maybe you should ride over and see if they're still there, but hurry, we don't have any time to waste."

-

Herman Langley led his men deep onto Clay's ranch and came to a good-sized valley where several hundred head of cattle were grazing on knee deep grass. In the distance he could see the sun glisten off a lake where several head of cattle stood with their noses buried in the water.

Herman pulled his horse to a halt and waited as his men gathered around him. Looking at his foreman, he said, "You boys ride down there and see if any of those cows has my brand on them."

"Yes sir," Johnny Barr, the foreman said as he turned his horse and rode toward the grazing cattle, motioning with his arm for the others to follow him.

Langley pulled a cigar from his inside jacket pocket and lit it. He inhaled deeply and let the smoke out slowly. By now his anger had quelled a little, but not completely. He and several other ranchers were sure Brentwood and his Indian friends were the ones stealing everyone's cattle, even though, so far, they couldn't prove it. He watched as his men rode slowly among the cattle, checking for brands. If they could find even one brand that didn't belong to Brentwood it would be enough evidence to bring charges against the man.

-

Brave Eagle's horse was lathered by the time he rode into Walks Tall's camp, calling out his name. He'd ridden hard and fast and would need a new mount before returning.

At the sound of his name being called, Walks Tall came out of his teepee and put his hand over his eyes to shade them from the sun and be able to see who was shouting his name. He'd been taking a nap and was still trying to shake the cobwebs from his brain.

Brave Eagle pulled his horse to a sliding stop just in front of the chief and jumped down. "Your brother needs your help, now!"

No more words needed to be said. Walks Tall called for his braves to mount their horses and told them, "Arm yourselves and take your best horse. Our brother, Clay Brentwood needs our help."

Brave Eagle followed Walks Tall to where his horses were grazing and Walks Tall pointed to the small herd and said, "Pick anyone you want."

In less than five minutes Brave Eagle was leading at least seventy armed braves back in the direction he'd come from.

During the time Brave Eagle was making contact with Walks Tall, Running Coyote found their neighbor and friend, Marion Sooner and the four cowboys who work for him, cutting out some young, unbranded stock, so they could be branded.

"What's wrong?" Marion asked as Running Coyote pulled his horse alongside him.

"Maybe nothing, and yet maybe a lot," Running Coyote said to Marion – then went on to tell him what had happened earlier.

"I thought I heard something that sounded like a couple of gunshots, earlier, but with this Texas wind, it was hard to tell, and when I didn't hear any more, I guess I didn't pay any more mind to it. Do you really think Langley would steal some of Clay's cattle? I know he can be hardheaded and overbearing. I even know about his dislike of Clay, but that is mainly because of Clay's friendship with Walks Tall and his people. Like a lot of people around here, he has this misconception about Indians."

Running Coyote shook his head back and forth. "He does have a hatred for Indians, that goes without saying. But will he take his revenge on Clay by actually stealing some of his cattle? I don't know, but I do know what he said he was going to do, and that's why I'm here. If he follows through on his threat, then we need to stop him. He has at least forty men with him, which could be a big problem if it comes down to a shootout, which we definitely do not want."

"So, what's the plan?" Marion Sooner asked.

Running Coyote took a deep breath, calculating what he wanted to say. "If Brave Eagle gets here with Walks Tall and his braves, I think when we get to where I believe Langley and his men are, and they are taking some of Mister Brentwood's cattle, we should stay out of sight – meaning me, Brave Eagle, Walks Tall and his people. I think you should go talk to him, alone; try to convince him to leave without taking any cows."

Marion Sooner nodded his head in agreement. "Yes, that sounds like a good plan. If he is doing something stupid, like taking cows that don't belong to him just because he is mad, maybe he'll listen to me, another white man."

About that time, Brave Eagle and Walks Tall, followed by the braves came riding over the hill and down to where Running Coyote and Marion Sooner were talking.

"Is it true, someone is stealing my brother's cattle?" Walks Tall asked.

"We don't know for sure, but there is a strong chance, that's why we asked you to come with your braves," Running Coyote told him.

"What is it you want us to do?" Walks Tall asked, waving his hands toward his braves.

After Running Coyote explained his plan, Walks Tall agreed it was a good plan. They didn't want to start a war with the whites if they didn't have to, and charging down on Langley and his men would do it, especially if any of the whites were injured. A large amount of the white people already thought of them as blood thirsty heathens.

A short time later, Marion Sooner called a halt to the men following him. "I can hear cattle bawling just beyond that hill," he said, pointing toward a medium sized hill just ahead of them. Stepping down from his horse, Marion said, "I'll go have a looksee."

Running Coyote also stepped down from his horse and hurried to catch up to Marion Sooner. "I'll go with you," Running Coyote informed him when he caught up.

-

After finding no cattle with his or any other rancher's brand on it; only Clay Brentwood's, Herman Langley, in his anger, ordered his men to cut out all of the young stock that had no brand on them. He had a running iron in his saddlebag and would brand them right here on sight, then take them back to his ranch and since they would have his brand on them, no one would be the wiser. And if they ran into anyone, he would tell them he was just taking back the cattle that had been stolen from him. The fact that all the cattle were yearlings, would more than likely, never come up.

-

Marion Sooner studied the situation for only a moment, then he looked over at Running Coyote and said, "This looks bad."

Running Coyote nodded his head. It did look bad. Langley was branding Clay's unbranded stock with his own brand, which meant the same thing as rustling. There seemed to be only about half a dozen of the young stock that had been branded so far, but more were being hauled over next to the fire. Running Coyote was glad Marion Sooner was here to see this because the sheriff or none of the white people in town would believe an Indian. "So, what should we do?" Running Coyote asked.

Marion Sooner sighed. "I need to get down there and try to stop him, if I can, before any more calves get his brand on them."

Langley looked up and saw the rider coming toward him and felt a rumbling in his gut. "Damn. Not now," he said to himself. Well, there was nothing to do but let whoever it is, come on. He hoped it might be the Ranger, Brentwood. He could kill the Indian lover and still take all the unbranded calves he could find.

Langley was disappointed when Marion Sooner rode up and looked toward the branding fires and asked, "What's going on?"

"What's it look like?" Langley asked. "I'm just taking some of my cows back that your Indian lovin' friend stole from me. You got a problem with that?"

"Now that you mention it, Langley, I do. You know as well as I do that it wasn't Clay Brentwood, or the Indians who work for him that stole your cattle – nor was it Walks Tall or any of his braves, either. It was white men dressed up as Indians to fool nearsighted men like you and several others I could mention," Marion told Langley.

Langley sat his saddle in a leisurely manner and said, "Oh, I forgot. You're another one of them Indian lovin' yahoos. I suggest you turn your horse around and go on back to where you come from before I get angry."

Marion Sooner could see Langley was on the prod and just two seconds away from pulling his six-gun and filling the air with lead. "Before you cut loose with that hog-leg, there's a bit of information you should know. While you were out here trying to blame innocent people for stealing your cattle, Clay, the sheriff, the mayor and the Indians who work for Clay, caught up to the real rustlers and arrested them – all white men. Your cattle are either in the pens back in Seymour, waiting for you to pick them up, or maybe someone drove them out to your place. Either way, you got your cattle back, so there's no need to steal any from Clay."

"I don't believe you," Langley said. "It was Indians who stole my cattle. I saw 'em with my own eyes."

"Then you'd best go see an eye doctor because you know what we found in those white men cattle rustler's saddlebags? Indian costumes – head feathers, war paint, the works."

Suddenly, Langley felt like a balloon with a hole punched in it. All the air seemed to be draining out of him. This couldn't be true. He had been so sure it was Indians. He looked at Marion Sooner, who stared back at him and knew the man was telling the truth.

Without an apology or a thank you, or any word at all to Marion Sooner, Langley yelled for his men to put out the fire they used for heating the branding iron and call off the branding. He told them they were going to town. And with that, Langley rode away with forty cowhands trailing after him.

Marion Sooner watched him go and gave a sigh of relief. It didn't matter that the man hadn't apologized. It only mattered that he was gone, and no one was shot. He would help Clay redo the Langley brands in a day or two.

CHAPTER NINETEEN

-

On the way into town, the sheriff brought Clay up to date on the man who came into town and demanded the ransom money, then rode away in the opposite direction.

"Like I said earlier, he waved at me as he rode past my blacksmith shop," Cyrus Clemmons chimed in.

"And you say he was heading east?" Clay asked.

"Yes sir. Looked like he was headed for Wichita Falls," Cyrus stated.

The mayor shook his head back and forth. "If he gets to Wichita Falls before you catch up to him, he could go anywhere from there and you'd never find him."

"Wichita Falls is a little less than a two day ride. That doesn't give you much time," Cyrus said.

Clay looked at the sheriff and asked, "Do you think you boys can handle these outlaws without losing them, again?"

With an embarrassed look on his face, the sheriff said, "They won't get away from me this time. Why do you ask?"

Before answering the sheriff, Clay turned and looked at He Who Bites, who had just ridden up, shaking his head back and forth. "There was no money to be found."

"But… but there has to be," the mayor sputtered. "He had it with him."

He Who Bites looked at the mayor and said, "You're welcome to go search for yourself. I even looked for places where he might have buried it, but there was no sign of him doing that, either."

"Then where is it?" the mayor asked.

"That's not for me to say," He Who Bites said, turning his attention to Clay, not wanting to reveal his thoughts about the women.

Clay read the meaning in his friend's eyes and said, "You could be right."

"Who could be right?" the mayor asked.

As much as Clay didn't want to out and out accuse anyone of taking the money, he said, "I'm not pointing the finger at anyone, but there were only two other people out there. You do the math."

For a moment the mayor was stunned that the ranger would even suggest such an outrageous idea, but the more he thought about it, the more he believed it could be true. "Well, if they did, it was only to bring it back," the mayor said, with a confidence he wasn't totally sure of. His wife liked having money.

"Yes, I'm sure you're right," Clay said, glad to be able to change the subject. Turning back to He Who Bites, he said, "I need you to go back to the ranch and make sure everything is all right. And I need you to tell Loralie that I still have one outlaw to bring in. Tell her I'll be along as soon as I have him in custody."

He Who Bites looked at Clay with a questioned look on his face, and Clay quickly explained the situation about the man who had stolen the ransom money.

He Who Bites nodded his head, then turned and without another word, rode west toward the ranch. They watched as he crossed the river, and put his horse into a steady lope.

Clay turned back to the sheriff and said, "I'll be heading on into town and pick up a few things, then head for Wichita Falls, if you still think you'll be okay with handling these outlaws."

"You go ahead. Just get the town's money back," the sheriff told him.

As the sheriff, the mayor, the bank president and the blacksmith watched Clay ride toward Seymour, they each wondered about the money the women may have taken. Was it really the way the mayor had stated it, that they were only bringing it back? And if they had, would they willingly come forward?

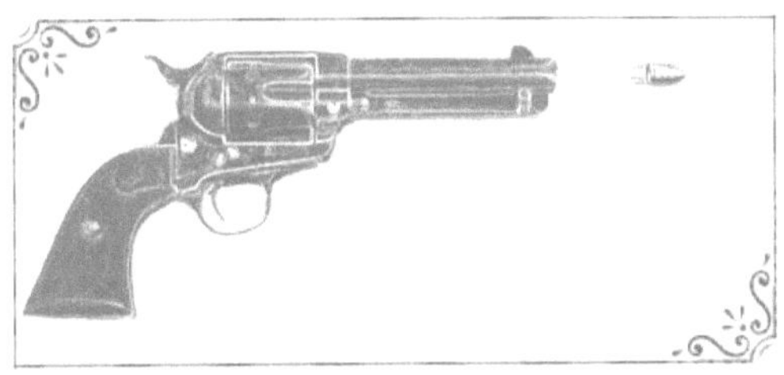

CHAPTER TWENTY

As Clay rode toward town, his mind was teaming with thoughts. How much of a head start did the man have? What was his name? What did he look like? These were all questions he should have asked before leaving.

With these and other questions racing across his brain, Clay turned the black stallion around and rode back. Fortunately, he wasn't yet out of sight when he'd made his decision.

The sheriff was surprised to see Clay coming back and rode out to meet him. "What's wrong?"

"I need a few questions answered before I go off on a wild goose chase," Clay told him.

Five minutes later, Clay was once again headed for Seymore. Everyone had been eager to share what information they had, even one of the outlaws, who provided Clay with the man's name, Bill Musgrove.

By the time Clay rode into Seymour, he had formulated a loose plan in his mind and was ready to put it into play. The man had at least a five-hour head start on him and he would have to wear out at least two horses to try and catch up to him before he reached Wichita Falls. But… if he was to take his train, he could go much faster, and on a direct route, and save his horse.

Harold was just stepping down from the engine when Clay rode up and stepped down from the black stallion.

"Mister Brentwood! I'm surprised to see you in town. What's up? Do I need to get the engine fired up? She's ready to go."

Clay took a moment to digest all the questions, then said, "Yes, we need to head for Wichita Falls as quickly as we can."

Without asking why, Harold turned and climbed back aboard the engine and began firing it up.

When the engine was running smoothly, he pulled three times on the whistle, and yelled down to Clay who had just loaded Midnight into the boxcar he kept for hauling his horses, "Got a new stoker and this is his signal that I need him. He's a good man. His name is Shorty and he can shovel coal all day long."

Clay nodded his head and had just climbed aboard his private car and looked out the window in time to see a short, bald headed man, wearing overalls, running toward the engine. He was built like one of those wrestlers you see at a circus, with huge arms and shoulders. Clay had no doubt the man could do exactly as Harold said he could.

Clay had just settled down into his seat when he felt the train lurch forward and heard the wheels spinning on the tracks. Harold was wasting no time getting started.

As the train left Seymour, and headed east, Clay gave more thought to his plan. If Harold highballed the train, as it looked like he was doing. There was a good chance Clay would be in Wichita Falls before the outlaw. The only problem with this logic was if the man wasn't going to Wichita Falls. What if he turned off to either the north or the south?

North didn't hold much appeal unless the man just wanted to disappear and eventually wind up in Denver. But if he turned south and headed for Dallas, he also had a lot of possibilities in that direction, too. He was taking a big chance and he knew it. It was his gut feeling that he was right that kept him headed for Wichita Falls.

Looking out of the window, Clay could see the road leading eastward, but it wouldn't be long before he could no longer see it. Darkness was less than an hour away.

Suddenly, Clay's stomach began to growl. He grinned when he realized he hadn't eaten anything since early that morning and then it wasn't much.

As Clay looked through the pantry and the onboard ice cooler, he was once again, thankful for Harold. Somehow, there always seemed to be food, coffee and water.

The cooler had a box on top that held a large, square chunk of ice that kept the things in the lower part, cool. In the lower part, Clay found, eggs, bacon, several potatoes and some fresh vegetables. There was also a bottle of wine and a container of water.

After a meal of bacon, eggs, fried potatoes, toast with butter and strawberry jam, Clay sat in his seat, sipping his second cup of coffee as he watched the darkness outside. Not much to see but shapes that stood out in the moonlight. He hoped one of those shapes turned out to be a man riding hard toward the east.

He was about to turn away when he saw the glow of a campfire in among a small stand of trees.

For just a moment, Clay couldn't breathe. Could that be the man he was after? Could he be that lucky?

Taking a deep breath, Clay tried to think rationally. His first instinct was to pull the emergency cord and stop the train – take Midnight from his car and ride over and see if this was the man he was after.

But after thinking about it, he decided that might not be the best action to take. The train was still close enough that whoever was in the camp would take notice of a train screeching to a sudden stop and if it was the man he was after, the man would be alerted and be ready for him. He would probably shoot him as soon as he got within the firelight.

Getting up, Clay swallowed the rest of his coffee, then put the empty cup into the sink.

Clay's private car was the last car in the line. There were two boxcars between him and the engine and the only way to get there was to climb on top and make his way forward.

Fortunately, there was enough moonlight that Clay could see where he was going and made good time, even though he had to jump from the top of his car to the top of the boxcar in front of him, then again to the top of the one attached to the engine.

When Clay got to a place where he could see Harold and Shorty, he yelled out to them, but the engine noise drowned him out. After several tries, Clay gave up and climbed down the ladder on the front of the boxcar and stepped the short distance, into the engine compartment.

Both men jumped like they'd been shot when Clay yelled out Harold's name.

"What in blazes are you doing here?" was Harold's first reaction. "And how did you get here? You didn't come over the top of the cars, did you?"

Before answering Harold, Clay leaned out of the engine compartment and looked back toward where he'd seen the campfire. It was no bigger than a dot, but still visible.

Stepping back into the engine compartment, Clay held up both hands, indicating for Harold to wait.

Not sure what was going on, Harold sat still and allowed the train to continue on at its present speed of twenty-five miles an hour.

After the train rounded a small hill and straightened itself out, Clay took a second look back toward the campsite, but saw nothing but the hill.

He straightened himself up and stepped close to Harold so he wouldn't have to yell so loud. "Take your time and slow the train down to a stop – but do it as quietly as you can. I need to get off."

Harold nodded his head to show he understood, then pulled a lever slowly backward.

When the train finally came to a halt, Clay guessed they were a good mile beyond where he'd seen the campfire and nodded his head in approval.

"Why are we stopped out here in the middle of nowhere?" Shorty wanted to know.

Clay explained seeing the campfire and his guess that it might be the man he was after. "I'm going to unload Midnight and ride back down the road. If it is him, he won't expect anyone to come looking for him from that direction. Maybe that will give me the advantage I need."

"And if it ain't him?" Shorty asked.

"Then I won't be gone long."

"And if it is?" Harold wanted to know.

"If it is, I still shouldn't be gone long – especially if I can get the drop on him."

"So, how long do you want me to wait before I come back, looking for you?" Harold asked, giving a twist of his head.

Clay thought for a moment before saying, "Good question. I'm not sure. Let's see, from here to the road is let's say, a quarter of a mile, and the camp is a good mile or so behind us. Without looking like I'm in a big hurry, I'd give it half an hour.

"Depending on how the meeting goes, another ten minutes, then another half an hour to get back. To be on the safe side, give it an hour and a half."

"And if things don't go the way you plan?" Shorty asked, scratching his bald head. "What if we hear gunfire?"

"Then play it by ear. If you head back and see someone that doesn't look like me, heading your way, put this train in high gear and get out of here."

"And if you're laying back there, dead or wounded?" Harold asked.

Clay thought for a moment. He knew Harold would be reluctant to leave Clay alone if he was wounded. "Again, play it by ear, but don't let that man on this train. He's dangerous and would more than likely not hesitate to kill either of you."

Harold looked at Clay and said, "We'll keep our heads. You just be careful and if it is him, don't give him a chance. Do whatever it takes."

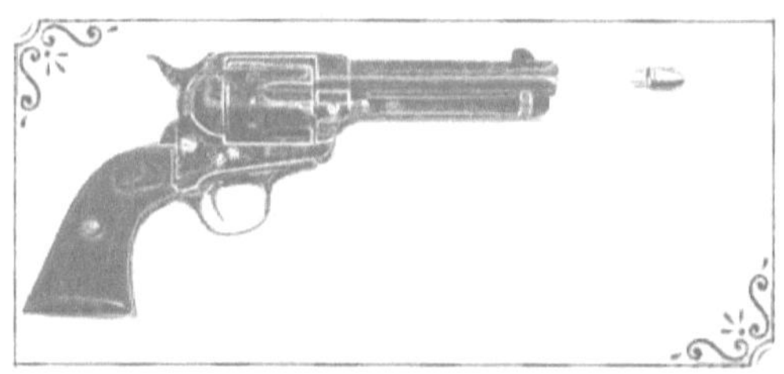

CHAPTER TWENTY-ONE

Rusty was one of the cowboys who worked on Clay's ranch. He'd shown up one day, nearly half starved, and fell off his horse near the well. They had taken him in and found out later that he'd been on his way to California when he was way-laid and left for dead. It was his horse, not him who had chosen Clay's ranch. That had been slightly over a year ago and California had been long forgotten.

Rusty knocked on the back door of the ranch house and when Mrs. McIntyre opened it, Rusty doffed his hat and said, "Just thought you might want to know, they're coming back.

Mrs. McIntyre stepped out onto the back porch and put her hand up to shade her eyes and saw them in the distance, only there were a lot more than had left the ranch a

few hours ago. Now there seemed to be at least a hundred or more as was evidenced by the large dust cloud they were causing.

Loralie had heard the knock at the back door and also went to see who was there. She stepped out onto the back porch and looked at the large dust cloud coming toward the ranch and felt her heart begin to beat faster.

Rusty saw the look of panic on Loralie's face and said, "No need to worry, ma'am, it's just Walks Tall and his braves. Running Coyote must have asked for his help in chasing off them cattle rustlers. I think they're coming for a visit so they can take a look at you."

Loralie had heard of Clay's Indian half-brother but she'd never actually met him and by now they were close enough that she could see the tall Indian riding next to Running Coyote and Brave Eagle. The sight of him caused the air to catch in her throat.

Rusty grinned. "Spitting image of Mister Brentwood, only he's an Indian. Kind of weird ain't it."

Loralie could only nod her head. The likeness was remarkable. They could pass for twins.

It wasn't until they reined in near the well in the center of the yard that Loralie noticed Mister Sooner was with them.

She stepped off the porch and walked out to greet him. "It's good to see you, Mister Sooner," she said when she got near. "Please tell me everything is all right, and no one got hurt."

"All right," Marion Sooner said. "Everything went smoothly, and no one got hurt. And by the way, it's, Marion, not Mister Sooner.

The man known as Walks Tall stepped up next to Marion Sooner and reached out and took Loralie's hand and lifted it to his lips, kissing the back of her hand, then said, "I am Walks Tall, chief of the Buffalo Chasers and half-brother to Clay Brentwood. We are Comanche. If ever you are in trouble, we will come. We are honored to have you as a sister."

Walks Tall released Loralie's hand and stepped back, smiling at her.

Marion Sooner would have paid good money to have a picture of the look on Loralie's face. Not only was her face flushed, she was breathing hard and her eyes were as round as saucers.

Straining to regain her composure, Loralie said, "Clay has spoken highly of you and also calls you brother, but I never realized the two of you could look so much alike. Please forgive me for being a bit overwhelmed. And thank you for coming to our aid, today. Please ask your braves to step down. I'm sure they are hungry."

Walks Tall smiled at Loralie, again. He was happy his brother had picked this woman to mate with. Not only was she pleasant on the eyes, he knew she would stand next to Clay no matter what."

"Thank you for your kind offer, but we need to get back to our camp. Our women and children will be worried. Maybe another time, after Clay has returned. We would be happy if he brought you to our camp. We like throwing parties."

"I would like that," Loralie told Walks Tall, truthfully.

Walks Tall nodded, then turned and swung up onto his horse and rode out through the gate at a high gallop with all his braves following him.

"He's something, isn't he," Marion Sooner said as he watched the Indians leave.

"I can't believe how much alike he and Clay look," Loralie said, shaking her head. "And how gallant. Did he also go to the Jesuit school?"

"I think he did," Marion said, not knowing for sure.

Loralie looked at Marion Sooner and said, "Oh my, with the Indians showing up like they did, I've forgotten my manners. Please come in and have a drink and something to eat. I want to hear all about what happened."

"Not much to tell. I'm not real hungry and I'm sure Rebecca will have supper ready by the time I get back, but I will take that drink."

After a brief explanation of what had transpired, Marion Sooner walked out onto the front porch and watched as his horse was led from the barn, where he'd been cared for.

As Marion settled down on his saddle, he said, "When Clay gets back, you make him bring you over to meet Rebecca. I'm sure the two of you will get along just fine."

Loralie promised she would, then watched as their nearest neighbor rode through the front gate and soon disappeared.

Back inside the house, Mrs. McIntyre and Cindy were waiting by the dining table when Loralie walked into the dining room. She looked at the chair where Clay always sat and wished he would be home, soon.

Mrs. McIntyre poured a glass of wine and offered it to Loralie.

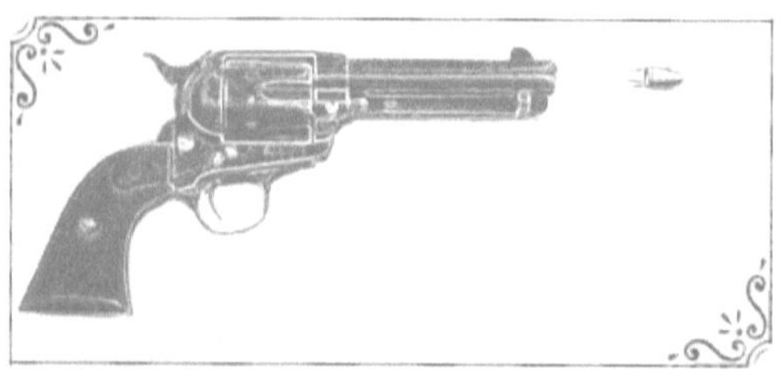

CHAPTER TWENTY-TWO

It was dark and most men didn't travel at night, so Clay rode with caution. Midnight's ears stood up when they neared the campsite. Clay could see the glow of the fire through the trees and pulled Midnight to a halt. "Hello, the camp," he called out.

From somewhere inside the group of trees, but not close to the fire, a voice called out, "State your business and why you're riding at night and not camped somewhere."

Thinking quickly, Clay said, "I was headed for New Mexico, but several miles back I was attacked by some Indians and they drove off my pack horse. I lit out like my tail was on fire and I guess they were more interested in my pack horse. When my horse was about done in, I slowed down to a walk to give him a breather. About a mile down the road, when I was sure I wasn't bein' chased, I stopped and gave him some water and rubbed him down with a piece of cloth I keep in my saddlebag. Do you know if there is a town anywhere close by? I sure could use some coffee and something to eat. My belly feels like my throat's been cut. Plus, my horse needs fed."

There was a long silence, then Clay heard the man's voice, again. "Why are you going to New Mexico?"

Clay smiled to himself. He was buying Clay's story, hook, line and sinker. "I'm hopin' ta buy some land and start a horse ranch."

Bill Musgrove could see the outline of the rider in the moonlight and decided he didn't look like a threat. Plus, if the man was planning on buying land in New Mexico, he might have money on him.

It didn't matter that he already had a lot of money from what he'd stolen back in Seymour, the thought of more money, intrigued him. "Come on in but ride slow and keep your hands where I can see them," Bill called out.

Instead of raising his hands over his head, Clay held the reins in his left hand, up in plain sight where the outlaw could see it, and his right hand, out to the side, shoulder high. With his feet, he urged the black stallion toward the camp, at a slow walk.

When Midnight got close to the fire, he stopped and waited the next command. "Can I step down?" Clay asked, staring straight ahead, not sure where the outlaw was.

"Just do it real slow like," the voice said, coming from Clay's left – the opposite of where his pistol rested.

Clay lowered his left hand and let the reins drop to the ground, while keeping his right hand still out at shoulder level. Taking the saddle horn in his left hand, Clay swung his right leg over the saddle and stepped down, turning to look toward where the voice had come from.

The man who stepped out of the trees, pointing a rifle at him looked as though he'd seen better days. His suit looked like it had been a good one at one time, but now it was dirty and needed some mending here and there. The man was in need of a bath and a shave, but his eyes were clear and took in everything in front of him. In fact, the man was also looking over Clay's shoulder to see if anyone else might be coming toward the camp.

"Step away from your horse and keep your hands up," the outlaw told him.

Clay did as he was told, and as the man got closer, Clay could see they were about the same size.

Clay smiled his friendliest smile and said, "That coffee sure does smell good – and is that bacon I also smell?" Clay licked his lips like he hadn't eaten in some time.

Bill Musgrove decided the man didn't look like a lawman, nor did he look like a threat and decided to test the water so to speak and have a little fun at the same time. "Coffee's a dollar a cup and beans and bacon is two dollars."

Clay couldn't decide whether the man was pulling his leg or just plain greedy. Finally, Clay decided to go along and see what happened. "That would be three dollars," Clay said as he reached into his pants pocket and pulled out a roll of money and pulled off three dollars and handed it toward the outlaw. He still hadn't given up his pistol that was hanging against his right leg.

Bill Musgrove shook his head and laughed out loud. "Put your money away. I was just joshing you. I'm sure if the tables were turned you wouldn't charge me just because I'd had my grub stolen by Injuns. Go ahead and get yourself something to eat and that's a fresh pot of coffee. And I suppose you can lower your hands." By now, Bill thought the man was just what he'd said he was and wasn't concerned; although, the tied down holster on the man's leg should have raised a red flag, but it didn't.

"Much obliged," Clay said as he lowered his hands and squatted down next to the fire and picked up a plate that was sitting there just off to the side.

Being cautious because he knew the man was an outlaw and deserved no trust, and more than likely wanted the roll of money he was carrying, Clay had just picked up the tin plate when he saw the rifle barrel coming toward his head from his peripheral vision.

Rolling to his right and at the same time, tossing the plate toward the outlaw's face, Clay pulled his pistol and pointed it at the man as he came to his knees. "Hold it right there. You make a stupid move and I'll put a bullet in your brain."

Bill Musgrove struggled to keep his balance after missing his swing at the man's head and by the time he was back upright, he was staring down the barrel of a forty-four, and the look in the man's eyes told him he'd made a huge mistake.

"So, what happens now? You gonna rob me? Well lots of luck with that because I don't have any money. What little I had, I spent it on this grub you'll be eating," Bill said with all the sincerity he could muster.

Clay stood up and said, drop the rifle on the ground and step to your left six paces."

Bill did as he was told, but still couldn't make out the man's motives. "Eat my food, drink my coffee and take anything else I might have, but I ask that you not shoot me nor steal my horse."

Clay told the outlaw to squat down in a sitting position and lace his fingers together on top of his head – and when the man had complied, Clay squatted down and poured himself a cup of coffee.

It seemed to Bill Musgrove like a long time had passed before the man spoke, but in reality, it had been no more than five minutes.

Clay nodded his head and said, "Just a poor cowboy traveling across Texas, is that it?"

"Something like that," Bill said.

"Uh huh," Clay said. "And all the cowboys wear expensive suits to work in, now-a-days."

Bill could see the man wasn't buying his poor cowboy story, but still wasn't sure who the man was or why he was here. If he was a lawman, he should have been coming from the west, not the east. "You a law man or something?" Bill asked.

Clay thought for a moment, searching for the correct answer. In his eyes, he was no longer a Texas Ranger – he was retired – but in Bill McDaniel's mind, once a Texas Ranger, always a Texas Ranger. Plus, McDaniel had refused to accept his badge back.

"Texas Ranger. I'm a Texas Ranger and Mister Bill Musgrove, you're under arrest for cattle rustling, kidnapping and robbery."

Bill Musgrove was flabbergasted to learn the man not only knew his name, but the crimes he'd committed.

"And what makes you think I'm this man, Bill Musgrove? My name is Lawrence Milhouse," Bill said, trying to bluff his way out of this. "And no, I'm not a drifting cowboy in search of chasing cows all day. I was hoping to apprentice a law degree with an attorney in Albuquerque, but when I got there, he'd passed on. And now I'm trying to get back to Boston, which is where I'm from."

Clay could almost laugh. The man was good. He'd lied with a straight face. Instead of becoming an outlaw, he should have gone to New York and become an actor. "So, Mister Milhouse, you won't mind if I have a look in your saddlebags or the other bag laying next to your saddle."

For just a moment, Clay could see the anger in the man's eyes and knew he was dealing with a rattlesnake, then the smile was back.

"You look like a reasonable man," Bill said, turning on the charm. "And the truth is, there is some money in that bag next to my saddle – a lot of money as a matter of fact. I know this sounds like a made-up story, but the truth is, I found the bag laying in the road, maybe two miles back. It's found money, so I might not mind sharing it, if you get my drift."

"Are you trying to bribe an officer of the law?" Clay asked, watching the man become even more agitated.

"Bribe a Texas Ranger? Of course not. I'm just saying that from what I hear, you boys don't make a lot of money for risking your neck on a regular basis, and since I have no idea who this money belongs to, I just thought, us being new friends and all, well, I was thinking, why not share? We could both use a bit of extra cash. You, to do whatever you need to, and me, to get back to Boston."

"Well now, that's real friendly like. So, since you have no idea who the money belongs to, I suppose you wouldn't mind coming back to Seymour with me, since I believe it might belong to some folks back there."

"You think you're pretty smart, don't you, what did you say your name was, Brentwood? Well, Mister Brentwood, I know enough about the law to know you can't prove I stole that money. Like I said, I found it laying in the road a few miles back. You do whatever you want with the money, but I'm still going back to Boston. And to be honest with you, I think you'll wind up keeping the money for yourself."

"You're right. I can't prove you did anything wrong, but the people back in Seymour can, which is where you're going, first thing in the morning. Stand up and put your hands behind your back."

Bill Musgrove got slowly to his feet. He was mad through and through. Somehow, some way, he would have to kill this ranger before they got back to Seymour.

CHAPTER TWENTY-THREE

-

Beatrice Dalton and Gloria Travis had talked themselves into keeping the money the rustlers had stolen. Both agreed they would put it to good use. Beatrice could expand her business interests and Gloria could have the wedding and honeymoon she'd always wanted, and still have money left over.

The only problem with this kind of thinking was, neither of them were criminals and both were soon having second thoughts. The truth was, it was not their money. It had been stolen from the bank and belonged to the people of Seymour – the store owners, the small farmers, and yes, the rich cattle ranchers, as well.

With the new decision made, the women headed for the sheriff's office. Beatrice held the bag of money tightly to her chest as though she never wanted to turn it loose. They were about to cross the street when Herman Langley and his men came riding down the middle of the street – half each, heading for the two saloons while Langley reined up in front of the sheriff's office.

When the street was empty, Beatrice and Gloria walked across the street and also stopped in front of the sheriff's office.

"Mister Langley," Beatrice said.

Herman Langley was still sitting on his horse and lifted his hat just above his head and said, "Beatrice, Gloria. Would either of you happen to know where I can find the sheriff?"

Beatrice smiled and pointed down the street.

When Langley turned to look in the direction, she was pointing he saw the sheriff, the mayor, the bank president and the blacksmith coming toward him. In front of them he counted ten bedraggled looking cowboys walking toward him like they couldn't walk much farther.

Langley wasn't sure what this was all about since the mayor and the blacksmith were leading ten horses. As they got closer, he studied them more closely. Were these the men he saw stealing his cattle? It sure didn't look like the men he saw; but then again, he was told they were dressed up to look like Indians – something he would ask the sheriff about.

Instead of stopping at the jail, the sheriff herded his prisoners on down the street to a windowless building that looked like it had been unoccupied for some time. In fact, it had been empty for nearly a year. There, he ushered the outlaws inside and turned them loose, then stepped outside and closed the door.

The sheriff stationed four of the posse as guards, front and back and both sides. He was taking no chances this time.

As the sheriff put his foot into the stirrup and swung his leg over the saddle, Herman Langley rode up and asked, "Are those the men who've been rustling our cattle?"

"They are," the sheriff replied.

"Then why didn't you lock them in the jail?" Langley wanted to know.

"Because the jail hasn't been repaired, yet," the sheriff said, pointing to the blown away wall of the cells.

Herman Langley realized he'd missed a lot being out trying to run down the men he thought were stealing his cattle.

"And you're sure these are the men?" Langley asked, wanting to be reassured it hadn't been Indians. "The men I saw looked like Indians, to me."

The sheriff grinned and said, "Yea, they had us all fooled, but if you ride on down to the livery barn and have Cyrus show you what's in their saddlebags, I'm sure you'll be as convinced as I am that these are the men who've been rustling your cattle."

"Think I'll do that, Sheriff. Yes, I will do that," Langley said, turning his horse in the direction of the livery stable.

The sheriff thanked the rest of the posse but told them they weren't released, yet. He told them to drop by his office shortly to get their times to guard the prisoners. It would cost a little more this way but figured the ranch owners wouldn't mind helping pay for the extra help – after all, they did get their cattle back.

When the sheriff got back down to his office, he found the mayor, the banker and the two women inside, waiting for him. He also noticed the bag sitting on his desk.

"The mystery of the stolen money has been cleared up, Sheriff," the bank president said proudly. "The ladies took it when the head of the rustlers was killed and as you can see, they returned it safe and sound."

"Well, that's just fine. Thank you, ladies." the sheriff said as he walked around his desk and sat down. Looking up at the mayor, he asked, "Anything else?"

The mayor looked at the floor, then back up at the sheriff and said, "No. You have the prisoners locked up – we have the bank's money back. Except for Mister Brentwood apprehending the other outlaw, the one who also stole a lot of money from the bank, and returning him, I think we're doing just fine."

As the mayor, the women and the bank president were about to leave, the sheriff said, "Just two more things."

The mayor turned back and asked, "What two things?"

The sheriff laid both hands on his desk and said, "First, when will the circuit judge be coming through so we can get this thing with the rustlers settled? It's costing the town money every day. And second, I need to talk to the city council about the repair of our jail wall, or better still, the building of a new jail."

The thought of building a new jail almost flabbergasted the mayor. "A new jail... I... I don't know about that. That would be very expensive."

The sheriff grinned. The man was not only cheap, but a penny pincher as well. A person would think it was coming out of his pocket. "What about turning that warehouse where the prisoners are, now, into the new jail. It wouldn't be nearly as expensive, and it would give us room for more cells."

The mayor thought that might be the answer. The building had been empty for some time and it for sure wasn't bringing in any money. "I'll bring that to the council's attention at the meeting, tomorrow."

"And the circuit judge?" the sheriff asked.

The mayor studied the question for a moment, then said, "I'll put in a wire to the capital. They will know."

The sheriff watched them leave and for the first time since this whole fiasco had begun, he was feeling good about things. Maybe he would stay around for a while longer.

The sheriff checked the stove and the coffee pot – both were cold. He checked the wood bin and found it empty. And after finding the coffee bin empty, too, he left the jail and headed for the hotel restaurant. Besides wanting a cup of coffee, he was hungry. He would order food to be taken to the prisoners.

CHAPTER TWENTY-FOUR

Clay smiled when he heard Harold bringing his train back down along the tracks. "On your feet Mister Musgrove, we're going for a train ride.

Bill Musgrove had sat down next to the fire after being handcuffed and now stood up and looked at Clay, shaking his head. "You sure are going to be embarrassed when you find out I'm not this Bill Musgrove you keep talking about. As I told you, my name is Lawrence Milhouse," Bill said, trying to keep up the ruse until he could find a way to get loose.

"How'd you know a train would be coming along?" Bill asked as he walked toward his horse and waited for the ranger to help him up.

Clay helped Bill Musgrove climb aboard his horse, then pulled his pistol and pointed it at Bill. "Just a little insurance to make sure you don't try something stupid, like trying to get away while I get on my horse.

"And to answer your question, that's my train. I own it."

Bill looked down at the Texas Ranger and said, "There's more to you than meets the eye, Mister Texas Ranger… Yea, a lot more, I'm guessing."

Clay stepped over to the small fire and kicked dirt on it to put it out, then stepped aboard Midnight and ordered his prisoner to ride toward the train at a slow pace.

With his hands cuffed behind his back, Bill didn't stand much chance of racing off into the darkness and he knew it. "Just relax and bide your time," he whispered to himself.

Harold and Shorty were waiting next to the train with rifles in their hands when Clay and his prisoner rode up. "That him?" Harold asked.

"It is," Clay said as he stepped down from Midnight just as Shorty opened the boxcar door and pulled out the ramp so the horses could get in.

Clay helped his prisoner down from his horse, then led the horse up the ramp. Midnight knew the drill and had already boarded the boxcar and was nibbling on some hay from the feeding trough Clay had installed for long trips.

After unsaddling Bill's horse, he did the same for Midnight and hung them on the bar in the front of the boxcar.

When Clay was back on the ground, Shorty made quick work of replacing the ramp and closing and locking the boxcar door.

"What do you plan on doing with him?" Harold asked, pointing at Bill Musgrove.

"I'll tie him into one of the seats in my car," Clay told him. "It's only a short trip back to Seymour."

Harold and Shorty watched as Clay took his prisoner aboard the train and tied him to a seat, then went back to the engine.

Clay felt the jerk as the wheels spun to get traction on the rails and when the train was moving smoothly, he took his seat and looked out the window, wondering how Loralie was doing? He hoped there hadn't been any trouble.

The sheriff was sitting, leaned back in his chair with his hat down over his eyes and his feet propped on his desk when he heard the train whistle. "What the?" he said as he got to his feet. It was late at night and no trains were due to come through that he knew of.

The sheriff walked out onto the sidewalk and looked down toward the train station and what he saw caused him to hurry in that direction.

Clay Brentwood's small train came to a halt directly in front of the train station platform. Through the window Clay could see the sheriff hurrying in his direction. "Good," he said. "I can get rid of my prisoner and head for home."

Harold and Shorty had just stepped down from the engine when Clay left the train with his prisoner. He saw Harold and Shorty and called over his shoulder, "I'll be wanting to head out to the ranch as soon as I turn my prisoner over to the sheriff, so, if you could bring his horse, I'd be much obliged."

"I'll see to that," Shorty said.

"We'll be ready, Sir. And if you don't mind, we'll spend the night in the bunk house and come back to town tomorrow."

"Sounds like a good idea to me. I'm sure Mrs. McIntyre will make sure you have a good breakfast before you leave."

"I was planning on that," Harold said in a low voice to Shorty.

"Me too," Shorty countered.

The sheriff took one look at Bill Musgrove and said, "That's him. Did he have the money with him?"

Clay held up the sack with the money in it and said, "I didn't count it, but I doubt he spent much of it."

"I'll make sure you get the best room in the hotel and I'll have them wake up the cook," the sheriff informed Clay.

"What about me? I could use a good meal," Bill said.

"You'll be lucky if you get bread and water," the sheriff told him.

Clay was in a hurry to get his business done and head for home. "Thanks for the offer but I'll be taking the train out to the ranch as soon as we're finished here."

The sheriff asked Clay if he would mind coming along while he took the prisoner to the warehouse where the other outlaws were locked in.

"Sure," Clay said. "It will be interesting to see how the others react when they see him after him running out on them with the money like he did."

"Wait a minute, Sheriff, you can't put me in there with them. My life won't be worth a plug nickel," Bill said in a voice a few octaves above his normal range.

"Guess you should have thought about that before you absconded with the money," the sheriff said, shaking his head, giving Bill a shove in the direction of the warehouse.

Clay and the sheriff left the warehouse to Bill Musgrove trying to explain to the other outlaws how he was just trying to protect their money.

At the sheriff's office, they stopped on the sidewalk and shook hands, then Clay headed for the train station and his ride back to the ranch.

Harold was waiting for him and said they would have to wait for a few days; a very important gauge had stopped working and he would have to order a new one from Dallas. He said he could ease the train over onto the side track, but that would be about as far as he could go without the new gauge.

Clay patted Harold on the shoulder and said, "They may be comfortable to ride in and make better time, but when it comes right down to it, they're still not as dependable as a man's horse."

"Will you be staying at the hotel, Sir?" Harold asked.

"Now why would I do that when I've got a perfectly comfortable bed on the train, and there's plenty to eat and coffee to drink. You go ahead and move the train. Midnight and I will leave first thing in the morning."

"Yes sir," Harold said as he turned toward the engine. He'd only gone a few steps when Clay called out…

"Hold on," Clay said. "Come aboard and I'll write you a check so you can pay for the new gage and give Shorty what's coming to him, along with some money for you."

"Yes sir!" Harold said as he headed for Clay's private car..

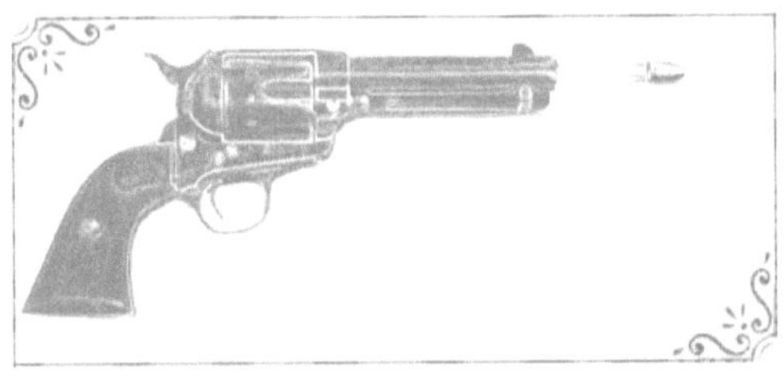

CHAPTER TWENTY-FIVE

-

Everybody on the ranch was asleep, except for Herman Langley who was pacing back and forth across the office floor in his sprawling ranch house. He was carrying his fourth glass of whiskey and was beginning to feel the effects of drinking on an empty stomach.

"It can't be true," he said to no one in particular. "White men dressed up as Indians. I still can't believe it."

Langley gulped down the glass of whiskey and felt it burn all the way down into his stomach, then walked over and dropped down into the large chair behind his desk. He reached out and picked up the half empty bottle of whiskey and filled his glass, again, and this time, took only a sip. He needed to think.

Herman Langley was a man who was used to getting what he wanted and he wanted the land where Walks Tall and his people called home. It was perfect for raising cattle. It had plenty of good grass and water. It was too good for a bunch of stinking redskins.

Proving Walks Tall and his people were stealing cattle had been the ideal way to get rid of them and claim the land for himself. His only opposition would have been that ranger and his neighbor, Sooner. They were thicker than thieves with Walks Tall and his people. It was said they even gave them cattle to eat during the winter when there wasn't enough buffalo.

Langley took another sip of whiskey and stared at the map laying on his desk. If he had Walks Tall's land, his ranch would more than double in size. He would have the biggest ranch in this part of Texas, and in a few years, the most powerful.

Langley leaned back in his chair and downed the rest of his whiskey, then closed his eyes. Between being tired and the lack of food in his stomach, the whiskey did its job and as he slipped into a deep sleep, the glass fell from his hand and landed on the floor with a loud crash, breaking and sending broken glass across the floor – but Langley never heard a sound.

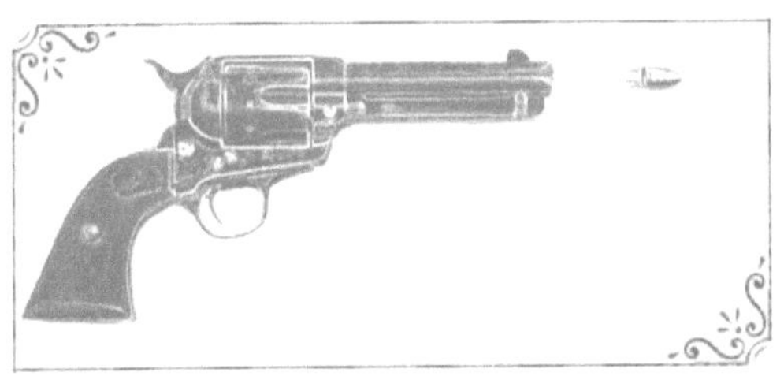

CHAPTER TWENTY-SIX

Loralie was closing the gate to the corral when Brave Eagle said, "I think Mister Brentwood is coming home."

Loralie looked through the open front gate and saw a lone rider in the far distance, but he was too far away to make out who it was. She turned back to Brave Eagle and said, "How do you know that's Mister Brentwood? I can barely make out that it's a man on a horse." Brave Eagle smiled and said, "It is him."

When Loralie looked back again at the small outline of a rider, her heart began to pound harder and she felt the excitement building up inside her. Could it really be him? Without thinking more about it, she knew if Brave Eagle said it was him… it was, and she wasn't about to stand around and wait for him to get here.

She grabbed a halter from the railing of the corral, opened corral gate and quickly put the halter on the first horse she came to and swung up on its back and raced out the front gate, leaving the corral gate for Brave Eagle to close.

Clay saw the small dust cloud coming in his direction and grinned. He knew who it was and put his heels to Midnight's sides.

The big horse felt his master's excitement and broke into a hard run.

When they pulled up to a sliding stop next to each other, Loralie leaped from her horse into Clay's arms, almost unseating him from his saddle.

After several minutes of hugging and kissing, Loralie leaned back and looked at Clay and said, "I've been so worried about you."

In mock surprise, Clay responded, "Worried? Why? I was never in any danger."

"Of course, you weren't," Loralie said. "And the sun only comes up every other day."

Clay sat Loralie back on her horse and, trying to change the subject, yelled, "I'll race you back to the ranch!"

And with that the black stallion leaped into a dead run for the front gate, leaving Loralie trying to catch up.

Fifty feet or so from the front gate, Clay pulled Midnight to a walk and looked back over his shoulder. Loralie was pushing her horse as fast as he could go, but Clay still had time to walk Midnight through the front gate at a leisurely pace. The big horse might be getting up in years for horses, but he was still a force to be reckoned with when it came to racing. Midnight loved to run and as long as he could, Clay would allow it.

Brave Eagle and several of the other people who worked on the ranch welcomed him back. Brave Eagle took both horses and led them into the barn where they would be given a good rub down, along with grain and water.

Inside the house, Mrs. McIntyre and Cindy both expressed their happiness at Clay being home.

From Clay's office, Ol' Son came racing toward Clay and leaped up on him, wagging his tail back and forth.

"Good to see you too, Ol' Son," Clay said, scratching the dog's ears and rubbing his back.

Ol' Son followed Clay into the kitchen where Mrs. McIntyre said she would be putting some food out.

Clay was surprised to see that she had fixed a nice roast with all the trimmings. He cut off a good-sized chunk of roast and slowly lowered it beneath the table where Ol' Son was waiting.

Ol' Son had just gulped down the meat when he saw his master's hand come under the table, again. This time he held a bone in his hand and Ol' Son gently took it in his teeth, then sprawled out on his belly and happily began to chew on it.

"You know you shouldn't feed him at the table," Loralie said in mock admonishment.

"Yeah, I know," Clay said with a grin as he filled his plate with the wonderful smelling food.

Mrs. McIntyre and Cindy joined them in the meal and when it was finished, it was Cindy who said to Clay, "If you want to go into the living room, I'll get you a brandy and you can tell us all about your adventure."

Clay didn't particularly like talking about chasing down outlaws and said, "A brandy sounds nice, but there wasn't much to it. He Who Bites and I tracked down the cattle rustlers and turned them over to the law. That's about all there was to it. So, now, if you don't mind, I'd like that brandy and then I really could use a bath and some rest."

When Cindy brought Clay his brandy, she asked, "Would you like to hear what happened here while you were gone?"

Before Clay could answer, Cindy said, "Miss Benson and mama each shot a man and we had to defend the place from forty or more men who wanted to take our Indians from us and hang them."

Clay almost gagged on his drink. Suddenly, a bath and sleep were the last thing on his mind. "What? Who?" Clay asked, turning to look at Loralie.

"I planned on telling you," Loralie said.

"When?" Clay asked, sitting his drink on the large oak table in front of the leather couch.

"After you've had a chance to clean up and rest," she responded with a girlish smile.

"I think right now would be a real good time," Clay said. "Are you all right? Did any of our people get hurt?" A thousand questions were racing through his mind.

"Slow down, cowboy," Loralie teased. "Sit back and enjoy your drink and I'll tell you all about it."

It took two glasses of brandy before Loralie finished telling the story of what happened, including the part where Mister Sooner went down and talked with the rancher who was about to take some of Clay's yearlings.

"Tell me somebody knew who that rancher was," Clay said when she'd finished.

About that time, Running Coyote came into the living room and said, "It was Herman Langley and his bunch."

"Langley," Clay said. "I should have known."

Running Coyote looked at Clay and said, "Seems like he's hated us ever since he got here. What got him so down on Indians? We've never done anything to him that I know of."

"Hating Indians is just the excuse he uses to cover up his real reason," Clay said, setting his glass on the table and waving off Cindy's attempt for a refill.

"So, if he doesn't really hate Indians, then what is it?" Loralie asked.

"Land," Clay said. "He wants the land where Walks Tall and his people live. It's prime land and would more than double the size of his ranch. I'm sure his hatred of you is because your people stand in his way."

"Which means he'll try to find any way he can to get us off that land, even if he has to kill us to do it," He Who Bites said from the corner of the room where he'd been standing, listening.

"That's about it," Clay said.

"What an evil man," Loralie said, shaking her head. "What can we do about him?"

"Not much, I'm afraid," Clay told her. "Not until he does something really stupid."

"Like stealing someone's cattle or hanging an innocent Indian?" Loralie asked.

Clay sighed and stood up, stretching. He was tired and needed some rest. "I'm afraid that hanging an Indian, right now, the way he's got the town riled up, would only get him a slap on the wrist, at most."

They watched as Clay mounted the stairs. "You'll tell us about what happened, in the morning?" Loralie threw at his back.

"He Who Bites can tell you about most of it," Clay said as he closed the door to his room and saw steam rising from his bathtub. Smiling, he knew He Who Bites would be in his element, giving a recount of this latest adventure.

Clay slipped into the tub of hot water and felt his body relax. He massaged the many scars on his body and was glad he'd escaped any more injuries. He wasn't sure how many more times his body could stand being shot or cut. It really was time for him to retire.

CHAPTER TWENTY-SEVEN

-

Early morning sunrise found its way into Herman Langley's office and forced its way under his eyelids, bringing him slowly awake. "What the?" he said as he sat up slowly and rubbed his hand over his face, still a bit disoriented. His mouth tasted like something he didn't want to think about and the pounding in his head made his eyes hurt. He was about to try and stand up when the knock on his office door sounded like a train wreck in his ears.

Johnny Barr, his foreman opened the door slowly and poked his head through the opening. "Mornin', boss. Any special orders you want done, today?"

"Yes! Stop yelling! Then go tell Min Sing to bring lots of black coffee up to my room, then fix me a hot bath; and when he's done with that, come in here and clean up the broken glass on my floor."

Johnny Barr had gotten to be foreman on Langley's ranch because he kept his mouth shut and followed orders. From the doorway, Johnny could see the empty whiskey bottle sitting on the desk and the washed out look on his boss's face. "Yes sir, he said as he backed away and closed the door as quietly as he could.

"And get my buggy ready. I'll be going to town right after breakfast," Johnny heard his boss yell through the closed door. "Yes sir!" he yelled over his shoulder as he hurried into the kitchen where Min Sing was already getting a pot of coffee ready to take upstairs.

Min Sing had been chief cook and housekeeper for Herman Langley for as long as anyone could remember. Someone had said Langley picked him up in St. Louis when he was coming west to look for land.

Min Sing was like many Chinese men, small in stature, but with an unbounding energy. Plus, he was the only one who wasn't afraid to stand up to the boss and speak his piece. Of course, no one ever knew what that was because, he always seemed to have a meat cleaver in his hand and rambled on in Chinese and no one understood a word he said, or challenged him, not even the boss.

When Herman Langley walked out of his house, he saw the buggy hitched and waiting by the hitchrail. As he climbed up on the buggy and sat down, Johnny Barr suddenly appeared and asked, "Anything special you want the boys to do, today, Boss?"

Langley thought for a moment, then said, "Move the cattle down to the lower forty and get a head count. I want to know how many we're missing, more or less."

"Are you sure about that? With all the cattle in the lower forty, it's gonna be a mite crowded."

Langley gave Johnny's information some thought and decided he was right. "You're right. Move half of them to the lower forty and the other half to the east pasture."

"Gonna take at least two days, and even then we won't be able to get the ones hidden in the brush," Johnny informed his boss.

"Do the best you can and give me your best guess on the ones in the brush."

"We gettin' ready for ah drive?" Johnny asked, surprised at the roundup.

Langley's head still hurt and he was tired of talking. "Just do as you're told," Langley said as he snapped the reins against the horse's hind quarters and left his foreman standing in the dust.

Johnny Barr watched as his boss drove away from the ranch – and when he was in the far distance, he turned and headed for the bunkhouse. "Mister Langley might pay well, but he sure ain't easy ta work for, no sir, not by a long shot," he said to himself. "All hands out here, now," he yelled as he got close to the bunkhouse.

The trip to Seymour took Herman Langley a little over three hours and he was in need of a little hair of the dog by the time he arrived. He left his horse and buggy at the livery stable, then headed for the nearest saloon.

This early in the day, there were only two people in the saloon when Langley came through the batwing doors and strolled up to the bar – the bartender and the town drunk, who was mopping the floor.

Langley knew the bartender and said, "Give me a cold beer," Mike.

Mike Handley had been the bartender in the Redeye Saloon for the past three years and was observant of his customers. Herman Langley's eyes were red and bloodshot and Mike knew he was suffering a hangover. "How about I fix you one of my special beer remedies? It's been known to cure what ails you."

Herman Langley was well aware of Mike's special remedy because he'd drank it before. No one knew for sure what was in it, and he would never reveal what the secret ingrediencies were, but everyone agreed, it worked. "Sure, Mike. I could use one of your special beers about now."

When Mike brought the special mug of beer and set it in front of the rancher, he asked, "So, what brings you to town?"

"Had a few too many last night and came in to get one of your special cures," Langley told him, then downed the drink and slammed the mug down on the bar and left, leaving Mike standing there, scratching the back of his neck.

When Herman Langley walked back out onto the sidewalk and stopped to look around, he was feeling much better and his head was much clearer. Mike's remedy worked fast.

Turning his head toward where the prisoners were being held, Langley saw the armed guard out front and guessed there would be others on the sides and at the back. Just how he would orchestrate the plan that had formed in his head, he wasn't yet sure, but he knew he had to do it. He needed the men who were locked up. They were ruthless and would do most anything for money.

Langley stopped at the bank with the pretense of checking his account and while he was there made a comment on where the cattle rustlers were being held.

Percival Brown was not only the bank teller, but also known as the town gossip and took the liberty of giving Langley more information than he really needed to know. Langley stood and listened, patiently.

"Well now, that's mighty interesting," Langley said when Percival finally shut up. "You say the one who run off with the ransom money was captured by that ranger fella and tossed in with the rest of them? Wasn't the sheriff afraid the others might kill him or at the very least, beat him within an inch of his life?"

Percival leaned a little closer to Langley and said, "I believe that's just what the sheriff wanted them to do."

"You don't say," Langley said, shaking his head. "And did they?"

Percival stood back up and moved some papers around on his workstation and said, "Not that anyone could tell. He seemed all right when they were marched over to eat breakfast at Lucy's Café this morning."

"That where they feed them, Lucy's Café?"

"Three times a day, and I don't need to tell you, the city council isn't too happy about the expense. Rumor has it the mayor and council will be asking you ranchers who had cattle stolen and got them back, to help pay the bills for keeping them incarcerated until the circuit judge arrives."

Langley let this piece of information roll around in his brain, then said, "Sure. Sure, I'll be glad to put in my share. In fact, I'll go over to the mayor's office right now and let him know I'm in."

Percival watched as Langley walked out of the bank, then turned to the bank president who had just walked out of his office and told him, "Now, there goes a good man."

The bank president watched as Langley turned and headed in the direction of the mayor's office and thought to himself, 'A good man? I wouldn't call him that.'

Winford Hershel had been in the banking business for more than twenty years and had come to Seymour three years ago to head up this bank. During those years he had come to be a fair judge of people. Herman Langley had been one of the people he'd taken a hard look at. Langley had walked into the bank on the third day after it had opened and told the cashier he would only deal with the bank president. When Winford came out of his office, Langley had ushered him back inside and told him he wanted to deposit ten thousand dollars, cash, like he was somebody special. Langley went on to tell him that he'd found a prime piece of property and wanted to purchase it – the only thing being, Indians were living on it. But if he had his way and he usually did, they wouldn't be there long, and the land would be his. In the meantime, he wanted to purchase the land next to it and wondered who owned it?

As the bank president, Winford Hershel kept a record of all the land surrounding Seymour – who owned, who wanted to sell and so forth. The land Langley was talking about was owned by a woman who had moved back to Minneapolis after her husband had been thrown and stomped on by a bronc. He was still alive, but that's about all you could say about him. He was confined to a wheelchair and needed constant care.

Before going to Texas, she had begged him to stay in Minneapolis and join the family business, but he had dreams of being a horse rancher and nothing or nobody was going to talk him out of it, even though he'd never ridden a horse before going to Texas.

Fortunately, his wife's family had money and they had been seeing to their daughter and her husband's needs ever since their return to Minneapolis.

Winford gave Langley what information he had and wished him luck.

As it turned out, Langley contacted the woman, telling her he was interested in buying the ranch, but had very little money. After several letters of negotiating, Langley bought the ranch for less than a third of what it was worth. Apparently, the woman just wanted to get rid of the albatross that, as far as she was concerned, had taken the life out of her husband.

When Langley took possession of the ranch, he'd bragged about how he'd taken advantage of the woman's desire to get rid of the property – even to the point of lying to her about his financial position.

From that day to now, Winford had had no respect for this man. And it was known all over town that he still, somehow, planned to run Walks Tall and his people off the land they had lived on long before any white people came here. No, Herman Langley was definitely not a good man, and more than likely, never would be.

Langley saw the mayor walking down the sidewalk on the opposite side of the street and called to him.

Mayor Dalton saw Langley coming across the street and cringed. The rancher was a blow hard and if he admitted it, he was a little bit afraid of the man.

"Mayor Dalton, just the man I'm looking for," Langley said as he stepped up on the sidewalk, next to the mayor.

"And what can I do for you, Mister Langley?" Mayor Dalton asked.

"I'm afraid you've got it all wrong mayor, it's what I can do for you and the fine people of Seymour," Langley said with a wide grin.

Always suspicious of something being too good to be true, Angus asked, "And what might that be?"

Langley took the mayor by the arm and guided him down to the saloon, where Langley suggested they talk over a cold glass of beer.

Dalton was not a heavy drinker, especially before noon, but he was afraid if he said no, the big rancher might get angry, and then who knew what would happen.

After sitting down at a table and ordering two beers, Langley looked around and saw there were only a few people in the saloon this time of day. When the bartender brought their drinks, Langley took a long pull, then wiped the foam from his mouth and said, loud enough for everyone to hear, "I heard about the jail bein' blown up and I want you to know that getting my cattle back was a real blessing. Since the new sheriff did such a good job, I'm willing to help rebuild the jail, bigger and better than it was."

The mayor was speechless as he sat and watched Langley retrieve his billfold and take out some money and laid it on the table.

"There's an even one thousand dollars," Langley proclaimed loudly. Has any other rancher come forward to help, yet?"

"No… no, not so far," Mayor Dalton said, still in shock over what Langley had just done.

"Well never let it be said that Herman Langley don't appreciate the law and what it does to help us ranchers," Langley said with a wide grin.

And with that, he gulped down the rest of his beer and stood up, sticking out his hand toward the mayor. Angus looked up at the large rancher and slowly reached out and shook hands with him. He was still in shock as he watched Langley stroll out of the saloon like he'd just saved the town.

"He did what?" Winford Hershel said when the mayor walked into his office and told him about Langley's generosity.

"You heard me right," Mayor Dalton said, spreading the bills out on the bank president's desk. "So, now I guess we need to open an account."

While the mayor and the bank president were discussing a side of Herman Langley they'd never seen before, Herman Langley was walking up to the guard standing in front of the building where the outlaws were being held.

The man standing guard watched as Langley approached him and wondered what the rancher was up to.

"You know who I am?" Langley asked when he stopped in front of the guard.

"Yeah, I know who you are. You're Herman Langley. You own a big spread southwest of town."

"So then, I guess you know that the men inside that building are the ones who stole my cattle."

The guard just nodded his head, wondering where this was headed. Langley was a big man in this part of Texas and known to be a hardcase.

"I understand they also robbed the bank where I keep my money," Langley said, staring straight at the guard.

Again, the guard just nodded his head.

"I'm guessing you're not supposed to let anyone in to see them, is that right?"

"Not without the sheriff's permission," the guard informed him, thinking he already knew this.

"Yes, about that," Langley said, rubbing his chin. "You see, I tried to see the sheriff to get his permission, and I'm sure he would have given it to me, but the thing is, he's out of town and I need to be getting back to my ranch. So, do you suppose you could bend the rule just this once? I only want to take a look at the scum who stole my cattle… Five minutes, that's all I'm asking." Langley was lying about the sheriff being out of town and hoped he didn't show up – at least until after he accomplished his mission.

The guard studied the situation for a moment, then said, "Mister Langley, I understand your predicament, but I've got my orders."

"That's very commendable," Langley told him, nodding his head. "What's your name, son?" Langley asked, still being very cordial.

"Lester. Lester Stockton," the guard told him.

"You wouldn't happen to be looking for work, would you?"

The guard swallowed and said, "Matter of fact, I am."

"You want a job with me?" Langley asked. "I pay top wages."

"I would like that just fine, Sir," Lester said, knowing what this was leading up to. "But I still can't let you go inside without the sheriff or the mayor's permission – and I'm pretty sure the mayor is in town."

Suddenly, Langley's attitude changed. "Look son, you ride for me, you ride for the brand and you do as I say. Now, I want five minutes with those scumbags in there."

Langley reached into his pocket and pulled out a roll of bills and pulled off, twenty dollars and stuffed it into Lester's pocket. "A little something to show my gratitude," Langley said with a smile as he turned and headed for the front door of the building.

"Five minutes," Lester told him as he hurried up to the front door and unlocked it.

Inside, it was semi-dark and it took a moment for Langley's eyes to adjust and when they did, he saw the outlaws standing in front of him, staring at him, wondering what he was doing here.

"Which one of you is Bill Musgrove?" Langley asked.

No one moved or even twitched an eyebrow.

Langley decided to try a different tactic. "How many of you would like to get out of here and have five hundred dollars in your pocket to go anyplace you want to?"

"I'm Bill Musgrove and I think I speak for all of us when I say we all would. What's on your mind?"

CHAPTER TWENTY-EIGHT

-

Clay Brentwood smelled bacon as he came down the stairs, feeling refreshed and in clean clothes. Of course, his feeling good today had nothing to do with the fact that Loralie had sneaked into his room during the middle of the night.

As Clay walked into the dining room, he saw Loralie sitting at the table with a cup of coffee in her hand and a smile on her lips. "Good morning, Mister Brentwood," she said, raising her cup up in a salute.

"Good morning to you, too, Miss Benson," Clay said, taking his seat at the end of the table.

Colleen McIntyre was just coming into the dining room with a platter of food and saw the exchange between Clay and Loralie. She smiled to herself, knowing the look on their faces and feeling a bit of tingling in her stomach. She and Running Coyote had exchanged similar greetings in the past. Turning and seeing Running Coyote also sitting at the table, smiling a knowing smile, she felt her face turning the color of a bright red desert flower.

She set the platter on the table, then turned and hurried back into the safety of the kitchen, almost bumping into her daughter, Cindy, who was bringing in the large pot of coffee.

"Be careful, mom, this coffee is hot," Cindy told her mother, barely skirting a possible collision.

Running Coyote had to put his hand to his mouth, pretending to stifle a sneeze, to disguise the laughter inside him. He'd seen Colleen's reaction to Clay and Loralie's greeting and knew what she was thinking. If he was the blushing kind, he too might be turning red.

As promised, over breakfast, Clay filled them in on what happened after He Who Bites went back to the ranch.

Loralie shook her head back and forth. "Clay Brentwood, you never stop amazing me."

Wanting to change the subject, Clay asked, "So, Riley, what have you and Running Coyote been up to besides running off outlaws and getting my cattle back from Langley and his bunch?"

Riley looked at Running Coyote, who nodded his head. "Well, Sir," Riley said, "durin' yer absence, we put all the cattle in one place ta keep ah better eye on 'em and picked up ten new wild horses, and Boss, you won't believe it, but Miss Benson here, she done gentled them up so's a child could ride 'em."

Clay looked over at Loralie, whose face was already turning pink. "I have no doubt she did. I've seen what she can do with horses."

He turned his attention back on Riley and said, "You'd best be careful or she just might take your job."

Riley almost choked on the mouthful of food he was trying to swallow. "But, Boss…"

Clay waved his hand at him. "Just kiddin',"

This was one of the reasons Riley liked working for Clay – he was good natured and liked a good joke, once in a while.

"Do you want me ta send some men out there to keep an eye on 'em? Riley asked. "You know, in case Langley changes his mind?"

Clay thought for a moment, then remembered the bank president telling him there were cattle buyers in town. "Yes. Six should do it.

Riley, you go into town and have Harold bring the train out, we're going to take some cattle to market." Turning to Running Coyote, Clay said, "Take some men and bring a hundred head of good stock over to the loading pens."

Both men had finished their breakfast and were ready to go – and without a word, stood up and left the room without questioning him. He was the boss.

Clay saw the questioning look on Loralie's face and said, "Winford Hershel, the bank president told me there were buyers in town looking for prime stock and I'm going to get some into them before the other ranchers do. Should get top dollar that way."

Loralie was disappointed that Clay was leaving again, but said, "Sure. You go ahead. We'll be just fine here until you get back."

Clay saw the look in Loralie's eyes and said, "If everything goes the way I think it should, we should be back no later than tomorrow afternoon."

"Of course," Loralie said. "I just didn't expect you to leave so soon after getting back."

Clay stood Loralie up and took her in his arms. "You of all people should understand, you have to strike while the iron is hot. What if it were horse buyers?"

"I know. I know. I'm just being a female. I like having you here," she confessed.

"And I like being here," Clay said, then leaned down and whispered in her ear – "Especially the nights."

Loralie's face turned as red as her hair and she pushed Clay away, slapping him playfully on the shoulder. "Get out of here. Go sell your cattle, then get back here as fast as you can."

Clay couldn't help seeing the twinkle in Loralie's eyes and he reached out and kissed her on the lips, and said, "Yes, ma'am."

CHAPTER TWENTY-NINE

Harold had replaced the broken gauge and it was late in the afternoon when Clay's train, loaded with cattle, pulled up next to the loading pens near the Seymour train station. His men began unloading the cattle while Clay walked into town to find the buyers.

There was a crowd of men standing in front of the sheriff's office and the sheriff was talking to them.

When Clay walked up and the sheriff saw him, he rushed over and said, "I don't know how you knew and don't care. I'm just glad you're here."

Clay looked at the sheriff and said, "I don't have the slightest idea what you're talking about. What happened?"

The sheriff gave a big sigh and said, "They did it again."

Clay got a tingling on the back of his neck, but asked, "Who did what, again?"

"The outlaws. They broke out of jail, again. Only this time they had outside help."

Clay was floored. How could this be happening right now? Loralie might go back to Tennessee if he got involved, again. "What kind of outside help? Anybody we know?"

"How about Herman Langley?" the sheriff told him.

"Herman Langley? What's he got to do with all this?" Clay asked, even though he was sure he already knew.

"All I know is, Langley was seen down there, talking to the guard out front, then the guard let him go inside and the next thing we knew, most of them raided the livery stable and got their horses while three of them robbed the bank, again."

Clay blew out a long breath of air as he absorbed this bit of information. Finally, he looked at the sheriff and said, "Which means the cattle buyers have no money with which to buy cattle."

"I guess so," the sheriff said, scratching his head.

"I just brought in a train load of cattle into town, to sell," Clay informed him.

"Then maybe you should go with us and get their money back," the sheriff told him.

"Of course," Clay said, "but first I need to speak with my foremen."

Clay found Running Coyote and Riley emptying the last carload of cattle and drew them aside where he informed them of the situation.

Running Coyote listened and said, "I need to come with you. I know where they are going."

Clay looked at Running Coyote for a moment before understanding filled his brain. "He wouldn't be stupid enough to try something like that, would he?"

"The man is crazy, Clay. Yes, even crazy enough to try something like that."

"I'm sure glad you fellas know what you're talkin' about cause I don't have ah clue," Riley told them.

Clay looked at Riley and said, "I need you to find the buyers and have them look at our cattle and get offers. Let them know the cattle goes to the highest bidder and you'll only take sealed written bids."

Riley grinned. "That's smart boss, real smart."

"You tell them we'll be bringing their money back," Clay told him.

Clay then turned to Harold and said, "I need you to go out to the ranch and let Loralie know what happened. Tell her I don't have any other choice but to go after them. Otherwise, the buyers can't buy my cattle."

"Don't worry, Mister Brentwood, I'll do my best to keep her temper in check. You just go do what you have to do."

When Clay and Running Coyote got back to the sheriff's office, the sheriff informed Clay he had a good forty men in the posse – some of them were cattle buyers wanting to get their money back.

"Which ones are they?" Clay asked.

After the sheriff pointed them out, Clay had a talk with them and convinced them to stay in town and look over his cattle, and if they liked what they saw, make a bid.

The sheriff had no idea which direction to go, but Clay said, "We do," indicating his head toward Running Coyote.

Winford Hershel stood on the sidewalk in front of the bank and watched the posse ride out of town, heading south. He was glad the ranger had come to town when he did and was doubly glad Clay was heading up the posse. "The man always seems to show up when he is needed," he said to himself before going back into the bank and hanging a closed sign on the door.

CHAPTER THIRTY

-

Herman Langley rode at the head of the outlaws when they entered his ranch and came to a stop in front of his house.

Several of the ranch hands came out to see who was there, and were instructed to show the outlaws to the bunkhouse and where to put up their horses. He further instructed the cook to fix something to eat for everyone.

"When you've finished putting your gear away and had a bite to eat, there will be a meeting in the barn."

Turning to the nearest cowboy who worked for him, Langley said, "Inform the others about the meeting, and tell them to get something to eat, along with meeting the new hands."

The young cowboy looked at the outlaws and saw trouble. They were rough looking and all of them were wearing guns. Not one of them looked like he'd ever worked cattle before, but he held his tongue. "Yes sir," was all he said as he turned and headed for the bunk house.

Langley went into his house and headed straight for his office where he opened a bottle of whiskey and took a long pull before filling a glass sitting on his desk. He sat down behind his desk and looked at the glass of whiskey. What he was about to do would make him the largest rancher in this part of Texas, but he would have to keep his wits about him to do it right. He picked up the glass and gently poured the whiskey back into the bottle.

The barn was filled with over fifty men when Herman Langley walked in. Right away, he noticed the ranch hands were standing in the middle of the open area, while the outlaws were standing off to one side. So be it, he thought to himself. Once this was over, they would be long gone, anyway.

He'd promised each man five hundred dollars, which would be worth it to get done what he wanted done, but maybe, just maybe, a few of them might get killed along the way, saving him a few thousand dollars.

"Men," Langley said, stepping up on a bale of hay and raising his hands over his head.

The men stopped mumbling amongst themselves and turned toward their boss.

"Tonight, we are going to do something I should have done a long time ago, and I know you're all wondering about the new men. I brought some extra help because the job I want done requires men tough enough to get the job done."

The men stared up at their boss, wondering what he was going to do now. Each man who worked for Langley knew he was capable of doing things that pushed the limits of the law and wondered if this was one of those times.

"I know some of you are cowards and do not ride for the brand, so when I tell you what I want done, you'll probably balk. So be it. You're free to pack your gear and leave. But for the ones of you who stay, there will be a five-hundred-dollar bonus come payday."

Langley was well aware of the outlaws robbing the bank, again, and he had plans for that money. How he was going to get it from them, he wasn't sure, but get it, he would.

"A five-hundred-dollar bonus sounds real good boss, but what do we have to do ta earn it?" his foreman asked.

Langley looked down at his men and said, "We're gonna run them, stinking, cattle thieving redskins off the land that is rightfully mine! That's what we're gonna do."

There was a stunned silence in the barn. All of the cowboys who worked for Herman Langley knew he harbored a grudge against the Indians, especially Walks Tall and his people who lived on the land adjoining Langley's ranch. It was prime land and was on the migration route for the buffalo, but they never thought he might go this far.

Bill Musgrove saw the surprised looks on their faces and the reluctance to go along with Langley's plan. He, himself, could care less one way or another about the Indians. As far as he could see, they were on their way out, anyway. More and more white people were coming from back east, looking for free land and the Indians who stood in their way would get pushed aside. Bill saw an opportunity to put himself in a better position with the rancher. "We're with you all the way," he said, indicating his men. "It's something that should have been done a long time ago."

Herman Langley looked at Bill Musgrove and grinned. He hated the man and all that he stood for, but right now he was of use. Maybe he would have the opportunity to shoot him during the battle. "Now, here are men with some backbone, ready to make a wrong, right. Who's with us?"

The thought of the extra money in their pockets just for chasing some Indians off a piece of land they were eventually going to lose, anyway, put all but three of them in a receptive mood. "We're with you, too, Mister Langley. What's the plan?"

Herman Langley watched as his foreman and two other cowboys backed away, then turned and headed for the bunkhouse to get their gear. "Cowards!" Langley yelled at them.

-

Before leaving town, Clay and Running Coyote had a discussion on the merit of going to Langley's ranch, first, to try and catch the outlaws before they left. That might result in retrieving the bank money, but in the end, without more proof, the sheriff couldn't arrest Langley, so, it wouldn't stop Langley and his men from raiding Walks Tall's camp and the possibility of a lot of innocent Indians being killed, including women and children. It would be in the interest of Walks Tall and his people if they were standing with them when Langley and his bunch arrived.

When the sheriff was informed of what both Clay and Running Coyote thought Langley was up to, he had a hard time believing it. "As I understand it, they've lived on that land ever since before the white man got here."

"That's true," Clay replied, "but Langley doesn't see it that way. In his opinion the Indians are nothing more than heathens and the white man has every right to take whatever land he wants, even if it means killing all the red skinned people who get in the way."

"And he thinks he can get away with it?" the sheriff asked.

Clay looked at the sheriff and said, "If he does this, what do you plan to do about it? Are you going to arrest him and give the land back to Walks Tall and his people?"

The sheriff looked at Clay and swallowed. "You know I can't do that. It's far out of my jurisdiction."

"That's right," Clay said with anger in his voice. "You or nobody else is going to raise a finger to stop him until there are laws that cover driving the Redman off his property, or even killing them all. The sad thing is, a lot of the people who could do something, feel the same way Langley does."

The sheriff shook his head and said, "You know, until a short time ago, I felt the same way they do."

"And now?" Clay asked.

The sheriff looked at Running Coyote and said, "After meeting Mister Coyote and his friends, and finding out some of them are far more educated than I am, and not the heathens I believed them to be, I'll do all I can to see Langley and people like him, no longer drive the Indians off their lands."

Running Coyote looked at the sheriff and said, "Thank you. There may be hope for you, yet."

The sheriff laughed and said, "I truly hope so, my friend. I truly hope so."

So, with the decision made, they headed south of town for a mile, then turned west, which would take them across part of Clay's ranch and then across part of Marion Sooner's place. It would be well after dark before they got to Walks Tall's land.

The moon was well up in the sky when Clay and the posse left Clay's land and crossed over onto Marion Sooner's property. Clay rode close to Running Coyote and told him it might be to their advantage if Marion and his men wanted to join the posse.

Running Coyote saw the wisdom in this and turned his horse in the direction of Marion's ranch house. As he rode away, the sheriff rode up next to Clay and asked, "Where's he going?"

"I was thinking if Marion Sooner and his men were to join us…"

"And Running Coyote is headed to his place to recruit him," the sheriff said, nodding his head.

"Well, I wouldn't want him to miss out on something like this. He dislikes Herman Langley almost as much as I do," Clay told the sheriff.

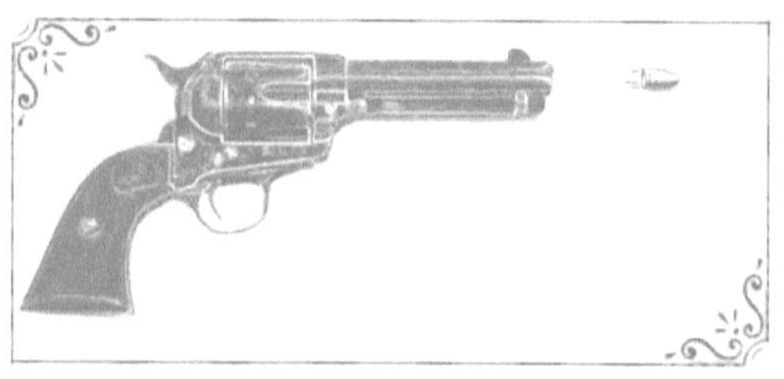

CHAPTER THIRTY-ONE

Loralie listened as Harold informed her of what had happened and of Clay's reasoning to allow himself to get involved, again.

"What did these people do before Clay got here?" Loralie asked, which only brought a shrug from Harold's shoulders and Shorty staring off into space.

They were sitting on the couch in front of the fireplace and Mrs. McIntyre and her daughter, Cindy had been standing in the doorway between the living room and the dining room, and had heard it all.

"There was a lot of lawlessness back then," Mrs. McIntyre informed them. "They should put up a statute for him for what's he's done, but they'll just say, "He's a Texas Ranger and that's what he's supposed to do."

"I suppose you're right," Loralie said.

After Harold and Shorty left and went out to the bunkhouse for the night, and Cindy went off to bed, Loralie and Mrs. McIntyre sat up late, discussing the problem of how to keep Clay home long enough for him to get married.

"Ya know he wants ta marry ya, or he wouldn't have asked ya and brought ya all the way out here," Mrs. McIntyre declared.

"I know. I know," Loralie said, "but what I can't understand, is why the sheriff and the rest of them in Seymour can't seem to do anything without Clay being involved. He told me he's retired from being a Texas Ranger, but yet, he goes traipsing off to only God knows where whenever they come begging him to do something."

Mrs. McIntyre nodded her head back and forth and poured more wine for the two of them. "No matter what he says, the man still feels an obligation, not only ta the people, but Walks Tall and his people. After all, they are his kin, ya know."

Loralie drank down half of the wine that was in her glass before saying, "I'm sure you're right, but that doesn't change the fact that he is needed here on the ranch and that they need to learn to handle their troubles, themselves. That's why they hired a sheriff. About Walks Tall and his people, I can understand that."

Mrs. McIntyre took a sip of her wine and set the glass on the table in front of her. "That sounds good, but the truth is, the sheriff has no jurisdiction beyond the city limits unless he's in hot pursuit, which we know ain't gonna happen. Whereas, Mister Brentwood bein' ah Texas Ranger, is free ta chas 'em all over the state."

"But if he's retired…" Loralie said.

"Tut, tut. Once ah Texas Ranger, always ah Texas Ranger. They don't ever actually retire," Mrs. McIntyre informed the woman who would soon be the true mistress of the house – that is if they could keep Mister Brentwood home long enough for a marriage to take place.

"Well I hope he doesn't take too long in catching them – and I hope that stupid sheriff can keep them locked up long enough this time, for a judge to sentence them."

"I'll drink ta that," Mrs. McIntyre said as she lifted her glass to her lips.

Everyone in Seymour more than likely thought the same thing. Even the mayor was thinking he had made a mistake hiring this man.

CHAPTER THIRTY-TWO

-

Clay and the posse were not far from Walks Tall's camp when, Running Coyote and Marion Sooner and his men caught up to them. "I hope what Running Coyote told me isn't true," Marion Sooner said as he rode up next to Clay.

"It sure looks like it is," Clay told his friend.

"Did he completely lose his mind, or somthin'?" Marion asked, shaking his head.

"That's what we're going to find out real soon," Clay answered.

"And he thinks he can get away with raidin' Walks Tall and his people – run them off their land and take it for his own, and nobody will say or do anything?" Marion asked as though no one had given this any thought.

"That's about the way I have it figured," Clay told him.

"And he helped break that bunch of thievin' no goods out of jail to help him make this raid?" Marion asked over his shoulder at the sheriff.

"Plus, they robbed the bank, again," the sheriff added.

"So, where do you think they are now?" Marion asked, continuing to satisfy his curiosity.

"That we're not sure of. But it's my hope we get to Walks Tall's camp before they do," Clay said.

"Does Walks Tall know about any of this?" Marion asked.

"Not unless Langley and his bunch have already gotten there," Clay answered.

"Then we'd best hurry," Marion suggested.

Clay looked at Marion and said, "I sent He Who Sleeps A Lot on ahead to warn Walks Tall and tell him we're on our way to help."

Marion looked toward the west and said, "We're not far from his camp and I don't hear any gunfire, so I guess we're still in the clear."

Marion had no more than gotten the words out of his mouth when the sound of yelling and gunfire filled the air.

"Sounds like the party started without us," Clay said over the roar of the gunfire. "We'll ride like the devil is chasing us until we get close enough to see what's going on, then slow down and take a look. No point in rushing in like yokels and getting our heads blown off."

As they came to the top of a small rise, they could look down into the Indian camp and were surprised at what they saw. The moon was out and they could see everything clearly. Langley and his bunch had ridden into the camp, hoping to catch the Indians asleep and take them by surprise. But that's not what happened.

Walks Tall and his people were in the tall grass surrounding his camp and when the outlaws got to the center of the camp, the Indians cut loose on them, killing at least ten or more in the first volley.

Langley and his bunch were confused and couldn't see anyone to shoot at so they were shooting at anything and nothing.

"They must 'a knowed we was comin'!" one of the cowboys yelled.

"How do we get outta this mess?" another cowboy yelled back at him.

From their vantage point, Clay and his men spread out and came down to the camp and circled the outlaws, with their rifles pointed at them. Walks Tall and his braves allowed Clay and his men to ride past them, then waited to see what was going to happen.

"Langley, if you and your men want to go on breathing, tell them to throw their guns on the ground and raise their hands in the air. You're surrounded and there's no reason for anyone else to die," Clay yelled at the top of his voice.

Suddenly the night got as quiet as a tomb. The men looked at Langley, waiting for him to give a command, although, the majority of the cowboys were ready to give up. They'd thought this was a stupid idea to begin with. They'd been enticed by the money Langley offered each one of them. It was the outlaws who couldn't see any good side to giving up – especially not if they were to get hung in the end.

Langley raised his hand in the air and said, "Throw down your guns, boys! We'll live to fight another day."

"Not us! Follow me, boys!" Bill Musgrove yelled as he turned and headed for the far side of the camp, shooting at anything that moved.

There were only a few of the town's people on that side of the camp and the Indians that were there had only bows and arrows. When two of the townsmen left their saddles with gunshot wounds, the others turned and ran. The Indians stayed low until the outlaws passed, then fired arrows at them, but they had already disappeared into the night.

Clay had no choice but to watch them ride off into the darkness. He counted six of them and doubted the ones who had died were the ones carrying the stolen money. If he had to guess, he would put his money on Musgrove.

"I might 'a known it was you," Langley spat out as Clay rode up next to him.

"You didn't really think you could get away with this, did you?" Clay asked.

"I did, and would have if you hadn't shown up," Langley said as he glared at Clay. "Once I had possession of the land, who was gonna take it away from me?"

Clay studied Langley and knew what he'd just said was true. A small group of people would complain and say what an awful man he was, but the majority would praise him for having the guts to do it. After all, the Indians were heathens and he had every right to take the land if he wanted it.

Langley looked around and saw that the Indians had come out of hiding and had them surrounded. He watched as the one called, Walks Tall walked up and stopped next to the ranger.

"Thank you, my brother," Walks Tall said to Clay.

Clay grinned and said, "You knew I couldn't let you have all the fun."

One of Langley's men swallowed and asked, "What are they gonna do to us, now?"

Clay turned and looked at the cowboy and saw he was scared. Deciding to have some fun, he said, "Well, I guess since you came here to kill him and his people, it would only be fair if we turn you over to them. What they would do, I'm not sure, but I do know they have a whole bunch of ways of torturing a man before he dies – like stringing him up and skinning him a little at a time until he begs them to kill him."

Clay watched as the young cowboy's face turned white and he began to breathe hard.

"You… you wouldn't let 'em do that to us, would you, Mister Langley?"

"Don't you pay any attention to him. He's just pulling your leg, trying to get you all riled up," Langley said, shaking his head.

"That's right," Walks Tall said. "We don't skin white people any more. They cry and whimper like women. Now we stake them out over ant hills and pour honey on their faces, then leave so we don't have to listen to their crying and begging."

"That ain't true, either, is it Mister Langley?" the young cowboy asked, almost in tears.

Walks Tall had to turn away so they wouldn't see him laugh and it was all Clay could do to keep a straight face.

Before Langley got a chance to say anything more, Clay got himself together and looked down at Walks Tall. "You planning on pressing charges?"

Walks Tall thought for a full minute before answering Clay, which made Langley begin to get nervous. "If I do, what will it get me? Nothing. The whites in town will say it is out of their jurisdiction, plus, we are just Indians and therefore, we have no rights."

At this, Langley grinned and looked at Clay. "He's right, Ranger. They're just heathen redskins and have no rights as far as the law is concerned… So, if you and your friends will back off, me and my boys will be leaving."

With a smug look on his face, Langley looked down at Walks Tall and said, "This ain't over, redman, not by a long shot. The next time you won't be so lucky and have your friends here to help you. You take my advice and pack up and move somewhere else.

You do that and you just might save the lives of your people… Otherwise…"

With that, Langley swung his horse around and led his men away from Walks Tall's camp, laughing as he went. He yelled over his shoulder, "Bring our dead with us. We'll bury them on my land."

To say that Clay was seething with anger, would be stating it lightly. He wanted to arrest him for breaking the outlaws out of jail, but knew that was useless, also. "You stay alert and keep lookouts. The man is crazy and wants your land, real bad," Clay told Walks Tall.

"We'll try to help keep an eye out for 'em, too," Marion Sooner said.

Walks Tall smiled and said, "Thank you. It is because of people like you that we know all white people aren't bad, just like all redmen aren't bad. We have men just like your Langley, who believe all whites are bad and want to make war on them."

The sheriff rode up next to Clay and said, "I don't mean to interrupt all this back pattin', but don't we have some outlaws to track down and some money to get back?"

Clay looked at the sheriff and said, "Where we're going will be a good way out of your jurisdiction, so I suggest you and the other men go on back to town. I'll put some of my men together and go after them. I am still a Texas Ranger, I guess, which gives me a lot more room to operate."

Several of the men from town offered to go along. Clay thanked them but said, "Nothing personal, but me and my men have worked together for some time now and I think I would prefer to keep my posse, small."

Walks Tall and his people watched as the white men rode away, wondering if he would be as lucky the next time.

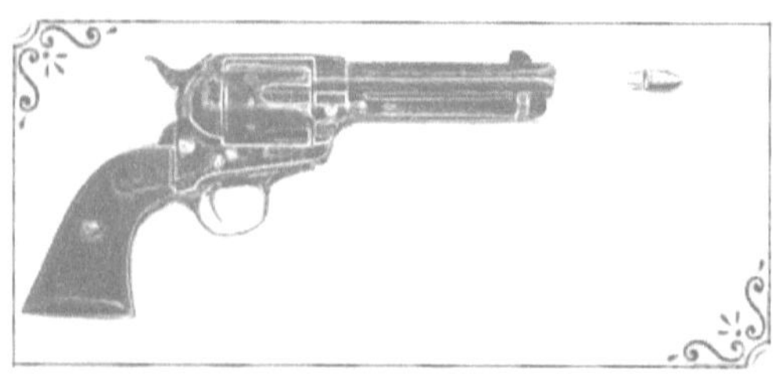

CHAPTER THIRTY-THREE

The outlaw's horses were covered with lather and blowing hard by the time Bill Musgrove called a halt near a small stream. "We'll hole up here long enough to rest the horses and give them a drink. One of you take my horse while I have a look at our back trail."

None of the outlaws argued with Bill. After all, he had been second in command and now that James was dead, Bill just naturally took command and none of the outlaws wanted to challenge him.

"We could sure use some coffee," one of the men said as Bill was walking away.

Bill stopped and looked back at the men and saw they were in need of rest. "Make sure the fire is small and can't be seen. And use dry wood to keep the smoke down."

Bill had to admit to himself, he too needed rest and the thought of coffee sounded good.

Bill had walked nearly a quarter of a mile before he found a small hill that would give him a wide field of vision.

The moon was on the downside of the sky, but bright enough that Bill took off his hat before dropping down on his stomach and looking over the top of the rise.

The only movement he saw came from a deer that was making its way across the plains. The thought of deer meat made his mouth water, but two things prohibited that. First, the deer was too far away for a clean shot – and second, if anyone was following them, the sound of a rifle shot would alert them. They would just have to wait until they came upon a town or a ranch where they could get a meal and fresh horses. He knew he needed to put as much distance as he could between him and the ranger – who he knew would be coming after the money.

After watching for a good half an hour, Bill decided they were safe, at least for the time being. He stood up and headed back toward the river and the coffee.

As he sat leaning back against a tree, sipping the hot brew, his mind drifted to what to do about the money. If the truth were known, he wanted to keep it all. It would not only get him back east; it would also be enough to set him up in a business of some kind. But he knew that wouldn't be possible unless he could somehow get rid of the five men who wanted their share and wouldn't think twice about killing him if he did anything stupid."

One of the outlaws, Luke Nevil, was a tall rawboned man in his late thirties who rode for anyone who would pay him. What he had to do for the money was of little matter as long as he got paid. Luke walked up and looked down at Bill. "We need ta get movin'. We're all hungry and none of us has any food that I know of. Plus, we need ta find a place where we can split the money Then we can all head in different directions and confuse that ranger - and hope we're not the one he follows."

There it was. They were thinking about the money so he would have to be very careful if he was going to get away with all of it.

Bill stood up, downed the rest of his coffee, then walked over and bent down and rinsed his cup in the stream. When he stood up, Nevil was standing a few feet away, waiting for him to say something.

"You're right," Bill said. "We need to get something to eat and some fresh horses – and yes, definitely split up the money."

As Bill started to step around the outlaw, Nevil stepped in front of him. "What's wrong with splittin' the money here and now, then we could go our separate ways before that ranger gets too close."

Bill stopped dead in his tracks, knowing what the outlaw said was true. The only problem he had, was, he didn't want to part with the money.

Finding no other way out of the situation, Bill pulled his pistol and shot Nevil in the heart, and when the outlaw fell to the ground, he pulled the man's pistol from his holster and placed it in his hand.

He'd just stood up and stepped away from the body when the others came running over.

"What happened?" they wanted to know.

Thinking quickly, Bill Musgrove holstered his pistol and said, "He informed me he was going to kill me and take over. I had no choice but to shoot him. He already had the drop on me, but I guess I was a little quicker."

This was something outlaws could understand and accept, which they did. Again, with outlaws not having a lot of compassion, they dragged his body off into the trees and left it for the animals, after taking what they wanted from him, such as his boots, pistol and gun belt. One of them wanted his hat.

Back at the small fire, Bill Musgrove took charge, again and told them to mount up. "We need to find a place where we can get some food and fresh horses."

The thought of food and fresh horses caused them to forget about the money, at least for the time being.

As they rode away toward the west, Bill Musgrove wondered who else he was going to have to kill so he could keep the money. It didn't really matter. He would kill them all if that's what it took.

CHAPTER THIRTY-FOUR

Clay and his men went back to the ranch to get something to eat, along with some rest. Tomorrow, after an early breakfast, they would get fresh horses and whatever else they thought they would need for the trip. He Who Bites would be able to pick up the outlaws tracks easier come morning when he could see better.

The biggest problem Clay could foresee, was facing and telling Loralie he was leaving, again, to go chase down the same outlaws he'd already captured before. None of this would be happening if Seymour had a sheriff with a lick of sense.

When Loralie saw them ride in, she went out to the barn to greet them and inform Clay she'd been making plans for their wedding. The wedding was planned for Friday of next week. She would have the house decorated by then, plus, that was the day the minister from town could come out. Invitations had been sent and Manuel had started to dig the pit to roast a half a beef. All Clay needed to do was pick out a beef calf to butcher, and show up.

Loralie arrived at the same time Mrs. McIntyre did, except she was there to greet Running Coyote. Cindy showed up seconds later and was looking for Riley.

Clay rarely allowed anyone to see to Midnight because the black stallion had been known to be a little cantankerous around people he didn't care for. More than one ranch hand had teeth mark scars to prove it. But he liked Manual's son and followed him into a stall when Clay handed the boy Midnight's reins. He would have seen to Midnight himself, but he could see the eagerness in Loralie's face and hurried over to her.

She always seemed to surprise him by her willingness to kiss him in public, which she did as soon as he was close enough.

"We need to talk," Clay said as soon as Loralie allowed him to come up for air.

"Yes, we do. Me first," Loralie said, dragging Clay outside the barn. Taking his hand in hers, she began to walk, swinging their arms back and forth like some young couple taking a stroll in the moonlight.

When they got to the well, she released his hand and turned to face him. "Do you still love me?" she asked.

Clay was taken back a little, but managed to say, "Of course I still love you. We're going to be married, aren't we?"

"Friday, next week as a matter of fact. It's all been planned. All you need to do select a cow to cook over the fire and show up," Loralie stated.

From the look on Clay's face, she could tell he was stunned. "What's the matter? Cat got your tongue?" Loralie asked with a big grin.

When Clay was finally able to speak, he asked, "How did you… I mean… When did…"

Loralie reached up and kissed Clay, again. This time, soft and gentle, then stood back and said, "You didn't think I was just going to sit around and wait for you to get back, did you? I came out her so we could get married, and since you were too busy chasing outlaws, me and Mrs. McIntyre and her daughter, Cindy, put our heads together. Now it's all set. Like I said, all you have to do is show up."

Clay walked over to the well and dropped the bucket into the water and drew up a fresh bucket full, then took the cup from where it hung on one of the uprights and took a long drink.

Loralie put her hands on her hips and stomped her foot. 'You're leaving again, aren't you!" she said through gritted teeth.

"Drink?" Clay asked, extending a cup of water to her.

"No! I don't want any water! Now you tell me straight, Mister Clay Brentwood, are you leaving again in the morning?"

Clay took Loralie by the arm and guided her into his office where he poured himself a stiff drink of whiskey.

"No, Clay. You can't be leaving again. I've made all these plans," Loralie said. "What happened?"

Clay sat Loralie in one of the two stuffed chairs sitting in front of his desk, and took the other one. "It's complicated," he said.

"I've got all night," Loralie said as she folded her arms across her chest and glared at him.

It took two stiff drinks to get it all out and when he'd finished, Loralie shook her head back and forth. "You mean to tell me, they escaped from the sheriff, again, and then you just sat there and watched them ride away from Walks Tall's camp?"

Clay sighed and set his glass on his desk and said, "That about sums it up."

"And you think you can catch them, bring them back and still be home in time to get married?" Loralie asked.

"That's the plan," Clay said, hoping that would satisfy her.

"And what if you don't make it? What am I supposed to do?" Loralie asked, point blank.

Trying to make lite of the situation, Clay said, "I could leave one of the ranch hands here and he could act as a stand in – you know, like a proxy. That way we could still be married whether I'm back in time, or not."

The look on Loralie's face said she couldn't believe he'd just said what he had, but she came right back with, "And is your ranch hand supposed to fill in on our wedding night, too? That might be interesting. Do I get to choose the ranch hand?"

"All right. All right," Clay said, raising his hands up in the air. "I promise, if I am not dead, I will be here for the wedding. And just so you know, I was just kidding about the ranch hand."

Loralie looked at Clay and he knew she meant business when she said, "If you don't show up, I won't be here when you do get back. The wedding is planned for Friday next week at four o'clock in the afternoon. If you're not here by ten minutes after four, I will be on your train and Harold will be taking me back to Tennessee. Now, if you truly want to marry me, go catch those outlaws and then get back here. You've got, ten days."

And with that, she left Clay's office and went up to her room.

Clay's first reaction was anger. He didn't like being given ultimatums and was on the verge of telling her not to wait, but to go back to Tennessee. He was a Texas Ranger and it was his job to chase down outlaws. A man didn't pick and choose which outlaws he went after. An outlaw was an outlaw. In this case his own cattle, along with the cattle of his fellow ranchers had been involved, along with the bank robbery. They all had money in that bank and he wasn't about to let some owl hoots run off with it. Besides, hadn't he dropped everything when she was in trouble and asked for his help? She knew what she was getting into when she came out here. They'd talked about it.

Clay walked over and sat down in his chair and began to laugh. She was just being the fiery redhead she always was. She was just frustrated at the thought of him not being here for the wedding. Women took big store by their weddings. It was very important to them. Not that it wasn't important to him, too, but women fussed over things more than men did.

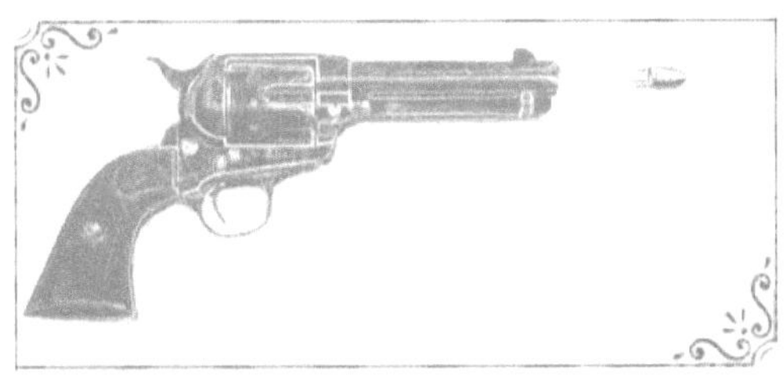

CHAPTER THIRTY-FIVE

-

He Who Bites, Riley, Brave Eagle and one of Clay's ranch hands, Slim, were waiting on him when Clay walked out of the house the next morning. Clay saw two pack horses had been loaded and were ready to go. Along with an extra horse for each man, Clay saw the black stallion was saddled and next to him was the buckskin mare he liked as a second horse. Ol' Son sat on the porch, wagging his tail, slowly. He would like to be going with them, but knew he no longer could.

Loralie hadn't come down for breakfast and Clay had mixed feelings about that. He'd liked to have told her everything would be all right, but it was her choice not to come down. Maybe it was better this way. That way there would be no arguing before he left.

Clay was about to put his foot in the stirrup when Loralie came running out of the house, shouting his name. "Clay! Clay, don't leave yet!"

Clay turned around just in time to catch her as Loralie leaped into his arms.

"I'm sorry about last night," she said with tears in her eyes. "I was just scared that you wouldn't be back in time for the wedding and I'm so looking forward to us getting married."

Clay started to say something, but Loralie reached up and put her finger against his lips.

"I know you're not only a rancher, but also a Texas Ranger, a lawman, and people look to you to help them when they're in trouble. And this time it involves you and your friends. So, you go do what you have to do. I'll pray you get back in time for us to get married, but if not, we'll just reschedule."

"Does this mean you won't be going back to Tennessee?" Clay asked with a grin.

"You're stuck with me, cowboy, and don't you forget it. Now go catch them outlaws and get back here so you can make an honest woman out of me."

And with that, she kissed him on the lips, then turned and ran up onto the porch so he could not see the tears beginning to run down her cheeks. Ol' Son walked over and leaned against her leg, wagging his tail slowly, back and forth.

-

Just on the west side of Walks Tall's camp, He Who Bites picked up the outlaw's trail. They had been in a hurry and hadn't bothered to try and hide their tracks, so the posse had been able to ride at a ground eating speed. By noon, they arrived at the edge of the small stream where the outlaws had crossed.

He Who Bites took his time studying the campsite. He even went as far as wading across the stream and finding where they crossed. The horses hoof prints were clearly embedded in the mud.

Back at the campsite, He Who Bites faced Clay and the others and said, "They continue to go west."

"How long have they been gone?" Riley asked.

He Who Bites said, "The tracks are several hours old, maybe twelve hours or more. I would say they didn't spend the night here, but only long enough to rest their horses a little."

"Any idea what there is west of here – ranches, towns, water?" Riley asked. "I ain't never been this far west and it looks pretty desolate to me."

Clay looked off to the west and said, "The next decent sized town west of here is Lubbock, and that's a good three to four-day ride if you have plenty of water with you. If you don't you might not make it. That's no man's land out there and as far as I know, there isn't enough water to sustain anything but the snakes and other critters that live there, but not a herd of cattle, so I doubt if they'll run into any ranches."

"We still plannin' on goin' after 'em?" Slim asked.

"I am," Clay said. "It won't be easy, and any man who wants to go back will not be looked on harshly. If it wasn't that I need to return the money, I would probably let them wander around out there and suffer their own fate, but that's the town's money and they need it to survive." He would never let the town of Seymour go bankrupt. He could afford to buy the bank, make loans and help keep the town solvent, but that was not information he tossed around, lightly.

Clay stepped down and got two large waterskins from one of the pack horses. As he stooped next to the stream to fill the skins, Slim dropped down next to him and began filling another waterskin. "I ride for the brand, and where you go, I go."

Riley walked up next to the stream, also, holding a waterskin. "You boys ain't goin' nowhere without me," he said with a wide grin.

By the time Clay and the others were hanging the waterskins on the pack horses, He Who Bites and Brave Eagle had gathered large bunches of grass that grew near the edge of the stream and had tied them on the packs.

"Water is not the only thing the horses will need out there," Brave Eagle told them.

Slim looked at the two Indians and had a new appreciation for them. He'd never been around Indians much and was impressed by what he learned from them.

"They'll do ta ride the river with," Slim whispered to Riley, who grinned and nodded his head. He too had come to appreciate their knowledge – but most of all, their friendship and loyalty.

"Hey, where's the next waterhole? My canteen's empty," one of the outlaws yelled through the dust cloud a hot, westerly wind was pushing across the desert.

Bill Musgrove was riding at the head of the column and looked up ahead, through the dust and sighed. What he saw was more of what they were riding through – a lonely, desolate land that gave no quarter. The temperature had to be close to a hundred and showed no signs of cooling down before nightfall. If there was any water out here in this God-forsaken piece of hell, only the snakes, lizards, and Indians would know where it was. At every high point, he'd looked for signs of a ranch or a town, but had come to realize the chance of that were zero and none. A short while later, he felt his horse stumble.

Pulling his horse to a halt, he called out, "Give the horses a rest and any water you can spare."

As he stepped down from his horse, he noticed that along with his horse, all the other horses were standing on trembling legs and their mouths were dripping foam. They were all, covered with dust.

"We gotta find someplace where we can get in outta this, plus we need some feed and water for our horses, or we ain't gonna make it," one of the outlaws said as he walked up close to Bill.

"Any idea where that might be?" another outlaw asked.

"Since I've never been this far west, your guess is as good as mine," Bill told him. "If any of you know this area, and where a ranch or a town is out here, speak up. I'll be happy to follow you," he said to the rest of them.

When no one said anything, another of the outlaws spoke up. "Maybe we should go back."

Bill looked at him and said, "You planning on walking, because your horse sure isn't going to carry you. Look at him, he's done in."

"We should 'a brought more water than we did, and extra horses," someone said.

"Yeah, Bill, why didn't you tell us ta do just that?" a voice from the back called out.

"Don't go blaming me," Bill said to all of them. "I have no more knowledge about this part of Texas than you do. Besides, we were in a bit of a hurry to get outta there, if you'll recall."

"So, what are we gonna do now, just wander around out here til we die of thirst?"

Bill's mouth was dry and his tongue felt several times larger than it should be as he looked ahead of them. In the distance, maybe half a mile or so, there was a small bunch of hills grouped together. It just might be what was needed for the idea that was forming in his brain. "We're going to walk our horses over to those hills," he told them, pointing toward the hills.

"What's over there?" one of the outlaws wanted to know.

"Maybe, life," Bill said as he started walking in the direction of the hills, his horse plodding along behind him with his head hanging down. He could see a few small trees, and with trees, there was a slight chance of water being there, also.

-

"We're gaining on them," He Who Bites told Clay. "See how the horses tracks show their feet are dragging and taking shorter steps. I doubt if they have any water, so the horses are moving slowly. It won't be long now before we catch up to them."

"In that case, let's take a break and water our horses and give them a little grass to eat. We want our horses in good shape when we catch up to the outlaws," Clay said.

Brave Eagle pointed to a small group of elm trees off to the left – ones the outlaws had passed by in their hurry to put distance between them and the ranger. "It won't be much shade, but better than staying out here," Brave Eagle told them as he led them toward the trees and what little cover they would provide.

The small group of elm trees surrounded a pool of water not two feet across and would provide only water for one horse at a time. Even with that, they had to wait a few minutes for the pool to refill itself. Pools of water like this existed; fed by underground waterways, but few knew about them. Many a tenderfoot had died of thirst no more than thirty or forty feet from such water. Other waterholes in this area were filled with alkali and not fit to drink. They were lucky to find this one.

Riley took advantage of the time and made a pot of coffee and a pan of beans. "We got ta keep up our strength too, if we're gonna be fightin' outlaws," he told the others with a grin spread across his face.

A little over an hour later, they tightened the cinches on their saddles and climbed aboard.

With He Who Bites in the lead so he could look for the outlaw's tracks, Clay and the others followed along.

As he rode along, Clay pulled his binoculars out of his saddlebag and put them to his eyes. They were strong binoculars and he could see for a long way, but to his dismay, all he saw was heat waves dancing across the dry, barren ground - not even a jack rabbit or a road runner. In the far, far distance, he thought he could see what amounted to a dust storm, but it was still a long way ahead of them. It'll be gone before we get to it, he thought to himself.

Sighing, he put the binoculars back in the case and hung the strap over the saddle horn in case they were needed, again. This was only day one, and how long it would take to catch up to the outlaws, he had no idea. And when they did, how long would it take to capture them and put them in irons? Then there would be the ride back. Ten days could go by real fast.

Clay shook off this kind of feeling and lit a cigarette. They would find them and he would be back at the ranch in time for the wedding – he'd told her he would.

During their trek across the dry, hard packed ground, every two hours, Clay called a halt and they gave their horses a little water, plus, with a water-soaked rag, they wiped the horse's noses, and the inside of their nostrils to get the dust out.

Riley grinned and said, "You sure know a lot about trackin' outlaws, don't ya?"

"Without our horses, we'd be afoot and we sure wouldn't last long. I doubt those men we're chasing were smart enough to do this, which is why we'll catch up to them before long," Clay said, giving the black stallion a pat on the forehead.

"Maybe they'll be so worn down they'll just give up," Riley replied.

"We can only hope," Clay said as he tightened his cinch and climbed aboard the buckskin mare, giving Midnight a rest.

As the outlaws rode behind the hills, they found a few stunted trees, but no water. Bill Musgrove stepped down and loosened the cinch on his saddle and advised the others to do the same.

"You plan on holin' up here for a spell?" one of the outlaws asked.

Bill waved his arm toward the land beyond where they were and asked, "You see a better place?"

"Maybe there is, farther on," the outlaw answered.

Bill stood looking out across the land for a good while before he answered. "You go on ahead then. Maybe you'll get lucky, but me, I'm staying right here where I can get a good shot at the men chasing us. They'll be out in the open and I'll have the protection of these hills. Now who do you think is going to win that battle?"

"And they'll have food and water and horses!" another of the outlaws piped in.

"Bill looked at all of them and said, "I rest my case."

After a brief confab, the outlaws all agreed that Bill's plan had merit. They were hungry, thirsty and just plumb tuckered out – and their horses were in no better condition.

"We'll go along with you, Bill," Arlo told him before they led their horses into the stand of trees where there was at least a mouthful or two of dry, brown grass for the horses to eat.

Bill Musgrove studied the backside of the hills for positions to defend themselves from, then walked over and looked at the land they'd just come from. He could see no dust trail, yet, but he knew the ranger was coming and it would be just a matter of time.

When the horses were eagerly eating what sparse amount of dry grass there was, the outlaws walked over to where Bill was standing, studying their back trail.

"See anything?" one of the outlaws asked.

"No, not yet, but it won't be long. I expect they'll be here before nightfall," Bill told them.

"I sure hope so," Arlo said. "We could use some of their food and water."

Bill studied the men he rode with and wondered why he'd ever come west.

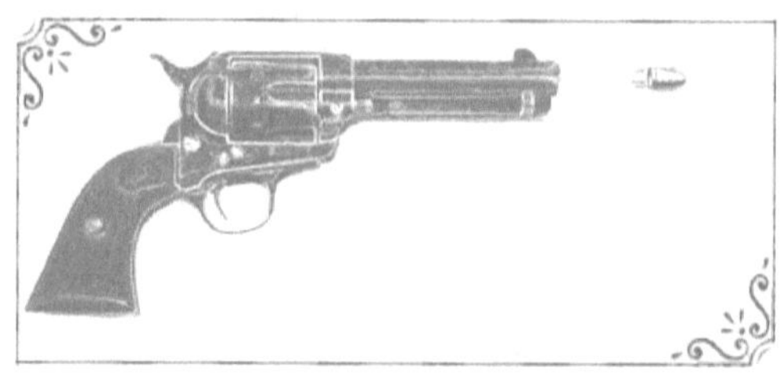

CHAPTER THIRTY-SIX

Herman Langley was still seething when he and his men reached the ranch. He yelled for the cook to fix some food for everybody, then broke out several bottles of whiskey. They needed something to mellow them out. On the way back, he'd heard several of them discussing the possibility of packing their gear and riding on. He couldn't have that. He would need every man he could get for the next time, which wouldn't be long.

After they'd finished eating, and several empty whiskey bottles lay on the floor of the ranch house, Langley stood up and announced he would raise the price to six hundred dollars a man for anyone who would ride with him on another raid. "That land rightfully belongs to me!" he shouted. "And I aim to take possession of it."

In their drunken stupor, six hundred dollars sounded like a fortune, and they all agreed to follow Langley back out to Walks Tall's camp, and this time make sure they did what they went out there to do.

189

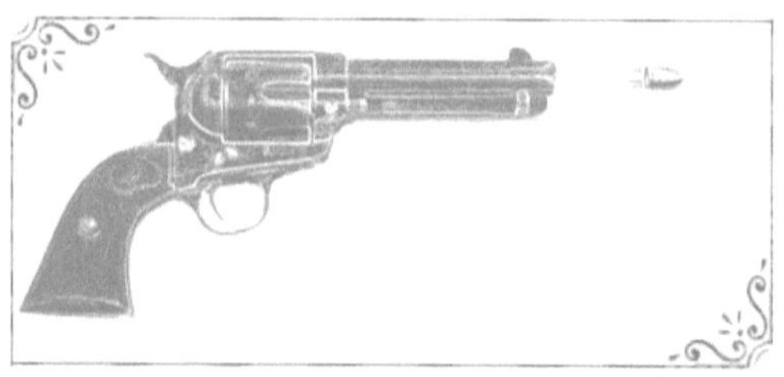

CHAPTER THIRTY-SEVEN

-

Still some distance away from the hills, He Who Bites called a halt and asked for Clay's binoculars. Clay handed them to him and waited while He Who Bites surveyed the hills.

After several minutes, He Who Bites handed the binoculars back to Clay and said, "They are waiting for us."

Riley had ridden up and he asked, He Who Bites, "How do you know that? Did you see 'em?"

"No. I saw no one," He told Riley. "Sometimes you do not need to see a man's face to know he is there."

Then how do you know they're up there waitin' on us?" Riley asked, a bit confused.

"I saw the sun glinting off three rifle barrels," He Who Bites said with a crooked smile and a tilt of his head.

Clay looked up at the sky and saw the sun drifting toward the western horizon at a very slow pace. "This time of year, it won't be dark until around nine o'clock. How far do you suppose we are from those hills," Clay asked?

He Who Bites studied the distance, then said, well over a quarter of a mile. I would guess less than half a mile."

"Which is beyond rifle range," Clay said.

"That would be true," He Who Bites agreed.

"Do you suppose they have spotted us, yet?" Clay asked.

"One of them looks at us as we speak. I saw the sun reflect off his binoculars," He Who Bites replied.

"Fine," Clay said as he stepped down from the buckskin and began to remove the saddle. "Let's make camp right here. Build up a big fire so they can see it. Do all the laughing and joking you can. I want them to hear us. I want them to know what fine shape we're in. Come dark, I want us to turn in, but we'll post lookouts so they can't sneak up on us."

"I don't understand," Riley said.

Clay grinned and said, "I want them to know we have food and water and maybe even food for the horses. And I want them to know we know they're out there and we're in no hurry. I'm sure by now they're in bad shape and want what we have. It will cause them to make mistakes."

"And you think, come dark, they'll try ta sneak up on us and catch us unawares?" Riley asked.

"Maybe," Clay said, "but if they do, we'll be ready for them, but if they don't, I've got a plan of my own."

"And what might that plan be?" Brave Eagle inquired of his boss, thinking he already knew the answer.

"Let's have some supper while I work out the details in my head, then I'll tell everybody," Clay told him.

"What 'er they up to?" one of the outlaws asked. "You think they know we're waitin' on 'em?"

Bill Musgrove shook his head and tried to spit, but his mouth was too dry. "Oh, he knows we're out here, all right. He's just playing with us because he rightly suspects we have no food or water. He's trying to bait us into making the mistake of rushing him."

"What if we wait til it's dark, then sneak up on 'em," the outlaw wanted to know.

Bill shook his head at the man's stupidity. "That's just what he wants us to do. From here, they're out of rifle range, so the only way to get a shot at 'em is for us to leave here and try to get close to them, which will put us out in the open, and he'll have men posted out away from the camp, waiting for us to do something stupid like that," Bill informed them.

"What if we wait until dark, then ride outta here?" Arlo asked, knowing the idea would get shot down.

"Bill lit a cigar and took a couple of puffs, then coughed as the raw smoke hit his throat and said, "And just how far do you think we could get. Come morning, they would ride us down like a pack of wolves after a herd of sheep. We'd be out in the open, tired, thirsty and hungry, and not thinking clearly. We'd be defenseless."

"About what I figured," Arlo told him. "Just wanted the rest to know and understand our situation."

Bill Musgrove puffed on his cigar as he studied the long, lanky cowboy called, Arlo. He didn't know much about him other than he had somehow become part of the gang. He stayed by himself most of the time and was a good hand with a gun. The man looked to be in his mid-thirties and had hard eyes.

Bill dropped the cigar butt on the ground and stepped on it, ending its short life, then walked over and leaned his elbows on the top of an outcrop rock, then he lifted the binoculars to his eyes, again. Every one of them would be an easy target if he could only get a little closer. He was tempted to try and get closer, after dark. If he could take out the ranger, maybe the others would leave, or on the other side of the coin, come after them with a vengeance. Besides, at best, he would only be able to get two of them before he was himself, under attack. He would wait until morning, and then decide what to do.

Before going over to their cold camp, he set four guards out to watch in case anyone from the posse tried to sneak up on them.

The men in Clay's posse took turns sleeping so that by about an hour before daylight they had all had some rest.

The moon was behind a cloud and the fire was no more than embers, which allowed Clay and his men to move around without being seen by the outlaws, unless they were watching the camp with binoculars, which Clay doubted at this time of the night, they would be. In quiet whispers, Clay gave instructions to Riley, Slim and Brave Eagle and watched as they moved off into the darkness.

Clay and He Who Bites walked over and saddled all the horses, and loaded their gear on the pack horses, then sat down to wait for daylight.

Maybe they would be so distraught they would just give up, like Riley had said. That sure would make things easier. But knowing outlaws like he did; especially ones who had nothing but a hangman's noose waiting on them, they would rather go down fighting than face a rope. He guessed he couldn't blame them for that.

CHAPTER THIRTY-EIGHT

Langley had not drunk as much as the men had. He wanted a clear head when they headed out.

Just as the sun was trying to clear the eastern horizon, Herman Langley began rousting the men out of their bunks and sending them to the big house for coffee and something to eat. "Eat hardy boys, we've got a big day ahead of us," he told them.

By the time the sun had cleared the eastern horizon and was making its way up into the sky, Langley's men had finished eating and had loaded a wagon with posts to use as boundary stakes for Langley's new land, along with saddling their own mounts.

They rode out of the ranch at a leisurely pace with a lot of headaches and grumbling among them.

Langley paid no attention to the men and their aching heads; he was thinking of what they would do today and what the repercussions might be. Not that it would matter in the end, but when the ranger found out, he would try to do something about it, Langley was sure. But by then it would be too late. Out here, possession was nine tenths of the law and he definitely would have possession of all of Walks Tall's land. And the nice thing about it was, Walks Tall would not be able to protest, even if he could, because he would be dead.

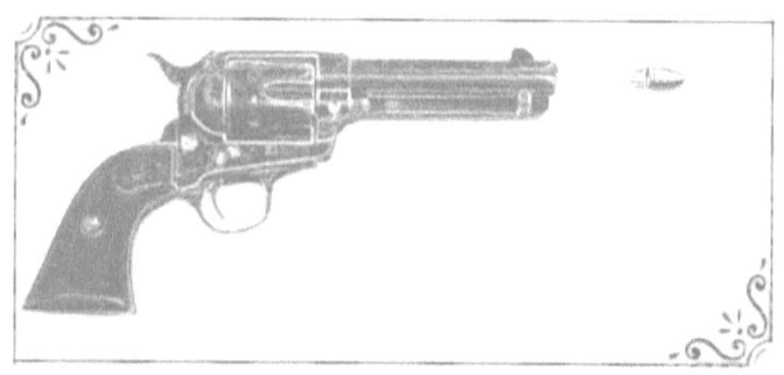

CHAPTER THIRTY-NINE

-

Loralie Benson stood at the open gates of Clay's ranch and stared out across the prairie and the loneliness it represented. Ol' Son sat on his haunches, next to her. It was his job to protect her when the master was gone.

"You all right?" Running Coyote asked as he walked up and stopped next to Loralie.

"I'm fine," Loralie told him. "I'm just watching the horizon in case they might be coming back."

Running Coyote knew Loralie worried about Clay when he was gone chasing outlaws, but there was nothing anyone could do but wait until he'd done what he went to do. When it was over, he would come home. "Don't worry, they'll be back in time for the wedding."

"That would be nice and I certainly hope so, but that's not what I'm concerned about right now. I woke up with the feeling they were about to face a terrible danger."

Running Coyote didn't know much about those things, but knew he'd had premonitions from time to time and most of them had come true. He also knew his people set great store when it came to dreams. "Don't let your dreams get the best of you. As you already know, Clay knows his way around a fight. Plus, the men with him are no strangers when it comes to that, either.

"Yes, I know," Loralie said with a sigh. "But I also know, things can happen."

All Running Coyote could do was, nod his head. She was a woman, and women worried about their men and children.

He reached out and took Loralie by the arm. "I think Colleen is fixing breakfast and I'm sure there is hot coffee."

Loralie glanced over her shoulder one last time as she allowed herself to be escorted back to the ranch house. She saw no tell-tale dust rising into the sky to signify they were on their way back, which made her worry. The dream had been so real-like.

Cindy was standing on the front porch and smiled when Loralie approached. "After breakfast, can we go riding? Maybe exercise some of your horses? We could talk about the wedding plans while we ride."

Loralie noticed Cindy already had her riding clothes on. "Sure. Why not." Maybe riding and talking about the wedding would get her mind off her dream and whatever danger Clay might be in.

CHAPTER FORTY

-

The sun was in the eyes of the outlaws when Clay and He Who Bites stepped aboard their saddles and began to ride slowly toward the hills the outlaws were hiding behind.

From Arlo's position behind a large boulder, he had to shade his eyes against the rising sun to make sure two men were riding toward them. "Hey, Bill, we've got two riders headed this way."

"Only two?" Bill Musgrove asked as he walked over and looked around from behind a boulder at the bottom of the hill. From its position, the sun hit him squarely in the eyes and he could see nothing until he pulled down his hat to shade his eyes. Only then could he see the two riders coming. Bill moved to a spot where he could place his rifle on the top of the big rock to help steady the rifle, and possibly get a shot at them.

Bill took his time and sighted down the barrel, but realized they were still out of range.

"Com 'on, just a little closer," he said to himself.

Arlo looked down and saw Bill aiming his rifle and he called down from where he sat. "They need to be a lot closer for us to do any good with these rifles. Maybe if we had a Sharp's buffalo gun, but not these rifles."

It angered Bill that Arlo thought he had to point that out. "Just wait," Bill told him. "They'll be in range soon, and then we can cut down on them."

"Where's the others? I thought there was five of 'em," another one of the outlaws asked.

Bill pulled his binoculars from the case and lifted them to his eyes. "Damn!" he said. The sun was till low enough in the eastern sky to make it impossible to see through their camp in long range glasses.

The outlaws were not the only ones judging the distance. Clay was calculating how close they could get and still be just out of rifle range. "This is close enough," he told He Who Bites, as he pulled back on the reins.

"What are they doin', now?" Bill called up to Arlo.

"They're just sittin' there, lookin' this way," Arlo yelled down at Bill.

"And you're sure it's just two of 'em?" Bill asked.

After a long pause, Arlo called down, "Just the two of 'em."

Bill turned around and scanned the area behind them, but saw no one. Then suddenly his face contorted into anger. Their horses were gone! How could that have happened without them hearing it?

Turning back, the sun had risen just enough so he could get a good view of the two men sitting in front of him, and in the distance, he saw three men leading their horses into the campsite behind the ranger and Indian.

As he was standing there, seething, he heard the ranger call out, "Looks like you boys are afoot."

At that, the other outlaws looked to where the horses were supposed to be, but they were indeed, gone.

The Texas Ranger's voice pulled their attention back to him and the Indian sitting next to him.

"So, here's my suggestion. Since you can't go anywhere afoot and you probably don't have any food or water with you, the best thing you can do for yourselves right now is to surrender. We have both food and water.”

“Why don’t you come on over and try to take us,” Bill yelled out – trying to bluff his way out of the situation.

“Now why would I want to ride into rifle range and become targets when I can do one of two things. I can sit here and eat my food and drink my coffee until you boys get thirsty and hungry enough to give up – or, I could just pack up and leave you boys out here to die. Which do you think I should do?” Clay asked.

Bill motioned with his arm for all the outlaws to come down off the rocks, and as soon as they had joined him, he said, “First off, we out number them six to five and I say, we pretend to give up. We hold our rifles out to the side and when we get close, we cut down on them. They won’t be expecting us to do anything like that and when the smoke clears, we’ll be the ones with food, water and fresh horses.”

By now, the outlaws were so hungry and thirsty they would agree to anything.

“All right, we’re coming out!” Bill yelled as he stepped from behind the boulder, his rifle held out to his side at shoulder height.

“They’re going to try and ambush us,” He Who Bites said when he saw all of them holding their rifles off to the side.

“Hold it right there!” Clay yelled as he lifted his rifle to his shoulder and pointed it at Bill Musgrove. “All of you, drop your rifles and toss your pistols and knives on the ground… Now!”

The outlaws all stopped and stared at Bill, who was trying to guess what would happen if he shot the ranger. Would the others fight or turn tail and run?

Before he could make a decision, a voice behind him said, “I think you should do as you’re told.”

Looking back over his shoulder, Bill saw an Indian and two white cowboys pointing rifles at them. “How did you get back there?” he asked, astonished they had been sneaked up on so easily.

“Do as the man said,” Bill told his men, then quietly, he said, “It’s a good three days back to Seymour. Somewhere between here and there, we’ll find a way to jump them.”

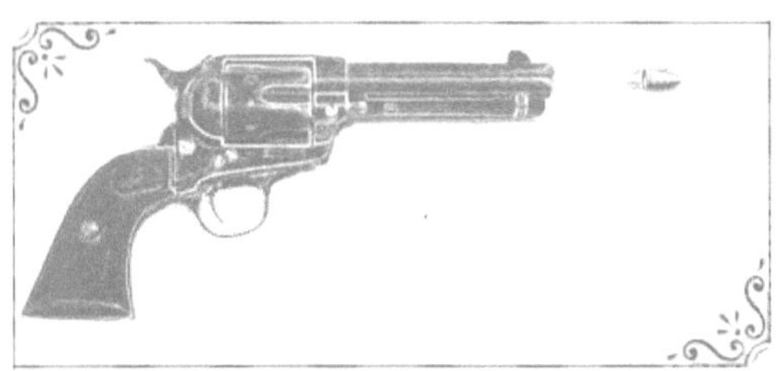

CHAPTER FORTY-ONE

Herman Langley stopped his men about a mile from Walks Tall's camp and gave his men final instructions. "This time, there will be no posse or ranger to stop us. We give no quarter – to man, woman or child. Remember, they're just heathens."

With that, he gave orders for the men to spread out and circle the camp. He would give them an hour to get into place, and when they heard his gunshot, they were to charge in firing. "The man who brings down Walks Tall gets an extra hundred dollars and a permanent job on my ranch."

To ensure no slip ups or anyone going soft about killing Indians, Langley had given his men more of the hair of the dog on the way out here. None of them were drunk, but had enough courage in them to get the job done.

Langley watched as they rode off to find their positions and wait for his signal. Each one had a bottle of whiskey to keep him in the mood for killing. And as long as they got the job done, he wouldn't mind if a few of them were killed during the fight. It would save him money.

Clay was in a hurry to get back and had decided to leave as soon as it was daylight. The outlaws were trussed up good and their horses were tied together with ten-foot lengths of rope. If they tried to escape, it would be all or none. And Clay doubted they could get far.

Brave Eagle was riding up front and saw something he didn't like. He raised his hand into the air and brought the group to a halt. When Clay rode up next to him, Brave Eagle pointed. "Walks Tall's camp is just beyond that hill, and look…"

Clay didn't like what he saw, either. Several cowboys were sitting their horses, a rifle in one hand and a whiskey bottle in the other. He'd just uttered Langley's name when they heard a pistol being fired.

The cowboys, unaware they were being watched, raised his rifle and kicked his horse in the sides, yelling, "Yee Haw!"

"Langley and his men are raiding Walks Tall's camp, again," He Who Bites said to Clay.

Clay turned and looked at Slim. "You keep an eye on these yahoos! The rest of you come with me!"

As Clay and the others raced across the prairie in pursuit of the cowboys, Slim backed his horse away from the outlaws and pointed his rifle at them. "Don't nobody do nuthin' stupid and you'll live ta see another day. Now, all of you, one at a time, step down from your cayuse and step away from it and sit down on the ground. Like I said, any one of you does somethin' stupid, there'll be one less for me ta guard."

There was something about the way Slim spoke that made believers of the outlaws and they did as they were told.

Slim rode around, keeping his rifle on his charges until he could reach down and take the lead rope of the horses. He then backed his horse up, taking the outlaw's horses out of reach. He'd just staked them down when it sounded like all hell had broken loose.

Gunfire thundered across the sky and Slim was tempted to go help his boss and his friends, but, because Clay had told him to stay here and watch the outlaws, he stayed where he was.

As Clay and the rest rode over the crest of the hill, one of the cowboys they were chasing looked over his shoulder and saw them. He raised his rifle and took a shot at them, but his shot went wide.

Brave Eagle's shot didn't, and the cowboy was lifted from his saddle and thrown to the ground.

"Spread out!" Clay called as he raced the black stallion into the fray.

Langley's cowboys were thrown into confusion when Clay's men began tossing lead at them and emptying saddles.

"It's that ranger, again," one of them yelled. Let's get outta here. I ain't dying for no Indian!"

He, and the others within the sound of his voice turned and rode as hard as they could, away from the fight. Knowing the majority of them were good men, just following orders, Clay and his men let them ride away.

Clay had ridden into the middle of the camp at breakneck speed and when he got to Walks Tall's teepee, he jumped down. Sitting next to the teepee with his head bent down and blood running from his shoulder was his half-brother, Walks Tall.

Clay dropped down on one knee and lifted Walks Tall's chin. His half-brother opened his eyes and looked up at him. "I knew you would come," he said just before his eyes went wide.

Clay whirled and at the same time pulled his pistol. As he pointed his pistol and pulled the trigger, he felt a bullet sear his left shoulder, tearing a slit in his shirt but not penetrating the skin.

Sitting on his horse with blood staining his shirt over his right lung, Langley looked down at Clay and asked, "Where in blue blazes did you come from?"

Clay was coming to his feet when Langley lifted his pistol for another shot at Clay.

Clay fired two more times – both bullets entered Langley's heart at almost the same time. The two slugs lifted Langley from his saddle. He hit the ground hard, rolled over on his stomach and laid there, unmoving.

The other cowboys of Langley's group saw their boss die at the hand of the ranger and immediately raised their hands in the air, surrendering.

Clay looked at Riley and nodded his head. Riley nodded back and took over rounding up the Langley bunch, who they turned loose because they had just been following orders, plus the fact that none of the Indians had been killed. They had been instructed by Riley to make tracks and never return to this part of the country.

A couple of Clay's men had been wounded, but nothing serious. Which one of Langley's men had done it, they didn't know and no one was confessing.

As Clay helped Walks Tall to his feet, Walks Tall said, "We are a pair to draw to, brother."

Clay looked at his half-brother and said, "I didn't know you played poker."

Walks Tall grinned and said, "We'll have to play sometime. I can use the money."

When Clay and his men came riding into town with the outlaws in tow, people came out of houses and stores to stare – not at the outlaws, or Clay and his men, but at the Indian riding proudly next to Clay with his arm in a sling.

After turning the outlaws over to the sheriff and returning the money to the bank, Clay and Walks Tall walked into the doctor's office and sat down.

Doctor Hartley had been the doctor in Seymour almost from the day it became a town. He was below average height, and had put on a pound or two in the last few years. His hair was streaked with silver and the wrinkles on his face reminded you of a road map, but his eyes were bright, he still had his own teeth, and he didn't need glasses.

The doctor looked up and grinned. He knew both men and said, "What happened? You two brothers get into a squabble over some woman and shoot each other?"

Clay grinned, remembering the doctor knew about them being brothers, before he did.

"Something like that," Walks Tall said, nodding his head. "Herman Langley raided my camp and shot me, and my Texas Ranger brother showed up and shot Langley, who was shooting at Clay. Langley won't be needing your help, but I have a bullet in my shoulder, and he has a scratch on his arm."

The doctor rubbed his chin. "I don't know what the town will say if they knew I treated a heathen redskin."

"Would it help if I drew my pistol and threatened you?" Walks Tall asked with a grin.

"Well sir, that just might help," he said as he opened Walks Tall's shirt and looked at the bloody hole in his shoulder.

Doctor Hartley looked at Clay and asked, "You gonna snitch on me if I work on the Indian first?"

"I'll just sit here and have some coffee until it's my turn. That is, if you have any that ain't three days old," Clay said.

"Fresh pot no more'n an hour ago, and there's some pain medicine on the shelf above the pot, if you'd be inclined."

"Now, just how do you plan on paying for my services? The doctor asked as he led Walks Tall over to a table covered with a sheet and told him to lay down.

"Do you need a buffalo hide?" Walks Tall said with a grin. He had money and paid for both him and Clay.

An hour later, Clay and Walks Tall left the doctor's office and headed for the sheriff's office. People along the sidewalk stopped and stared at them and whispered after they'd passed. It wasn't everyday you saw an Indian Chief walking down the street of Seymour.

The sheriff looked up when the two men came in. He wasted no time getting down to business. "Thank you, again, for bringing them back. I guarantee they won't get away, again. And you say Herman Langley is dead? You're sure about that?"

Clay looked at the sheriff and asked, "You know something I don't know? I shot him three times in the chest. And I watched as his men loaded him on his horse and hauled him away."

The sheriff shook his head and said, "That's strange because half an hour before you rode into town, I saw him coming out of doc's place. I admit, he was walking kind of tender like, but he was walking. He climbed into a rented wagon that one of his men was driving and they headed out of town, going in the direction of Langley's ranch. Drove right past where I was standing on the sidewalk. He even tipped his hat to me."

Clay heard every word the sheriff said, but it was hard to believe that a man shot three times in the chest with forty-four slugs could be alive, let alone, up and walking around.

"If you'll excuse me, I have to see for myself," Clay said as he turned and headed for the door.

Clay could have argued until his face was blue, but it would have done no good. Walks Tall said he was coming along and would not be talked out of it. After all, Clay had to admit, it was him and his land that Langley was after.

The sheriff had told them they were both crazy. Two wounded men riding out there with Langley and God only knew how many of his men they would have to face.

"You have to remember, if Langley isn't God – Almighty, he was shot, too!" Clay shouted back at the sheriff as he slammed the door so the sheriff couldn't say anything else.

The sheriff threw up his hands and said, "Go ahead and be damned fools. Go out there and get yourselves killed. It's out of my jurisdiction, so I can't help you – but don't say I didn't warn you."

But neither Clay or Walks Tall heard him, they were already headed for the doctor's office.

CHAPTER FORTY-TWO

-

The doctor confirmed that it was Langley who had come to see him, and he had nothing worse than three bruises on his chest.

"How can that be, Doc?" Clay wanted to know. "I shot him three times in the chest with my forty-four pistol."

"I'm sure you did, and that's what caused the bruises." The doctor chuckled, then said, "The man had a piece of oak wood, backed with a piece of steel plating under his shirt and coat. Maybe you should have shot him in the head, but considering how stubborn he is, that might not have worked, either."

By now it was late afternoon and neither Clay or Walks Tall wanted to ride out to Langley's place and try to brace him and his men, in the dark.

Clay rented two separate rooms and after cleaning up as best they could, they went down to the hotel restaurant for some supper.

People stopped by their table to congratulate them for capturing the outlaws and bringing the money back, but many just wanted to say they'd met and talked with a real Indian chief.

Before going to his room, Clay got in touch with his train engineer, Harold, and told him he needed him to go out to the ranch and tell Loralie he had only one more little thing to clear up and he'd be home in plenty of time for the wedding.

Harold said he would do as Clay asked, but inside he wasn't sure it would be as easy to go out and arrest Langley as Clay thought it might be.

The following morning as the two men rode out of town, they found out they were sore and stoved up, more than they thought they would be. "At least it wasn't my shooting arm that got hurt," Clay said with a grin.

"So," Clay said, "When we get out there, let me do the talking. I'd like to bring him in without gun play, if possible."

"Whatever, little brother," Walks Tall told Clay with a straight face, as if he believed that would be possible.

As they rode close enough to be within hailing distance, Clay and Walks Tall pulled their horses up and looked at the ranch house and barn. From every window, they saw rifle barrels.

"No need to be any shooting, Langley. You just come on out here and let's do this peaceful like," Clay called out.

When Langley built the ranch house, he'd put in shutters with rifle ports in case of Indian attacks. He chuckled to himself, there was in fact, an Indian out there. The fact that there was only one made little difference to Langley. The truth was, both of his enemies were out there and he wanted to see both of them, dead.

"And just what charge do you think you'll be arresting me on?" Langley shouted through the opening in the shutter.

"You raided an Indian camp and shot their chief," Clay called back at him.

"Hell, that ain't no crime. No court in Texas would condemn me for shooting an Indian."

"Then how about shooting and trying to kill a Texas Ranger?" Clay asked.

"I could argue that you were interfering in something that wasn't any of your business," Langley replied. "Plus, I could say I went out there with peaceful intentions. I was going to try and buy the land from him, even though Indians can't own land in Texas. And I might say you drew on me, first."

As Langley was ranting on, Clay studied the guns that were pointing at them and thought there was something peculiar about them. He reached into his saddlebag and retrieved his binoculars and raised them to his eyes. After a small adjustment so he could bring the guns into focus, he moved the glasses from gun to gun, then lowered them and looked at Walks Tall. "There ain't but three of them in there. The rest must have pulled out when the fight was over."

"Can your long eyes see through wood? How can you know this, brother?" Walks Tall asked, a bit confused.

As Clay put his binoculars back in his saddlebag, he said, "Only three of the rifle barrels have any movement. The rest are stationary. If there was a man holding it, the barrel would move from time to time. Take notice of the rifle barrel in the upstairs window."

Walks Tall looked at the upstairs window and the rifle barrel protruding out, and sure enough, it moved every now and then. He looked at Clay and grinned.

"Now take note of the window in the barn hayloft. It moves quite often, indicating the man is very nervous. The same with the rifle barrel sticking out of the window next to the front door, which I assume is Langley."

"Yes, I see what you mean," Walks Tall said.

"None of the others have moved even an inch since we've been here. They're more than likely just propped up on something to make us think there are more in there than there is."

"Which cuts the odds down in our favor," Walks Tall said with a grin.

From inside the house, Langley could see the ranger and the Indian sitting there, talking. "What can they be talking about?" he said to himself. "Could they have figured out there are only three of us?"

The man in the barn hayloft was having a hard time waiting. They were in rifle range, so why didn't Langley shoot them, he wondered? He had taken sight on both of them and could have killed either one.

He wanted a cigarette and a drink of whiskey to help calm his nerves, but he had neither. Sweat was beginning to run down his forehead. "Com 'on, com 'on," he said to himself, over and over.

Suddenly, he could stand it no longer and took aim. In his nervousness, he jerked the trigger, sending his bullet slightly off target.

Clay saw the bullet glance off his saddle horn and off to the side of him, just as the sound of the rifle filled the air. "Move!" Clay yelled!

The black stallion needed no prompting and whirled and ran back the way they'd come.

Walks Tall reacted by jerking his rifle from the saddle boot and dove for the ditch next to the road. He watched as his horse chased after Clay and Midnight.

At the sound of the rifle shot, the man in the upstairs window of the ranch house, thought his boss had started the ball and fired three times, his bullets hitting nothing but the empty road.

A short distance down the road, Clay pulled Midnight to a halt and stepped down, taking his rifle with him. After making his way over behind a nearby tree, he shook his head and gave a small chuckle. Maybe his luck was improving. So far during all of this, he had only a small scratch, which suited him just fine. He had enough scars to last him a lifetime.

Looking back down the road, Clay could see Walks Tall, laying in the ditch and knew he was all right. Next, Clay studied the situation and saw that he could make his way along the tree line to where he believed he could get a shot at the man in the hayloft.

Langley was pacing back and forth, peeking out of the windows, trying to see someone to shoot at. He didn't know which one had fired the shot, but thought it might have come from the hayloft. The shooting had started earlier than he'd wanted, but now it didn't matter. The dance had begun and he wanted to see the end of it. He wanted the ranger closer so he couldn't miss. As it was, he didn't know if the ranger had been hit, or not. He'd watched him ride away – and had seen the Indian dive into the ditch, carrying his rifle. Maybe he was dead. He could only hope.

Clay had made his way up to close to where Walks Tall was laying in the ditch. "You all right?" Clay called out in a loud whisper.

Walks Tall nodded his head and asked, "How bad are you hit?"

"My saddle horn is scarred for life, but I'm okay."

Walks Tall nodded his head, again.

Out of his peripheral vision, Clay saw movement and looked toward the hayloft. The man had moved to the open doorway and was pointing his rife in Walks Tall's direction.

Without thinking about it, Clay reacted and put a bullet in the man's chest. The man dropped his rifle and had an astonished look on his face as he went head first out of the open door and landed on his back, on the ground. If Clay's bullet hadn't killed him, the fall surely would have.

"Clay gave a sigh. He hadn't wanted to kill the man, but he'd been given no other choice.

"Langley!" Clay called out.

"Yeah?" Langley called back.

"I had to shoot your man in the hayloft. And I know most of those rifles are just propped up in the windows. It's you and one other man, now, the one in the upstairs window. I don't want to have to kill either one of you, so come on out with your hands in the air."

Langley turned with a jerk when the cowboy from upstairs walked into the living room. "No use stayin' up there. He knew where I was. Besides, we can both take him and his Indian friend from down from here," Randy said with a surety Langley didn't feel.

Langley's face was pale and he was sweating profusely. He was holding a rifle and Randy could see the man's hand was trembling. "You're not turnin' yellow on me, are ya?" Mister Langley.

Langley took a deep breath and said, "No. No, I haven't turned yellow. It's just that the man has more lives than a cat."

Hearing no response from the house, Clay scouted the area some more and decided the man in the upstairs window was gone. Plus, if he moved to his right and stayed in the trees, he might be able to get to the back of the house without being seen.

Clay looked over toward Walks Tall and said in a loud whisper. "Count to a hundred, slowly, then open up on the front windows of the house. I'm going to try and get around to the back of the house."

Walks Tall grinned and nodded his head.

Clay counted in his head as he made his way around to the back of the ranch house and up to the back door. With great caution, he tried the door and it opened soundlessly as it swung open. He was inside the kitchen when Walks Tall's rifle shots filled the air, followed by shots from inside the house.

Clay stepped into the living room with his pistol in his hand and yelled, "Put your guns down! It's over!"

Both men spun around, leveling their rifles at Clay. The roar of both rifle shots filled the inside of the living room, along with two shots from Clay's pistol, leaving the air filled with the acrid smell of burnt gunpowder.

When the smoke cleared, Randy was sprawled on his back with blood spouting from his chest. He was dead. Langley, on the other hand was sitting with his back against the wall. Blood was staining Langley's shirt over his right shoulder where Clay's second bullet had struck him.

Langley's eyes were glazed over. He looked at Clay, standing in front of him, still with his pistol pointed at him. "How many lives you got, Ranger?"

"Enough to see you hang," Clay told him, trying not to wince from the pain in his left side. He didn't know which man had shot him, but at this point it made very little difference.

Form outside, Clay heard Walks Tall's voice. "Are you all right, brother?"

"Yeah, I'm fit as a fiddle. Come on in," Clay called back.

After binding Langley's wound and tying his hands behind his back, Walks Tall turned to Clay and saw the pain in his eyes and he was holding his left side. Blood was seeping between his fingers.

"You were hit?" Walks Tall asked as he pushed Clay's hand away and checked the wound. "Yes, you do have more lives than a cat," Walks Tall said with a grin. "It's not serious. The bullet barely tore a slice in your skin, causing it to bleed. You're going to live… it's a long way from your heart," Walks Tall said with a chuckle.

Finding a dishcloth in the kitchen, Walks Tall bound up Clay's wound so they could take their prisoner into town and turn him over to the sheriff.

When the sheriff saw Clay and Walks Tall come riding into town with Langley riding between them, he shook his head. "It's true," he said to the blacksmith, Cyrus Clemmons, who had just walked up and stopped next to him.

"What's true?" Cyrus asked.

"Brentwood never fails to get his man or men…" The sheriff said, feeling a bit jealous.

As Clay and Walks Tall stopped in front of the sheriff's office and turned Langley over to the sheriff, Langley asked, "What am I being charged with? I need to see the doctor. This ranger came onto my property and shot me from ambush. I didn't have a chance. I want to press charges against him."

"Whoa," the sheriff said as he escorted Langley into the jail. "One thing at a time. I'm sure we'll find plenty to charge you with. I'll have the doctor come down and take a look at you when he has a chance. In the meantime, go ahead and file all the charges you want, but I'm sure the judge will say he was only doing his job."

The hole in the back wall of the jail had been boarded up so that at least the sheriff could put his prisoner in a cell, along with the other six who were already there. It was a little crowded, but at least here, he could keep a closer eye on them.

By now, Clay was feeling anxious to be on his way but Walks Tall suggested he go over to the doctor's office, first.

As they were going out the door, Carroll Atkins, another of the ranchers who had believed Indian's were stealing their cattle, stepped up on the sidewalk. He saw Clay, and Walks Tall and walked along with them to the doctor's office, making small talk.

Inside the doctor's office, while the doctor was patching up Clay's bullet wound, Atkins walked over and stood in front of Walks Tall. He stuck out his hand and said, "I guess I owe you and your people an apology. I was sure it was you who were stealing my cattle, but Brentwood, here, proved us all wrong."

Turning to Clay, Atkins said, "And my apologies to you, too, sir. We had you all wrong."

"Just try not to jump to conclusions in the future. They're good people and make good ranch hands should you need any." Clay told him, extending his hand.

Atkins accepted the hand shake and said, "I'll keep that in mind."

The doctor walked Atkins to the door and they shook hands.

When the doctor walked back over to where Clay was sitting, he opened his palm and showed Clay a wad of bills. "He paid for my services, so that makes you free to go. I know you won't take my advice, but here it is, anyway. Stay down for a few days, let your body heal." the doctor informed Clay.

"Okay, Doc, I will take your advice and stay in bed for few days." And with a grin spread across his face, Clay left the doctor standing in the doorway, scratching the back of his neck, with a confused look on his face.

As the doctor turned and went back into his office, he noticed the wedding invitation laying on his desk and smiled.

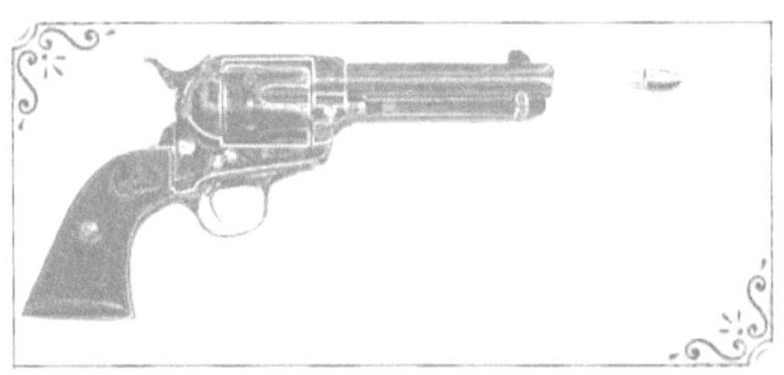

CHAPTER FORTY-THREE

-

At a point where Clay and Walks Tall had to split up – Clay heading toward his ranch and Walks Tall, heading toward his camp, Clay invited Walks Tall to come to the ranch with him and spend the night, but Walks Tall declined the offer, saying he needed to get back to his people and assure them everything was all right, but promised to see him on his wedding day. They shook hands and each man headed home.

As Clay rode up to the front gates of his home, he noticed they were closed, but before he could call out, they swung open.

As he rode through, Clay saw two of the Mexican men who worked for him, standing on each side of him, holding the gates open. Each man had a rifle in his hand.

Stopping the black stallion, he looked down at the one called, Ramon, and asked, "Anything wrong?"

"No, Senor', Miss Benson, she wants to make sure we don't get raided without us knowing it. So, we keep the gates closed and stand guard."

Clay looked at the courtyard and shook his head. The entire yard was decorated. It looked like a festival was about to take place.

As Clay rode up to the barn, Juan came running out. "Senor' Clay, you are back. The Senora' will be so happy to know you are back, and alive! And I am happy, too!"

Clay stepped down from Midnight and handed the reins to Juan. "Looks like we're going to have a party."

"Si, Senor'! There will be a big party tomorrow! There will be food and music and dancing and, you and the Senora' will be getting married! Did you forget?"

Clay laughed and rubbed the top of Juan's head. "No, Juan, I did not forget. Now, give Midnight a good rub down and plenty of grain to eat. He's had a rough few days."

As Juan looked up at him with a broad smile on his face, Clay reached into his pocket and pulled out a half a dollar and handed it to Juan. "Just between you and me," he told him. "It'll be our secret."

"Si, Senor'," Juan said as he stuffed the coin in the pocket of his pants.

On the way to the house, Clay stopped next to the well and looked around. They had done a lot of work during his absence. He couldn't believe the wedding was, tomorrow. He thought he had an extra day.

The inside of the house looked a lot like the outside. The living room was decorated from floor to ceiling – and the area in front of the fireplace had a large arch over it and it was covered with white flowers. Where all the flowers came from, he had no idea.

From the kitchen he heard pans rattling and women's voices. He turned and walked in that direction and as he got close, he heard Loralie's voice. "Do you think he'll be home in time for the wedding? I sure hate to waste all the work we've put in and bringing in the flowers."

As he walked into the kitchen, Mrs. McIntyre was saying, "He said he would…" She stopped in mid-sentence when she saw Clay standing just inside the kitchen door.

"Is somebody looking for me?" Clay asked as Loralie turned and saw him, her eyes going wide.

"Clay!" Loralie yelled as she ran over and started to hug him, then stopped and looked at him. She saw the dried blood on his shirt, and asked, "Are you all right?"

Clay reached out and pulled her to him. "Of course, I'm all right."

"But… there is dried blood on your shirt, and you look worn out. Are you sure you're all right?"

Clay pulled her close to him and hugged her tightly. "It's just a minor wound. If you're worried about whether I can make it to the wedding tomorrow, stop worrying. I'll be there with bells on."

Loralie pushed back from Clay and looked up into his face. He looked tired, like he hadn't had any sleep, in days. "You look very tired."

"Yeah, that's what the doc said after he fixed the slight wound on my side. And he went on to say, I needed to get some rest – maybe stay in bed for a few days," Clay told her with a wide smile and raised eyebrows. "What would you say to that?"

Loralie laid her head against his chest and played with the button on his shirt. "I think we can arrange that," she said with a giggle.

"Hurrumph!" Mrs. McIntyre said. "If ya don't mind waitin' at least until tomorrow!"

Loralie stepped back, her face turning red. "I guess I got carried away. The excitement of Clay getting home."

"Of course," Mrs. McIntyre said. "Welcome home, Mister Brentwood. Now, we have work ta do if we're gonna be ready by tomorrow. So, if you're not in need of medical attention, I suggest you go inta yer office and have a drink while I have Cindy draw ya ah hot bath and lay out some clean clothes."

Clay looked down at himself and had to agree, he'd seen better days. "That sounds like a fine idea, Mrs. McIntyre."

Clay patted Loralie on the cheek and said, "I guess I'll see you later, darlin'," and headed for his office, chuckling under his breath as Loralie stood there, pouting.

Supper that evening was chili that had been cooking a good part of the day. There were corn tortillas and a big bowl of peppers sitting on the table, but only the men ate any of the peppers.

After being out on the trail so much, lately, the chili tasted wonderful and the peppers hit the spot, making his mouth feel lively and awake.

When the meal was finished, the men were shushed from the room and retreated to Clay's office, since most of the rest of the house was off bounds – wedding preparations were still underway with last minute details.

Clay, Riley and Running Coyote were sitting on the couch, discussing what had gone on during Clay's absence. Clay and Riley were enjoying a glass of brandy, while Running Coyote sipped from a glass of buttermilk.

Running Coyote informed Clay that all the horses and cattle had been bunched up and could be accounted for. He went on to say all the yearlings had been branded so that any rustlers who thought about using a running iron on them would be out of luck.

Riley levered his, long, lanky body off the couch and told his boss, he was just plumb tuckered out and was in need of some bunk time.

Riley had just walked out the front door, when he turned back and said, "Boss, I think you need to come outside."

Clay and Running Coyote could hear the thunder of a great number of horses as they came to a halt in front of the house.

Grabbing a rifle from the wall, Clay ran for the front door, ready to defend himself and his people from whoever had shown up.

"Whoa, Boss, I don't think you're gonna need that rifle," Riley told him as he stopped near the door to look out and see what the ruckus was all about.

Clay grinned and turned back to the inside of the house and tossed the rifle to Running Coyote and said, "You can put this back on the wall."

Loralie, Mrs. McIntyre and Cindy had just rushed into the room when from outside, they heard, "Ho, Brother! We bring meat and presents!"

Clay stepped out onto the porch, followed by Riley, Running Coyote, Loralie, Mrs. McIntyre and Cindy.

The area in front of the house was filled with close to a hundred Indians, whooping and hollering. One of them rode up, pulling a travois that held half a buffalo, ready to be put on the spit over the big fire that was already roasting a side of beef.

"Is there room for our buffalo meat, Brother?" Walks Tall called out.

"If there isn't, we'll build another fire," Clay called back as he took Loralie by the hand and stepped down off the porch.

Walks Tall jumped off his horse and with the grace of a leader, walked over and stopped in front of Loralie, giving her a wide smile. "Sister," he said as he took her hand and brought it to his lips.

After kissing her hand, Walks Tall looked at Loralie with a mischievous look in his eyes and said, "If you ever get tired of this one, come see me. I will see that you are treated as you should be."

"Thanks," Clay said. "We aren't even married yet and already you're trying to steal her away from me!"

"I just think she deserves the better man," Walks Tall said with a grin.

Clay knew his half-brother was playing with him. Most Indians like a good joke and love to play pranks. "If it's a wrestling match you're looking for?" Clay challenged.

Walks Tall backed off a few paces, placing his hands up, palms forward. "Whoa, little brother. I do not want to embarrass you in front of your wife to be on the day before they are to be wed…"

"And just be glad you don't. I wouldn't want to disgrace a chief in front of his people," Clay threw back at him, with a wide grin on his face.

"I sure do hope you two are funnin' with each other," Loralie said, looking back and forth from one to the other.

Both men smiled at Loralie, and it was Walks Tall who said, "I love to tease my brother. I hope you were not offended."

Loralie looked at Walks Tall and thought, again, how much he looked like Clay. "Offended? No. I guess I have a lot to learn."

Walks Tall turned his attention to Clay, and said, "With your permission, we will set up our camp just outside the gates, then we will dig a firepit for our buffalo meat."

Clay nodded his head. "Of course. You know you and your people are always welcome here."

Walks Tall, looked at Loralie, but directed his words to Clay. "If I may borrow the bride to be, my people would like to meet her and get to know her, since she will soon be a sister."

Clay looked at Loralie, who nodded her head and stepped over close to Walks Tall. "I very much want to meet your people, especially if we are going to become, kin."

It was close to midnight before Loralie was able to get back into the house. Her arms were loaded with dresses made from skins, necklaces, moccasins, trinkets carved from, wood, bone and rock.

Mrs. McIntyre met her at the front door and helped her carry her wedding gifts over to a long table that had been set up in the living room for just that purpose.

"My, there are some beautiful things here," Mrs. McIntyre said as she laid things in neat piles.

"Yes. They are a very talented and loving people," Loralie told her. "I never had a sister before, now I think I have around fifty."

Both women broke out into laughter.

"Well, now, you'll be needin' ta be gettin' up ta bed. You've got ah big day ahead of ya tomorrow. If you think this this is bad, just wait til tomorrow. Half the town will be comin' out here – all of 'm wantin' ta see the woman that put a rope on Mister Brentwood."

"Are you sure?" Loralie asked. "There's still some cleaning up to do."

"Shush," Mrs. McIntyre told her as she gently pushed Loralie toward the stairs. "What little there is ta do, me and Cindy will have it done in no time. Now, off with ya."

Clay came out from his office about that time and said, "I agree. You look like you could use a little beauty rest."

Loralie put her hands to her face and asked, "Oh, I must look awful."

"I was just kidding," Clay threw in, as he guided her in the direction of the stairs.

As Loralie drifted up the stairs in a dream world, she remembered wondering as a little girl, about what her wedding day would be like. But it was nothing like this.

CHAPTER FORTY-FOUR

-

The sun was up and shining brightly as Clay came down the stairs. He was hungry and could smell the coffee and the bacon – and when he walked into the dining room, his two foremen were already there. Clay looked at them and said, "Mornin'."

Both men greeted him with head nods of their own. Loralie still had not come down.

Riley sat his coffee cup on the saucer next to his plate and as Clay sat down, he asked, "So, Boss, you still have a few more hours of freedom. What'cha gonna do with 'em?"

While Cindy poured Clay some coffee, Mrs. McIntyre sat a plate in front of Clay that was filled with, fried eggs, bacon, fried potatoes and a stack of flapjacks.

"There's Blackstrap molasses in the small pitcher, and some fresh made butter on the small plate," Mrs. McIntyre informed Clay.

"My God, woman, you'd think I was gonna ride bucking broncs all day," Clay told her, looking down at his plate.

"Is there anything on yer plate ya don't like?" Mrs. McIntyre asked.

Clay looked up at her and said, "Well, no. I was just…"

Mrs. McIntyre held up her hand and said, "Then I suggest ya get busy before it gets cold."

And with that she headed into the kitchen.

"So, what are you going to do this morning? I understand the wedding isn't until four this afternoon," Running Coyote stated.

"Shucks, it's his weddin' day. He don't have ta do nothin, if 'en he don't want ta," Riley said, poking Running Coyote in the ribs. "He'll be needin' ta save his strength fer later. I reckon that's why Mrs. McIntyre gave him such ah big breakfast."

Clay shoveled in a mouthful of food so he wouldn't have to comment on their ribbing, which did little good because both men sat there, staring at him, waiting for an answer.

Clay took a sip of coffee, then set it back down on the saucer. "For your information, I believe I have all the strength I need. As for this morning, I plan on riding out and looking over the cattle – take stock, it you will. I assume you've posted men out there to keep watch on them? Right?"

"They've been on six-hour watches ever since we rounded them up," Running Coyote told him.

Clay had just finished his breakfast and his second cup of coffee, when the front door opened and Bill McDaniel, head of the Texas Rangers and four other rangers came walking into the dining room.

McDaniel walked over and stopped in front of Clay, putting his fists on his hips. "Glad you're up. We need you saddled up and ready to go within the next half an hour. We've got some bad hombre's we need to bring down – and I need every ranger I can get my hands on."

Clay looked up at his old boss and thought, if he went off now with Bill, Loralie would have every right to leave and never come back.

Loralie had been standing at the dining room door and had heard everything McDaniel had said. She walked up and looked up at Bill McDaniel and said, "I can't believe this. You know Clay has retired, and even if he wasn't, you do realize we are getting married in a few hours. He can't go traipsin' off with you to go chasin' outlaws. It's our wedding day for God's sake."

"Really?" Bill McDaniel said, his eyes going wide and a look of shock on his face.

"Yes, really!" Loralie said with a lot of anger in her voice.

Bill doffed his hat and said, "Well then, it's a good thing I was just funnin', ain't it?"

Bill stuck out his hand and said, "It's my pleasure to meet the woman who's gonna put ole Clay here on the straight and narrow. My name's Bill McDaniel and I'm head of the rangers. Me and a few of Clay's friends who could get away, decided we just couldn't miss out on such an important day in our friend's life. And when we get a chance, I can tell you a few things you may not know about that man you're going to get hitched to, Miss Benson."

Loralie stepped back. "You know my name?"

Bill McDaniel glanced over at Clay, then back to Loralie. "It might surprise you how much I know about you. And believe me when I say how pleased I am that you decided to take our boy, here, and make an honest man of him."

Trying to change the subject, Clay stood up and shook hands with the new comers and asked, "Have you boys had breakfast, yet?"

"Right glad you asked," Billy Young said. "I was beginning to think you were going to let us starve."

They all waited until Loralie sat down before they took off their hats and sat down.

There was a lot of banter and small talk about the olden days, and Loralie picked up a few things she would tuck away in her memory. They were also curious about all of the Indians camped out in front of the wall that surrounded Clay's home.

"Seems ta me they could 'a raided the place during the night, beings that you left the gates wide open," Billy Young informed them.

"The chief of that bunch out there," Bill McDaniel said, "is Clay's half brother as I understand it. That right, Clay?"

"Yes. And they're friendly, so you don't have to worry about your scalps," Clay told them with a chuckle.

When they'd all finished eating, Sam Dyer, one of the other rangers excused himself and left.

He returned shortly with several boxes piled in his arms. "Wedding presents."

Loralie stood up and said, "Oh my. Follow me and I'll show you where to put them."

As they walked toward the long table in the dining room, Loralie said, "Really. You didn't have to do this. But thank you very much."

"It ain't much, ma'am. Ain't ah one of us that ain't happy for you and Clay," Sam told her.

Loralie knew that the rangers were a small, close group who went well beyond what most law enforcement officers did when tracking down outlaws, but she hadn't expected this kind of loyalty, and it pleased her to no end. "Thank you," was all she could come up with.

When Loralie and Sam came back into the living room, Mrs. McIntyre was shooing the men out of the room, telling them, "You men go do whatever it is men do at a time like this. We've got some final preparations ta get done and if you're hangin' around, you'll just be in the way. Now, scooch."

As Clay passed Loralie, he smiled and said, "I guess I'll see you at four."

Loralie smiled back at him and said, "And don't be late."

CHAPTER FORTY-FIVE

-

When Clay, Riley and the Texas Rangers rode out of the compound, the Indian women already had the buffalo meat wrapped and down in the hot coals, cooking.

"Looks like this is gonna be quite a shin-dig," Bill McDaniel said as he rode up next to Clay.

Clay looked over his shoulder at the two fire pits and said, "If you go away hungry it will be your own fault."

Once outside the walls of Clay's home, Clay turned to Riley and said, "Show us where you took the stock and what you've been up to."

When Riley took the lead, with the others falling in behind, Clay looked at Bill McDaniel and said, "This is the first time you've seen my spread in some time."

"You're right," Bill told him. "You didn't have any cattle to speak of and you sure hadn't built that walled in fortress you call a home."

Clay chuckled at the memory. "As I recall, I was under arrest at that time."

Bill nodded his head and said, "Yeah, a lot of water has crossed under the bridge since then."

They had ridden for nearly half an hour before they came upon the first herd of cattle. It was a herd of close to a thousand head and they were mostly down near the small lake, eating the lush green grass that grew there.

Clay noticed right away that there were six of his hands riding near the herd, and each man had a gun at his hip, and a rifle in the saddle boot.

Clay also noticed that each one of them knew of their arrival and had their pistols in their hands.

Bill McDaniel also noticed and said, "Good men. Maybe some of them might want to be Texas Rangers."

Clay looked at Bill, then back over toward his men. He knew they had the right to do whatever they wanted to, but secretly hoped they would elect to stay here, if Bill made them an offer. "They're free to do as they please," Clay told him.

"You'll notice there are no unbranded calves," Riley said, proudly.

Clay looked beyond the herd and the lake and saw a quickly thrown together corral that was between two low hills with steep walls and a brush gate.

Riley saw his boss look that direction and said, "We have two of them. One at each place. If trouble comes, we can run 'em into the keep and stop the rustlers from gettin' to 'em. We also got us some trenches dug ta shoot from."

Clay looked at Bill McDaniel and grinned. "Like you said, I've got some good men.

By the time they'd seen the other herd, that also held close to fifty horses, and had the same set up, Riley pulled his pocket watch out of his vest pocket and said, "If there ain't nuthin' else, maybe we should be headin' back, Mister Brentwood. You've got some cleanin' up ta do before ya go stand in front of the preacher."

Clay looked at Riley and said, "Yes, it is time for us to be heading back."

As they turned to head back to the ranch house, Clay noticed some black clouds in the far west and got an uneasy feeling.

He hoped the wedding would be over before the rain got here. Better still, he hoped it would pass by them, completely.

When they rode through the open gates, Clay looked again toward the west and saw the clouds looked bigger. He judged the storm was still a few hours away, but it looked like a mean one. It would be a mite crowded but they could move everything inside the house if they needed to.

CHAPTER FORTY-SIX

Clay's room upstairs had windows that looked down into the courtyard. He'd had his bath and a close shave and was in the process of getting dressed when he ambled over and looked down into the courtyard. He shook his head. There had to be over a hundred people down there, all laughing and having a good time. The Mexican men who worked for him had pulled out their guitars and fiddles and were playing lively music for anyone who wanted to dance on the wooden dance floor that had been set up. Clay counted twelve couples dancing and several others standing nearby, tapping their feet and clapping their hands to the tune of the music.

Clay raised his eyes and looked toward the west, and cringed. The black clouds were still there, in the far distance, but they covered more of the sky than they had earlier. He could see lightning bolts from time to time. He judged the storm was still several hours away, but still, it would be on them before the festivities were over and they would have to move into the house.

Dressed in his newly tailored suit and new boots, Clay descended the stairs to a long, low whistle from Cindy. "You look very handsome, Mister Brentwood."

"Thank you, Cindy," Clay said as he walked to the front door and opened it, feeling a bite to the air outside.

Running Coyote saw Clay and hurried over to him. "I'm worried about that storm just to the west that is headed our way. I've already moved all the horses to the barn and corral, but it's crowded."

Clay nodded his head and looked around. Tables covered with cloths, sat under the overhang of the porch; enough to seat most of their guests, with a few tables out in the open. Clay knew the Indians would more than likely eat by themselves, so there would be more than enough tables to seat everyone else. When the rain came, if there wasn't any wind, the tables on the porch area would stay dry, but if there was wind...

Clay looked at his pocket watch. It was three-thirty, only thirty minutes before the ceremony. He looked at the western sky, again and decided they still had time. "Keep an eye on things and keep me posted," Clay told Running Coyote.

When Clay went back inside the house, the minister was standing in the living room with a glass of brandy in his hand. He was admiring the arch where the wedding was to take place.

Clay poured himself a small glass of brandy. He didn't want to drink too much before the wedding.

The minister, Carlyle Broomfield, turned when Clay walked up. "Very impressive," he said with a voice that sounded like it came from the bottom of a well. Carlyle stood an even six feet, and weighed two-hundred and ten pounds. According to the people of Seymour, he gave rousing sermons and had a good following. He was thirty-two and single – and it was whispered a few women sought his company. Although, nothing was ever proved.

Because they'd never actually met, the reverend stuck out his hand. Mister Brentwood, thank you for asking me to do this service. My name is Carlyle Broomfield, Reverend Broomfield."

Clay shook the man's hand and was impressed with the grip. He had a firm handshake and from the looks of him, well taken care of. "Pleased to have you here, Have you met the bride to be?"

"Sorry, no. I've only been in contact with Mrs. McIntyre. She's the one who hired me."

Clay looked at his pocket watch again and saw it was ten minutes to four. "The wedding is set for four o'clock, so we've only got about ten minutes before you do."

The minister looked around and said, "Yes, people are already coming in."

The minister finished off his brandy, sat the glass on the table along with other glasses, picked up his bible and went to where he was supposed to stand in the middle of the archway. "Mister Brentwood, if you will be so kind and stand here to my left so we'll be ready when it's time."

As Clay walked up and stopped where he was supposed to stand, his breath began to come in short bursts and he felt his stomach rumble.

Fortunately, Running Coyote showed up as best man and stood next to him and said, "Take several deep breaths. You're going to be just fine."

"You have the rings?" Clay asked.

"Of course, I do. They're right here in my ..." Running Coyote said, as he began searching his pockets which caused Clay to panic.

"Don't tell me you lost the rings!" Clay whispered, loudly.

"Naw, I was just kidding. I have them right here," Running Coyote said, pulling the rings from his coat pocket, grinning like the cat that just swallowed the canary.

"Don't do that. I'm nervous enough as it is," Clay said.

"Sure, Boss. Whatever you say, Boss."

About that time, Mrs. McIntyre and Cindy, Loralie's bridesmaids, came to stand facing Clay, on the minister's right side.

Where and when they got an organ, Clay didn't know, but suddenly, organ music began to fill the inside of the house and the minister said to the room full of people, "All rise."

Clay turned and looked at the top of the stairs and he froze. She was dressed in a long, flowing white dress, with pearl earrings and a pearl necklace to grace her throat. Her hair was hanging loose, but had small feathers woven into it, giving her a look that caused the visitors to gasp.

She descended the stairs like she was floating on air and came down the middle aisle between the people and stopped opposite of Clay. Beneath her white veil, Clay could see her sparkling eyes and bright red lips. There was a glow about her he would never forget.

The Reverend Broomfield cleared his throat and said, "Shall we begin?"

Everyone sat down as Clay and Loralie each turned to face the minister.

Just as he began with, "Dearly beloved, we gather here today to…" A loud roar caused by the wind, surged through the house, breaking the glass in the windows.

"Boss, we got us a big problem," Riley said as he began closing the wooden shutters that were intended to be used in case of an attack. There were small holes where a man could shoot through.

Clay ran to the front of the house and as he helped close one of the shutters, he saw the tables and most everything else flying around in the air. Over the far, western wall, Clay saw the funnel drop down out of the sky and head toward them.

"Get all the shutters closed and barred off as best you can," Clay shouted to his men, then ran back up to where the minister and Loralie were waiting, panic stricken.

"Reverend, do you think you can give us the quick version? There's a tornado coming and we don't have much time."

The people in the room were looking around, nervously, but stayed rooted in place.

Reverend Broomfield cleared his throat and said, "Clay Brentwood, do you take Loralie Benson to be your lawful wife, to love and to cherish from this day forward?"

"I do," Clay said.

"And do you, Loralie Benson…"

"I do," Loralie said before he went any further.

"Place the rings on each other's fingers."

When they hurriedly did, the reverend said, "I now pronounce you man and wife. You may kiss the bride"

After a hurried kiss, they both turned and ran to see what they could do to help. The roar of the wind was so loud now that it threatened to rip the shutters off the side of the house.

Clay was trying to keep everyone calm when Juan's mother came to him and asked, "Have you seen, Juan?"

Clay thought for a moment and said, "No. The last time I saw him was when I turned Midnight over to him when I got back from looking over the herds."

"You think he's still in the barn, all alone?" she asked as panic creeped into her voice.

Clay wheeled and ran for the back door, which was closest to the barn. The back door was rattling from the force of the wind. Brave Eagle was in the kitchen and had just secured a shutter when Clay entered.

"Make sure this door gets closed when I leave," Clay yelled over the wind.

"Where you going?" Brave Eagle asked.

"I think Juan is trapped in the barn! Plus, I need to check on the horses." Clay yelled. "Get the door!"

And with that, Clay jerked the door open and drove himself through.

Bending over and using all his strength, Clay made his way to the barn, having to duck twice to keep from being hit by tables flying through the air at a speed that would more than likely have killed him.

Clay opened the small side door and went into the barn, closing it behind him. Fortunately, that side of the barn wasn't being affected much by the wind.

Inside, it was dark and it took Clay a minute or so to adjust his eyes. "Juan, are you in here?" he yelled.

"Here, Senor' Clay, In Midnight's stall," Juan called back.

Clay ran down to Midnight's stall, and there stood Juan, with his arms around Midnight's neck. "He was afraid, Senor' Clay. The wind, it is very loud. Is my mother safe?"

Clay grinned. "Yes, your mother is safe, but she needs you to come into the house so she can see that you are all right."

"But what about Midnight? Who will take care of him?" Juan asked.

Clay rubbed Juan on the top of his head and said, "Oh, I think he'll be all right. The storm should pass before long. But right now, we need to get you to your mother," Clay said, his eyes scanning the interior of the barn to check the horses. They looked secure enough, just scared.

"Si Senor'," Juan said, then patted Midnight on the neck and said, "I will be back as soon as the storm is over."

The big horse whinnied and shook his head up and down.

Clay grinned and said, "I do believe that horse understands every word you say."

"Si, Senor', he does."

When Clay opened the small barn door, tables, chairs and a bunch of other stuff was flying around the yard, some landing on the roof, to be swept away, while other things were slammed into the side of the house and broken into pieces.

The back door leading into the kitchen was standing open just enough to let Clay know someone was there, waiting.

"This does not look good, Senor'," Juan told Clay.

"It's just a short run. I'll carry you," Clay told the young Mexican boy who was staring outside with eyes as big a saucer. "Don't worry, we'll make it," Clay said with more assurance than he felt.

Clay had just picked Juan up in his arms when everything became very quiet. There was no wind and whatever was swirling around, fell to the ground. "It's the eye of the storm," Clay said as he ran for the back door.

As soon as Clay stepped onto the porch, the door flew open and Clay ran inside to where Loralie, Juan's mother and several other people were standing.

Clay sat Juan down and he ran into his mother's arms. "Oh mama, I was so worried about you!" Juan told her.

With tears running down her cheeks, she looked at Clay and whispered, "Thank you, Senor'"

Before Clay could say anything, the eye of the storm passed and they were hit with pounding wind, again.

In the living room, there was nothing anyone could do but sit, huddled together and wait for the storm to pass.

Less than twenty minutes later, the tornado was looking for new territory to terrorize.

Like other people who lived in the west and were used to hard living, they went outside and in no time, had what tables and chairs they could find, sitting upright. The Mexican men were playing their music and liquor was being served. The meat was hauled from the pits and sliced up to go with the other food prepared by Mrs. McIntyre, along with food brought by the people from town.

An hour after the tornado had passed; the place was filled with laughter, music and loud voices.

Clay and Loralie had been the center of attention, especially during the gift unwrapping, to whoops and hollers. They had danced to a slow waltz.

After the dance they were approached by the mayor and his wife, who presented Clay and Loralie with a set of silk sheets. "Imported from New York," the mayor informed them.

Clay looked around and said, "I haven't seen the sheriff. Did he not come?"

The mayor sighed. "About that," he said. "The sheriff quit and went back east to where he said life would be much quieter. Right now, the outlaws are being guarded by one of the cowboys who was looking to pick up some extra money. He's only temporary, and, we, the people of Seymour," he said, waving his arms around the room, "wondered if you might be interested in the job?"

Clay looked down at Loralie who had a frown on her face and her nose was wrinkled up. "I don't think so, but thanks," Clay said with a wink at Loralie.

The mayor smiled and said, "About what I expected. You wouldn't happen to…"

"I would," Clay told him, thinking of a ranger who had a bad leg from one of his missions and could no longer go chasing outlaws. He was in need of a way to make a living for him and his wife and having a hard time of it. It seemed no one wanted to hire a man with a bum leg, but Clay figured he could do the sheriff's job in Seymour just fine. "His name is Dirk Rogers and you can get ahold of him through Bill McDaniel, who is standing right over there," Clay said, pointing toward his old boss.

Somewhere around ten o'clock, that night, Bill McDaniel walked up to Running Coyote and asked, "Have you seen Clay? I need to have a word with him."

Running Coyote grinned and nodded his head in the direction of the stairs.

Bill looked in that direction, then he too grinned and said, "Oh."

CHAPTER FORTY-SEVEN

-

What the mayor, nor any of the townsfolks knew was, earlier that day, while they were en route to Clay and Loralie's wedding, an event took place in town that would once again, put Clay and the town of Seymour in jeopardy.

Herman Ledbetter, the town drunk, who would probably betray his own brother for whiskey money, if he had one, just happened to be standing nearby when Rice Cooper caught up with the mayor. He had just come out of the saloon after moping the floor and having his early morning pick-me-up.

The sheriff stopped the mayor and handed him his badge. "I'm sorry, Mayor, but this just isn't the kind of work I'm comfortable with. I'm used to having at least a half a dozen deputies to do the work. I'm what you might call, a desk man. I hate chasing outlaws and I'm sore from head to foot from all this riding I've had to do. I'd never ridden a horse before in my life until I came here. Plus, I don't like the idea of people shooting at me – so, I'm going back east where it's safer."

The mayor tried to argue, but Rice held up his hand. "Do you realize ever since I locked that fella, Bill Musgrove, in the cell, he's been telling me he's going to escape and when he does, both Clay Brentwood and I are dead men. I'm sorry Mayor, but you'll have to find a new sheriff. I've already bought my train ticket and my train leaves in fifteen minutes."

And with that, Rice Cooper spun around and headed for the train station, leaving the mayor standing on the sidewalk with his mouth hanging open.

The mayor brushed past Herman without even noticing him as he walked down the street, talking to himself.

Late that afternoon, the eye of the hurricane graced the town of Seymour, Texas; not with the eye, but the outer wind, which created a great deal of damage. Roofs were partially torn off, a wooden keg had smashed through the front window of the mercantile store, along with damage to everything the high wind came in contact with.

Herman was standing on the sidewalk, desperately wanting a drink, when the cowboy the mayor had hired to keep an eye on the prisoners, left the jail and walked down the street to the restaurant to get some supper. Herman smiled and nodded his head as an idea squirmed its way into his whiskey soaked brain.

The people were all too busy to notice Herman Ledbetter walk across the street and go into the sheriff's office.

Bill Musgrove stood up from his bunk and stared as a grizzled old man walked into the cell area, carrying a ring with the cell keys on it.

Herman stayed a good distance away from the cell and asked, "You Bill Musgrove?"

"Who wants to know?" Bill asked, cautiously.

Herman just grinned and said, "The sheriff quit and left town on the train."

"And out of the goodness in your heart, you've come to let us out..." Bill said with a big smile.

"Maybe," Herman said. "I know you want revenge on that ranger for what he's done to you... So, my question is, what's it worth to you for me to give you these keys?"

The thought of watching the ranger die a slow death, filled Bill's mind. "Whatever you want, old man, whatever you want" Bill told him, now remembering the old drunk.

With thoughts of enough money to keep him in whiskey for a long time, Herman walked over close to the cell and stuck the ring of keys in Bill's direction.

With a swiftness Herman didn't suspect, Bill grabbed Herman's arm and yanked it hard. Herman's head hit the cell bars with a loud thud.

Herman was still in a daze when Bill snapped his neck and let him drop to the floor. "Too bad, ol' man, I don't have time for drunks."

After opening the cell doors, Bill yelled at the other prisoners, "Com'on, boys, we got us a bank to rob and a ranger to settle with!"

THE END

FROM THE AUTHOR

Thank you to all my readers. Your reviews and requests for more Clay Brentwood books is an inspiration to me. I'll keep writing them as long as you keep requesting them…

Jared McVay

MEET THE AUTHOR

At the current time, Jared McVay lives in Oregon where he writes his books, does storytelling, book signings, speaking engagements, and gets in a little fishing from time to time.

Before becoming a novelist, Jared was a professional actor – stage, film and television, and a ghostwriter for screenplays.

As a young man he worked as a cowboy, a rodeo clown, a lumberjack, barker for a carnival and a truck driver. During the 1950's he rode the rails as a hobo and during the 80's, a blue water sailor. He spent his military time in the US Navy Sea Bees, where he learned his electrical trade as a power lineman, then spent ten years as a lineman for Kansas Gas & Electric. But it was his love of entertaining people that led him into acting and writing.

Jared has five children, eleven grandchildren, fifteen great grandchildren and four great, great grandchildren.

When not writing or talking about writing, or answering e-mails from his fans, you can find him enjoying life with his girlfriend, Jerri.

THANK YOU FOR READING!

If you enjoyed this book, we would appreciate your customer review on your book seller's website or on Goodreads.

Also, we would like for you to know that you can find more great books like this one at

www.SixGunBooks.com

Stories so real you can smell the gunsmoke.[TM]